# TEACH ME

The Wolf Hotel #3

K.A.TUCKER

Editing by Hot Tree Editing

Cover design by Shanoff Designs

Published by K.A. Tucker

# CHAPTER 1

The hospital doors slide open to welcome in a nurse, her purse slung over her shoulder. Coming in for her shift, I'm guessing.

I really should get out of the car and go in there. Jed texted about an hour ago to tell me that my dad was awake. I *do* really want to see him.

But going in there means leaving Henry, something I'm just not ready to do.

"I'm already hours late, Abbi. I have to get to my plane." Henry delivers that softly, his hand squeezing my thigh.

"I know. I'm sorry, it's just.... How long before you're back in New York, do you think?"

We've just reconciled in his hotel room and now he's flying back to Alaska and I'm staying in Pennsylvania, and I have no idea when I'm going to see him again.

I fight the tears that are threatening.

And fail.

He reaches up to brush them away from my cheek. I'm so thankful that Henry's driver stepped out of the car as soon as he pulled up to the curb, giving us privacy.

"It's hard to say. I need to bring these engineers to the site to assess it for the ski hill I want to put in. Then I'm flying to Colorado to meet with the builders who put in the runs at our Aspen location."

I fight the cringe. I can't hear "Aspen" without thinking about the disastrous night back on the grand opening weekend, when I believed Henry was sleeping with another woman and I let my broken heart be distracted by Henry's masseuse, Michael.

The weekend that, technically, I cheated on Henry.

I regretted it when it happened because I'd used Michael. But now that I know Henry lied to me, that he never slept with Roshana Mafi....

I force that stomach-churning guilt aside for now. "Can't someone else do these things? I mean, you're the CEO. You own Wolf Hotels now." Or a controlling 61 percent of it, anyway.

He smirks. "This isn't just some other hotel. You know that. I don't trust anyone with it."

I nod, trying to contain my emotions. I know how important Wolf Cove—and Alaska—is to him. He spent his childhood summers there. He considers it home. "So, I guess...."

"We'll keep in touch."

I can't help the frown. Keep in touch? That sounds like something casual friends say.

"Hey." He grips my chin between his thumb and index finger. "This isn't going to be easy, Abbi. I warned you. We lead very different lives, and right now, you're stuck here. You could be stuck here for a long time." He softens that reality by drawing the pad of his thumb across the bottom of my lip.

He's right. That tractor that rolled over Daddy did a real number on him, breaking multiple bones and puncturing his lung. It could have been much worse but, still, it's going to be months before he's back on his feet and running the farm. "I know, it's just...." I settle my gaze on his steely blue eyes, still amazed at how they can sometimes look so cold and hard, and yet other times melt my heart with their softness and warmth. "What *is this*? What are we?"

Henry officially fired me this morning, more a joke than anything. I left so abruptly that I hadn't had the opportunity to hand in my resignation, but it was pretty clear I was quitting anyway. Either way, I'm no longer a Wolf employee, which means that dating me isn't against company policy. Even though Henry would say he can do whatever the hell he wants now that he has controlling share, I think it would still bother him to be so blatantly and openly disregarding his own corporate rules. He has a lot of pride in the Wolf name.

He sighs. "We'll figure things out as we go. You need to get in there and spend time with your family. And I need to get back to doing what I need to do. Okay?"

"Okay." I know Henry enough to know that's as far as this conversation is going. I nod. Do I need an official label for what we are? Or is it just enough to know Henry's in my life? That he cares about me. Because I know he does. He dropped everything to fly across the country with me because he didn't want me sitting in a plane for ten hours alone, given the tragedy. He's gone out of his way to make sure my dad has the best trauma surgeon in the country and that my family is set up in his hotel while we're here. He's been carrying around a picture of me—the one the Japanese photographer Hachiro took that day so long ago—in his portfolio.

I *know* he cares.

The question is, will it be enough?

"So... I guess I'll see you when I see you?" I reach up to graze his handsome hard jawline, admiring the feel of his soft, freshly shaven skin.

"Something like that." Henry turns his face to kiss my

fingertips, and then he leans in to capture my lips with his, his tongue finding its way in to brush against mine in a slow, erotic dance that's not outright scandalous but is probably inappropriate right in front of the hospital. "I love this mouth of yours," he murmurs, taking the back of my head in his hand to deepen the kiss.

*And I love you.*

I've felt those words sitting on the tip of my tongue, threatening to tumble out, since he stepped onto the plane yesterday morning. I've somehow managed to hold on to them though. It's too soon for me to tell him. We've only just reconciled.

Henry breaks away with a groan. "Okay, you really need to go or I'll be unzipping my pants right here."

My blood rushes with the thought, my fingers digging into his forearm. I didn't get nearly enough of him this morning. "Maybe I want you to," I tease, catching his earlobe between my teeth.

"I don't think fuckface and his parents would enjoy the show so much though."

"What?" I spin around to find Jed with Reverend and Celeste Enderbey standing on the sidewalk.

Staring.

The Reverend and Celeste have the decency to look away when we make eye contact, but Jed continues staring at me, a mixture of shock and hurt filling his face.

They saw me come in with Henry yesterday. Sure, I told them he was my boss when they asked. If they were wondering what was going on... I guess they have their answer. "I guess I'm going."

I reach for the door.

Henry's hand seizes my thigh, holding me in place. "Just so we're crystal clear..."

I turn to find a hard gaze on me. "When I say 'let's see

where things go' that means make sure he keeps his fucking hands off you. And that goes for every other asshole out there, too."

Maybe it's odd that my heart swells with his words, but I smile anyway. It's his way of telling me he cares. "I only want you, Henry. Always."

He opens his mouth, and I hold my breath, wanting him to tell me that he only wants me, too. That he misses me already.

That he loves me.

"I'll call you later."

My cue to leave. "Bye, Henry." I force myself out of the backseat. Thank God Jed and his parents have already gone inside. It allows me the chance to watch his car pull away in private, my throat thick with emotion for that man.

With a sigh, I turn to face the hospital doors.

And prepare for what my life back in Greenbank, Pennsylvania, is going to be like.

---

"Daddy, you're awake!"

I run to his bedside and take his hand in mine as I peer down at him. He's not a weak man by any means; a lifetime of farming has made him strong. And his bones are far from being old and brittle; he's only forty.

Yet he lies here frail and broken, his hand limp within mine.

"Abigail," he whispers. "Your mother said you made it home."

I feel Mama's heavy stare from across the bed. She's angry with me for leaving to see Henry. "I did. Last night. How are you? Do you hurt anywhere?"

Finally, he smiles. "I don't feel a thing. These meds are great."

My bottom lip wobbles a little; it's hard to see him like this. He's never been hurt before. Hardly ever been sick. "You shouldn't pick fights with tractors."

He makes to laugh, only to scrunch up his face as if in pain.

"None of that, now. You need to rest." Finally, I hazard a glance at Mama. Her eyes are lined with heavy bags and her short brown curls are matted. Aunt May brought her clothes, so she's changed out of her nightgown at least, but I know she couldn't have slept much in these chairs, her 370-pound frame too large to fit comfortably. "Why don't you go and get some rest? Henry said the suite will be available to us for as long as we need it. For as long as Daddy's in the hospital." Which could be weeks. Just another way in which Henry has been generous to my family.

"That won't be necessary. Reverend Enderbey has a cousin who lives just on the other side of the city. He said there's a room there for me."

I frown. "But the hotel is *five minutes* away."

"We've already taken too much of that man's generosity."

"Who's Henry?" my dad interrupts.

"Her boss. He was flying out this way so he gave Abigail a lift on his plane," Mama answers for me. She makes it sound like it was nothing more than a minor inconvenience.

Like there's nothing going on between Henry and me, though she damn well knows there is.

"Well, that was awful nice of him." He looks to me. "I'd like to thank him. Is he still here?"

"No, he's gone," Mama cuts in. "And Abigail is home to stay."

Why does that sound like a punishment?

Daddy looks to me. "Is this true?"

I sigh. "I'm staying for as long as you need me. I quit my job in Alaska and I'll defer school for a year to help keep the farm going."

He frowns. "I'm sorry for being so careless. I don't know what happened."

"Hush, now. All that matters is that you are alive and on the mend," Mama chides.

"It's the busiest time of the year, Bernadette."

She takes Daddy's other hand. "It'll be fine. We've still got Jean. Now Abigail's here. And Jed quit his job so he can help us with the farm until it's time to leave for school."

"What?" I burst out. That means I'm going to have to deal with Jed all day, every day, for the next six weeks.

"Isn't it great?" Mama smiles wide. "We've got plenty of help. The Reverend will be putting out a call during service this Sunday, but we've already got people offering to come and help with the animals and the hay." She pats his hand. "The Lord is good. This is his doing. He's watching over us."

His and Henry's, though I'm guessing Mama hasn't mentioned the fact that Henry pulled major strings, called in enormous favors, to fly in Dr. Eisenhower.

Daddy smiles back at Mama, seemingly satisfied with her answer, and then turns to me. "It's been so long since I've seen you, Abigail."

"I know. I missed you so much." I didn't realize how much until just now. I was so focused on getting away from Jed and Mama, I forgot that I'd also be leaving him behind.

"You look stronger. And your hair…." He frowns. "Is it just me or is it a bit darker?"

"Don't worry, that'll fade soon," Mama answers for me—again. "We'll have our Abigail back in no time."

I can't help the glare I throw her way. *No you won't,* I want to say. That Abigail is gone for good. If not for Daddy's current situation, I would say it, but I don't want to upset him.

"Tell me about Alaska. What was it like?"

Breathtaking.

Eye-opening.

Heartbreaking.

Life changing.

Finally, I settle on, "It was beautiful, Daddy. You really need to go there one day."

"You think I should?" There's a twinkle in his eye. Daddy hasn't gone more than one state over in any direction his entire life.

"Yes. They have lots of hunting up there."

"Really? And did you see any wild animals?"

I grin. "A grizzly bear, Daddy."

His eyes widen. "In the resort?"

I giggle. "No. Out in a clearing. Henry and I were collecting wood and—"

"Darling, I think you need your rest. You can hear all about Alaska when you're better."

A scowl takes over Daddy's face. "Would you let the poor girl talk, Bernadette? I haven't seen her in months!"

The shock on Mama's face must match the astonishment I'm feeling. Daddy never raises his voice.

The rhythmic beep of his heart monitor starts speeding up.

"See? You need to calm yourself down, Roger. Abigail, please go and fetch some water for him."

I duck out of the room in search of a nurse. I find Celeste Enderbey instead.

"How is he doing?" she asks in that soft voice of hers, automatically reaching for my hand. I've forgotten how small she is. Next to her, I feel like a giant and I'm only five foot five.

"He seems to be doing all right," I assure her. "I'm going to get him some water. You can go in."

"I will. I came to tell you that your Aunt May has already left. She had to get ready for the dinner shift."

"I figured as much." The Pearl is the hub of Greenbank, especially on the weekends.

"We need to be on our way home shortly, too. The Reverend would like to prepare for tomorrow's sermon." Jed's father's name is George, but Celeste has taken to calling him the Reverend when she's talking to anyone else, including us.

"Can I get a ride with you? I feel bad, leaving everything at the farm to Jean to manage."

"Absolutely." Her eyes graze over the Northgate College sweatshirt I've been wearing since yesterday, hanging open to reveal the fitted tank top beneath. Something Mama wouldn't approve of because it shows too much of my figure. "You seem… different."

Is this because of the make-out session she witnessed half an hour ago?

I'm not sure what she wants me to say so I just smile. "Gotta get that water."

Her hand tightens its grip. "Please forgive him, Abigail. You two are so good for each other."

I heave a sigh. I hate disappointing Celeste. She's such a kind and loving woman, so opposite to Mama in every way. Every time I ran over to the Enderbeys', I knew that I'd be greeted with a smile and her gentleness. I've secretly considered her a second mother for years.

Finally, she releases me and disappears into Daddy's room.

When I slip through the door five minutes later, the Reverend has joined them. Where Jed is, I have no idea.

"…we had to be patient, waiting for Jed to find his way

back to us. Now it's Abigail's turn and we must be patient again." The Reverend's hand is on Mama's shoulder. "The man values money and power above all else. He will get bored soon enough."

"But he's preying on her innocence like a—" She spots me and straightens abruptly, her words cutting off.

They're talking about me.

About me, not being enough for Henry. About Henry getting bored of me.

The Reverend doesn't have to glance back to know I'm there. In a much louder voice, he says, "We'll all be praying for a speedy recovery, Roger."

"We are so blessed to have you in our lives." Mama grasps his hands. "Thank you for all you've done to help us. Jed is a godsend."

"Your family will be well looked after during this time."

They all turn to face me, fake broad smiles plastered across their faces.

"Ready, Abigail?" Celeste asks.

"Sure." Ninety minutes trapped in a car with them. Can't wait.

"Actually, I want to talk to her for a minute, alone," Daddy says.

Celeste takes her husband's arm. "We'll wait for you outside."

Daddy looks to Mama, waiting. She doesn't take the hint. "You too, Bernadette."

For the second time in ten minutes, her face is full of shock. "But, what could you want to talk about that—"

"That's between me and my daughter."

With a huff, she maneuvers her body around the hospital room furniture and disappears out the door.

"Lord, has that woman always been so overbearing, or

does it just take being trapped in a hospital bed with her hovering over my every breath to realize it?"

I stifle my giggle because I'm not sure if I'm supposed to find that funny. "She means well."

He sighs. "Now take a seat and tell me what's really going on with this boss of yours."

What do I say to him? As much as my dad was kind to me over the whole Jed disaster, assuring me that Jed didn't deserve me, I know he's always liked Jed, and I know he loves having Jed around to help with the farm. Jed was always keen on learning about milking cows and fixing farming equipment, about how to grow grain, and when to bale hay. He's a natural at it. It's always just been assumed that he'd take over at some point.

Is my dad going to tell me that Henry will get bored of me, too?

Because I can't take hearing that from him. It's already in my head, plenty.

"Abigail...."

"I love him," I blurt out. "I don't love Jed, Daddy. Not anymore. Maybe I never really did, because it didn't feel anything like it feels with Henry." Right now, I don't even *like* Jed much, though I have to give him credit, he's here when my family needs him.

"Is what your mother said about the plane true? That he was 'going this way?'"

I shake my head. "He only arrived in Alaska the day before your accident. He's going back there now. And the doctor you had? He's the best trauma surgeon in America and Henry flew him in especially for you."

That earns a brow lift. "Does your mother know that?"

"She does."

A knowing look fills his eyes as he nods. "She doesn't want you with this man."

"I know, Daddy. But it's not her choice. It's not anyone's choice but mine and Henry's." And I'm not letting anyone get in the way of us being together again.

He gives my hand a light squeeze. "Just remember, it's coming from a place of love. We're all worried that he's gonna hurt you."

"I've already been hurt, plenty, Daddy. Remember? By Jed." The godsend, according to Mama.

A sad smile touches his lips. "I do remember. I'm glad to see you happy again."

I *am* happy.

And stronger.

And smarter.

And petrified.

"Go on, now. They're waiting. Your mother's probably hunting for a glass to press up against the door."

I giggle because he's right. "I'll come back for a visit as soon as I can."

He chuckles softly. "See you soon."

I find Mama and the Enderbeys waiting just outside the door.

Mama pounces on me right away. "What was that about?"

"He just wanted to ask about Henry."

"So then why send me out of the room?"

*Because I wouldn't get a word in edgewise, perhaps?* I simply shrug.

She turns to Celeste. "He's never done anything like that before. I'm telling you, something's not right with him since he woke up. I think he must have a head injury."

"Maybe you're right. But wouldn't the doctors have seen something in all the tests they ran?" she asks.

"Who knows? We're always hearin' about things that get missed. Remember that surgery rag a doctor left inside that woman? Closed her right up and sent her home with it inside! The woman was in complete agony before they believed her." Mama talks like she personally knows the woman, when I'm sure it's just a byline she saw in a newspaper once and filed into her memory for future reference, when the need arose. She loves doing that. I think she feels it makes her sound knowledgeable.

"You should definitely mention it to the doctor, then," Reverend Enderbey suggests.

"Yes, you're right. I will. So, you're off now?"

"We are."

"Come here, baby girl." She reaches for me, pulling me into a fierce hug. For all that she is, I don't doubt that Mama loves me very much. "I'm so happy to have you home. You'll find your room the same as when you left it. All your clothes are there, too, so you can find somethin' more suitable than what they made you wear up there."

She just can't help herself.

"And make sure you make it to service tomorrow, Abigail. And confession." Under her breath, but loud enough for me to hear, she mutters, "Lord knows you'll need that."

This time I don't bother hiding the eye roll.

*If you only knew, Mama.*

# CHAPTER 2

"Everything's all taken care of for the day." Jean wipes the sweat from his weathered brow onto his forest green work pants. He's shown up to work here in those same pants and burgundy plaid button-down every single day for years. The outfit's always clean in the morning and filthy by day's end. Either he has several pairs of the same, or he makes his poor wife do laundry every night.

"Thank you for keeping the farm going while we were away."

He waves my words away as if it's nothing, but the poor man looks exhausted.

"How's Isabelle?"

Mention of his granddaughter seems to brighten his spirits a bit. "She's a sweet little thing." He beams. "Looks like her mother did when she was a baby."

"Tell Jennifer I said hi."

"Will do." He ambles off toward his truck, an old red Ford pickup full of dents and dings.

And I sigh, taking in the view of the farm I've known all my life. It's my favorite time to be here, when the air is warm and smells of freshly cut hay, and the grass is a dark green;

when the flowers surrounding the vegetable gardens are lush and colorful. We cut them every week to dress the church for Sunday service.

I always found comfort here. Until this past February, that is, when I caught Jed cheating on me. After that, I dreaded coming back here. I flew all the way to Alaska just to avoid it.

Now? I don't know what this feeling is. Nostalgia for a childhood gone, perhaps. The double-story farmhouse I've called home all these years sits ahead of me to the left, quiet and worn. It's over a hundred years old, built by my great-great-grandfather and home to several generations of Mitchells. I can see that a few shingles are missing on the east side. Likely on account of a big storm that rolled through here a month ago, according to Mama. She mentioned damage to a barn roof, too. I'll have to go and check that out.

We have three barns and four silos. The original barn, dating back to the same time as the house, is farther off to the side, some five hundred yards from our home. We use it for equipment now. That's also where I make my soaps during the warmer weather, in a small workshop equipped with an electric stove and several tables.

The other two barns that house the animals and hay sit side by side, not too far from the house.

I make my way toward the front porch, dragging the backpack that I stuffed haphazardly in my rush out of Wolf Cove alongside me. While I had a shower at Henry's, I wouldn't say that time was spent actually getting clean.

"Abigail!"

Jed is jogging toward me from the path between our houses, his calf muscles straining as he navigates the uneven ground. He's always been fit, but I would never have called him muscular, not like Henry, or even the outdoor crew guys. He's obviously been going to the gym, though.

What else he's been doing this summer, I have no idea. He was quiet on the drive home from Pittsburgh, sitting up front with his dad while Celeste sat in the back and made painfully polite conversation, filling me in on all the happenings in the community and the church since I've been away.

She didn't once ask about Alaska.

When Jed reaches me, he's out of breath. It's a good quarter mile between our two houses. "Dinner's gonna be at five thirty tonight instead of six. Dad's got some catch-up to do for tomorrow."

"Oh, I'm good, thanks."

He frowns. "What do you mean? It's Saturday night."

And every Saturday night, we go over to the Enderbeys' for dinner. That's just the way things have always been around here.

Not anymore, though. At least, not for me. "I'm pretty tired from the last few days, so I'm just going to pull something together here and then go to bed, I think."

"Oh." He brushes his blond hair off his forehead. It's longer than he's ever had it before, and slightly tousled. "But she's making roasted chicken. And a strawberry pie, just for you. She's already rolling out the pie crust and everything."

My favorites.

"You have to eat, and she's going to all this trouble."

I sigh, feeling the noose tightening around my neck. I can't very well get out of this one, especially since the Enderbeys dropped everything in their lives to rush to Pittsburgh. They sat with Mama all day when I couldn't.

"'Kay. I'll be there."

Jed's face splits into a wide grin. "Great."

"You know you could have just texted me instead of running all that way."

"Yeah, I know. But I wanted to see you." His gaze skims over me, stalling first on my chest, and then on my thighs.

"If I'm gonna make it there in time, I need to go shower." I start to climb the stairs.

"So it was him who answered?"

"What?" I ask, though I already know what he's talking about. The guy who answered my phone when Jed called to tell me about the accident. I was wondering when this would come up.

"Yesterday morning. When I called you. When you were asleep."

No, that would be Ronan, who happened to be there consoling me over Henry as a genuine friend. But I'm not going to tell Jed that.

"It's not really any of your business."

"How is it not? Come on, Abigail! You've known the guy for a few weeks. We've known each other our entire lives. We grew up together, we know each other's secrets."

I glare at him pointedly. "Yes, because I walked in on one of them accidentally."

"It's over between Cammie and me. That's out of my system, completely." He takes a few steps toward me. "I was stupid and selfish and I took for granted the best thing in my life. You." He pleads with his eyes. "I love you, Abigail. And I'm gonna spend the rest of my life proving it to you."

*Oh God*. "It's too late, Jed. Move on."

"No, it's not." He has that stubborn set in his jaw. I used to think it was adorable.

Now I can't help but laugh. "I'm in love with Henry!"

"Your boss?" He sighs. "Abigail, that's not gonna last. Seriously, think about it. He's this rich hotel owner and you live on a farm. It may have worked while you two were together, but outta sight, outta mind with guys like that."

"That's not how it is with us."

"Oh yeah?" He folds his arms over his chest. Somehow it's so patronizing. "Then how is it?"

"We're... seeing how it goes."

Jed gives me a knowing look, and I want to slap him. "How old is he, anyway?"

"Thirty-one."

"He's ten years older than you? Why would you even want a guy that old? That's halfway to your parents' age."

Because he's gorgeous and sexy.

Because he knows how to touch me.

Because he's all I think of when I go to sleep and when I wake up and every hour in between.

"Gotta go now. I'll see you for dinner." *Unfortunately.*

"Just remember, I'll be right here, waiting for you. Just come back to me when you're ready. We're meant to be, Abigail."

"It's Abbi, and no, we're not." There's no point arguing with him. Sometimes I think Jed and my Mama are too similar.

I make it up one step when he calls out, "Oh, my mom forgot to ask. Since you're back in town, would you be able to help out with the first of the month food drive? You remember what needs to be done, right?"

"I think I can manage." I've only been running it since I was seventeen.

"Great. Oh, and the charity BBQ. She'd love your help with that, too."

The creaky porch steps hide my sigh. Just like old times.

---

I FLOP ONTO MY BED, my stomach swollen from Celeste's cooking. I may not have wanted to go and face the Enderbeys for what was bound to be more awkwardness, but at least I'll go to bed full.

Sliding my phone from my pocket—the Reverend doesn't allow phones at the dinner table and it was absolute torture every time my phone vibrated in my back pocket—I smile at the group message from Ronan and Connor.

**Connor:** *The Cove isn't the same without you.*

I do the math. It's only four o'clock there.

**Abbi:** *Are you guys still working?*

**Connor:** *Yeah, it's pissing rain. We could have used you here.*

I roll my eyes at Connor's not-so-subtle reminder of our one time together, that day in the truck, even as nervous flutters stir in my stomach. I still can't believe I left for Alaska a heartbroken virgin and returned with not only three notches in my belt, so to speak, but the memory of a threesome with two gorgeous men.

That's never going to happen again, but how do I tell Connor that without telling him that I'm with Henry now? That my heart has always been with Henry. I'm not sure what Henry wants shared with his staff.

Ronan knows, even though we've never once come right out and said it. He's always known. But I can trust him not to say a word. Connor, on the other hand, can't be trusted to keep quiet.

**Abbi:** *Send me a picture of our spot on the bay. I want something to remember it by.*

A few minutes later, I get a selfie of a grinning Connor stretched out on the sand at the staff beach, shirtless, a beer in his hand. Several other staffers are around him in bikinis and trunks. Allowing these kinds of texts is probably wrong.

**Abbi:** *I thought you said it was raining?*

**Ronan:** *He's a drunken, horny liar.*

Ronan's been pretty quiet in this text exchange. Then

again, he's always been kind of quiet in comparison to Connor.

A few minutes later, I get a separate text from Ronan with a picture of Kachemak Bay, the dark blue waters rolling in soft waves, the tree-lined shores stretching as far as the eye can see. I curl up on my pillow and study it, my sadness suddenly overwhelming.

As much as I *need* to be here for my family, I *want* to be back there.

**Ronan:** *What happened with Wolf?*

I sigh. It's the first time he's ever outright asked about him and I can't lie to him.

**Abbi:** *We're seeing where things go. He's on his way back to the Cove tonight.*

**Ronan:** *I take it he knows about us?*

**Abbi:** *He knows enough.*

Henry never asked for specifics. If he ever does.... My stomach tightens with the thought of giving them to him. What would he say?

**Ronan:** *Do C and I need to worry about our jobs?*

**Abbi:** *No. I made him promise. Just maybe help Connor find another "interest" so he doesn't keep sending me these kinds of texts.*

I don't know that Connor's even capable of having a normal, non-sexually charged conversation, and if that's the case... I feel like I'm saying good-bye to two really good friends who got me through one of the hardest times of my life. In a way, I guess I am. I think Ronan feels it too.

**Ronan:** *Keep in touch.*

I snort. The exact words Henry used.

**Abbi:** *You too, Ronan. And thank you.*

I let the phone fall to my pillow beside me as I take in my dusty rose-and-white room. It hasn't changed since I was ten, when Mama last updated it. I even have the same antique furniture and bedspread, ivory lace with pink rosettes. My collection of porcelain dolls, handed down by my mother and her mother before her, are lined up on my dresser, staring at me.

Is it too soon to text Henry? He left nine hours ago now. When he said to keep in touch, did that mean I could text him whenever I wanted? He should be landing in Alaska soon. I can't help myself anymore.

**Abbi:** *Let me know when you've landed.*

I grab a book from the nightstand—my copy of *Wuthering Heights*—and blowing off the dust, flip it open and try to distract myself with words while I wait for the ones I truly want to read.

An hour later, they come.

**Henry:** *Just got in.*

**Abbi:** *I miss you so much already.*

I don't care if that makes me sound like a whiny little girl.

**Henry:** *Do you have the iPad nearby?*

**Abbi:** *On my nightstand.*

**Henry:** *Open it up and connect it.*

I do, and forty seconds later, there's an incoming call. I hit Accept and I'm treated to Henry's handsome face.

"I hate texting," he mutters through a sip of Scotch, his drink of choice. He's sitting on the white leather couch in Penthouse One, his legs spread in that relaxed way. He's still wearing the jeans and t-shirt that he left me in.

"This is definitely better," I agree, though I much prefer in person, when he's looking me straight in the eye instead of at my image on the screen.

"Hopefully the connection holds." His eyes flicker beyond his iPad camera. "There's a big storm rolling in."

"Really? It was sunny there not even an hour ago."

"Who told you that?" His jaw tenses, like he knows exactly who told me and he's not the least bit happy about it.

"They're just friends. They wanted to know how my dad was doing."

"Have you told them about me?"

"Ronan already figured it out, but he won't say a word."

Henry seems to consider that, but the tension hasn't eased from his jaw. "Are you in your bedroom?"

"Yeah."

"Who's home with you?"

"Just Flipper."

Henry frowns.

"My dad's farm dog. But he's an outdoor dog. He likes to roll in sheep manure."

"Lovely." Henry's lips twist. He leans forward until his elbows are resting on his knees. "I've changed my mind, Abbi."

His words feel like a punch to my stomach. Oh my God. After all that, it's over already?

"I need to know what happened with you and Michael, and you and those two…." He shakes his head, sighing to himself as that glint of anger in his eyes flares. "Outdoor crew guys."

It takes me a few moments to realize that he's not ending things, and another few moments to calm the nerves in my stomach, the relief overwhelming.

He's not ending things *yet*.

"Why?"

"Because I need to know. *Exactl*y how it happened. And exactly *what* happened."

My mouth drops. *Exactly?* "I… I can't."

"Why not?"

"Because I'm…. I guess I'm afraid that you'll judge me. Or leave me."

"I won't judge you. Or leave you. Not because of something in the past. But I need to know. We can't have a future if I don't. How exactly did you end up with Michael? I saw the video feed, of you going into your cabin and then running out a few minutes later."

"Right." *That night.* "I walked in on Ronan with Rachel and Katie, in the middle of... *things,* so I left. That's when I ran into Michael. He asked me if something was wrong and I started to bawl my eyes out. It was raining, so he took me to his cabin." I hesitate.

"And?"

"I changed into his dry clothes and curled up under his covers because I was cold. He tried to make me feel better by working out some knots in my neck. Then his roommate came in with his girlfriend—Lorraine, my roommate—and we had to lie there and listen to them have sex."

"And then Michael made his move." Henry's mouth twists with disdain. "I should have fired him."

"No. He didn't, actually." I stare at my fingers, my guilt heavy on my chest. "*I* started it." I'm the one who took his hand and slid it down into my shorts. "I couldn't get the image of you and Roshana and her friend out of my head. I knew—or thought—you three were in your cabin together and it was driving me crazy. I felt so horrible about myself and I wanted to not think about that anymore." I can't keep the tremble from my voice.

There's a long moment of silence, until I'm forced to look up to check that the call hasn't been dropped. It hasn't. Henry's still staring hard at me.

"And the other two?" he finally asks.

"That didn't happen for a long time. Seriously, only like a week ago. They were always flirting with me, but they also took good care of me, Henry. They're... friends. They didn't let anyone else make so much as a lewd comment about me. They made me feel really good about myself after the way you and I ended things."

"So you fucked them both?"

"No. Just Ronan."

"How many times?"

"Twice." I swallow hard. "Connor watched once."

"Where?"

"Once, in your family's cabin."

Henry's hard frown of disapproval makes me wince. "And?"

"And in a work truck. We were caught in a rainstorm and we pulled over. It… it just kind of happened. And I let it."

God, he's so angry. I can see it in the set of his jaw. It's making me want to cry.

"Take your clothes off."

"*What?*" I wasn't expecting such a sudden change in direction, but I should know by now that Henry likes to do that. I don't even know if he realizes it, or if his mind is just working that fast all the time.

"You heard me."

"You're angry."

"Yes, I am. And I need to feel something else besides this anger, or I'm going to go over to the staff lounge and rip their fucking heads off, so set your iPad where I can watch and take off every last thing you're wearing. Right now." He says it so smoothly and calmly, it's all the more scary.

With a slight tremble in my hands, I set the iPad down on the dresser, then I start to peel off my t-shirt and shorts, followed by my bra and panties, dropping them all to the floor. It feels weird, standing naked in my room with Henry watching me from over four thousand miles away.

"Get on your bed, on your knees," Henry demands, raising his glass to his lips. He hasn't moved a muscle except to drink.

I scramble on top of it.

"Now tell me exactly what happened in that truck."

I close my eyes. He's forcing me back to that day—a day I don't regret but one when I definitely wasn't myself. Or at least not the Abigail Mitchell I've known all my life. But I'm not really her anymore, am I? Still, I definitely tested boundaries I'd never thought I'd push with those two loveable deviants.

It's not hard to remember details of what started out as a playful kiss and turned into three naked, sweaty bodies. It was so organic too, nothing rushed, no pressure. From Ronan kissing me, to removing my shirt and bra for Connor to catch a glimpse. And then it all went to hell. Or heaven, depending on who you're asking.

"So he's had his tongue in you?"

I nod. "And then I… for him. But we didn't have sex."

"But you did with the other one."

"Ronan, yes."

"While the blond watched."

I hesitate, but then I finally nod. "But I don't want them, Henry."

"Did you enjoy it?"

I hesitate.

"Be honest with me."

"Yes. But not like I do when I'm with you," I quickly add. "It was just sex. And I trusted them not to hurt me so it was easy. There were no feelings involved there. Not like with you." We all used each other, for one reason or another.

"Did talking about it now make you wet?"

"I…." I look down at my naked body, on display for him. "I don't know."

"Check." I don't hear the same anger in his voice that I did moments ago, so that's good. Maybe being naked is a good distraction after all.

He clearly wants to watch me touch myself.

I can see myself naked in the small square at the bottom

of the screen, which means Henry is getting a full view. Reaching down, I run my fingertip through my slit.

"Inside."

I do as asked, pushing my finger in, touching myself where Henry invaded me just this morning. I'm still a bit sore.

"Are you? Don't lie to me."

"Yes." Not a crazy amount, but more than enough.

He tips his head back, showing me that sexy neck and the Adam's apple jutting out. If I were there now, I'd run my tongue along it. Just the thought is bringing heat between my legs.

"I want you to bring me closer to you on the bed, and then I want you to fuck yourself for me. Right in my face."

I don't know if it's even the words he says anymore, but the way he delivers them, his voice gravelly and demanding, makes my thighs squeeze.

"Come on, Abbi."

I've only ever touched myself once in front of him, the night before I found out about his ex-assistant and everything started going to shit. We're not even in the same room together this time, making it slightly less nerve-racking.

I reach for the iPad and then slide back all the way until my back rests against my pillows. Spreading my legs, I prop it upright in front of me. "Is that good for you?" I ask shyly.

"Open up wider."

I stretch my legs until my feet are hanging over either side of my bed.

And then I reach down to slide my finger over the wet, pink folds I see on the screen.

Henry sits unmoving, watching as I take turns rolling my fingertips back and forth and around my clit, then pumping them in and out of me, like he would do.

"We need to get you some toys to help out," he murmurs, taking a sip of his drink.

"Why don't you join me?" I ask softly. Now that I can see precisely what I'm doing, I stretch the skin around my opening out a bit, teasing him.

He merely smirks through another sip of his drink.

And watches as my folds begin to swell and glisten, and my fingers become slick. Finally, I pass that point of caring who's watching, a point when I know I'm about to come. My muscles begin to contract.

"Fuck," I hear him hiss through my cries, my head hanging back as I ride the euphoric waves.

I reach for the iPad, pulling it up to my face, just the tops of my breasts visible to him now. "It's your turn now."

"You're right, it is," he says so calmly. "And you like to watch, don't you?"

"Yes." I *love* to watch. I love seeing Henry undress. I love seeing him naked. I love seeing his erection, long and thick and sliding through his fist.

He reaches back over his head to pull his t-shirt off. That perfect, cut body is beneath, his shoulders strong and rounded, his collarbone jutting out. If he were here in front of me, I'd be running my hands along the curves of his biceps right now

I bite my bottom lip, waiting impatiently as he unfastens his belt with leisurely fingers.

My nipples begin to pebble again as he draws his zipper down, allowing me the first glimpse of his erection below, stretching against his gray boxer briefs, desperate to get out. I can even see the wet spots where his precum dampened the cotton.

I won't be able to resist touching myself again before long.

He slides his hand down past the elastic band and I sit up

to watch as it curls around his length, the lightest sigh escaping my lips. And then he smirks. It's a wicked smirk. "Good night, Abbi."

The connection cuts off.

I just stare at the screen. Did he just…?

I fall back into my pillow with a groan. That son of a bitch. Grabbing my phone, I text him.

**Abbi:** *Please call me back.*

It takes hours for me to fall asleep that night, with no message from Henry.

---

I KNOW I'm not supposed to check my phone in the middle of Reverend's Enderbey's service while in church.

But I also know that it could be Henry making my phone vibrate in my purse, and Henry trumps pretty much everything.

I'm in the first pew as usual, but thankfully in the far right corner and against the wall, so not directly under his nose. Still, there are eyes practically burning holes into the back of my head with their intensity. I hear the questions in everyone's thoughts as clearly as if they spoke them out loud.

*Has she forgiven him?*

*Are they back together?*

Jed didn't help matters by insisting on sitting right beside me. Celeste is on the end, hanging on to her husband's every word. It's just like in the old days. I'm even wearing one of the modest Sunday dresses that Celeste—a master seamstress—made for me years ago. It's a pale yellow knee-length sundress with cap sleeves and a high, round collar. It's nice. It just... not me anymore. I had nothing else church-worthy, though.

Finally, I can't take it anymore. As covertly as possible, I slip my phone out and tuck it next to my thigh.

Sleep well?

"You…." I press my lips together before the "bastard" slips out.

Jed leans over. "What'd you say?"

I shake my head at him and turn my focus back to his father, my hand covering my phone to hide it from view.

"…this is a new world and with each passing day, it becomes harder and harder to guide our youth. Temptation is all around us—in the movies we watch, in the music we listen to. This world of technology is a hub for the darkest, most depraved sorts of acts. The violence… the alcohol and drugs… the materialism… the type of casual relationships that weaken family values."

I drop my gaze to my lap as I feel the Reverend's judging eyes pass my way.

"It becomes hard to judge what's right past what feels good, to understand what's smart past what's risky and fun. We need to lead our children back, away from that temptation to what we know in our hearts will always be the right choice…."

He turns to the other side of the congregation and I quickly type out:

Fantastic. You?

Henry responds almost immediately.

Never better. You home?

Why? You want to make up for last night?

Actually, yes. Before I have to start my day.

I grit my teeth. This sucks.

"Abbi!" Jed elbows me in the arm. The reverend is still talking, only I'm not listening anymore, unable to shake the image of a naked Henry tangled in his white sheets, grasping his erection. What I would do to be there beside him right now, to watch him do that. To help him.

My palms twitch at the thought. I've never actually spent an entire night with him in bed, I realize. When will we get that opportunity? Will we?

My phone vibrates again, but this time it's with a call. Henry thinks I'm home.

"Dammit," I mutter under my breath, hitting Decline. My ears perk up when I hear Reverend Enderbey saying Daddy's name.

"You've all been asking, so I thought I'd tell you that, by the grace of God, the swift actions of the Greenbank ambulance services, the exceptional care in the Pittsburgh hospital, and all of your prayers and thoughts, Roger will pull through."

*Not a single mention of Henry's help.* He thanks everyone else but not Henry? No doubt Mama told the Reverend about how Henry brought in Dr. Eisenhower, because she seeks counsel on *everything*. That he has not given thanks to Henry *at all* tells me that he doesn't want Henry being a part of my life any more than Mama does. That irritates me.

"Roger has a long road to recovery but he will get there with the help of his wonderful family and friends, and this congregation." He gestures toward me. "His daughter, Abigail, rushed home to be by his side. I know I speak for myself and Celeste, and especially our son Jed, when we say how happy we are to have you back home with us. We feel complete again."

I offer him a tight smile as my cheeks burn from the unwanted attention. Thankfully the organ music begins then, signalling the end of his sermon and the continuation of the service.

It takes a few minutes for my nerves to calm before I dare check my phone again to see a text.

Why aren't you answering?

A thought comes to me and I can't resist. Making sure

Jed's not watching over my shoulder, I quickly pull up the picture I took last night, of myself lying in bed, waiting for him. It took thirty tries but I finally managed to get one that I think I look decent in. Even sexy. I intentionally kept my face out of it though. I don't have the nerve for that.

I'm busy.

I attach the pic and send it, then turn my phone over.

He tries calling three more times, and each time I decline. Not until the service ends and I scoot out the side door, avoiding the crowd milling out the front doors, do I check again.

Do you really want to play this game with me?

I definitely know I don't want to play any game with Henry because he will most certainly win and from four thousand miles away, I will most certainly suffer.

I'm not at home. I'm at Sunday church. I took that pic last night while waiting for you.

Absolving yourself of your sins with all the other sinners?

Henry's already made it pretty clear that he's not a fan of the institution of the church.

Yes. Though it may take a lot longer, now that I've met you.

Based on what I heard last night, I think we'd both agree that you've done pretty well on your own.

I grit my teeth against the dig. He said he wouldn't judge me for it, but I'm not entirely sure.

Be home and awake for midnight your time.

Or what?

Abigail…

Will you play fair this time?

I guess you'll just have to find out. See you tonight.

I smile.

"Abigail!"

I stuff my phone in my pocket just as Jenny Shoemaker trots up. "It's so good to see you!"

*It is?* Jenny and I haven't talked since elementary school. She, Veronica Flynn, and Beth Pruitt formed this tight-knit clique freshman year that didn't let anyone else in. Then Beth started flirting heavily with Jed, so I've just stayed away from the lot of them. "How long are you staying for?" She tucks strands of her long blonde hair back behind her ear. She's always been really pretty in this wholesome way, with bright blue eyes and a wide smile. She's wearing this retro-looking red dress with tiny white polka dots and cap sleeves. It's feminine and to the knee, and yet somehow flirty on her.

"As long as it takes for my dad to get back on his feet." A few months, at least.

"Hey, didn't I hear that you were in Alaska, or something like that?" She's playing it coy, but by the twinkle in her eyes, she *knows* I was and I'm guessing she's heard about Henry.

"Yeah. Since May."

"That's *so* cool. I'd love to do something like that."

Jenny was captain of the debate team and the Mathletes club. She dated Donald Munchauser, a skinny guy who has since left to join the seminary. I don't know how well Jenny would fit in there. Probably as well as I did, which was not at all. "How's college?"

"Great! One more year, then teachers college, and I'm done. Can't wait. So, are you and Jed back together?"

I roll my eyes. I knew this would happen. "No. Absolutely not."

"I was wondering! 'Cause I heard you were dating your boss. That Wolf guy."

"He's not my boss anymore."

Her brows spike. "So, you *were* dating him though?" There's definite scepticism in her voice.

Henry didn't tell me I had to keep this secret. He just

didn't want to put a label on it. "We *are* together, yes." That seems safe enough. And, to be honest, I don't want to hide it. I want to scream it from the rooftops.

"So, when are you going to see him again? Is he going to come here?"

"I don't know. He's really busy."

From the look on her face, I don't think she believes me. I'm not at all surprised, but that irritates me. Plus I'm still annoyed that the Reverend didn't mention Henry at all in his thanks. That spiteful streak that used to be nonexistent flares deep within me. "But probably. I mean, he calls me every night." Every night equals one night so far but she doesn't need to know that. "And he flew here with me on his private jet, just to get me here as fast as possible."

"Really?" Jenny's blue eyes widen. "That's kind of romantic."

"It is. And did you hear that he made the best trauma surgeon in the country drop what he was doing to come to Pittsburgh and fix Daddy, all without even telling me? Henry's a big reason why Daddy is alive. He's incredible."

Jenny's hand settles on her chest, over her heart. "Oh my God. That's so sweet!"

"It is." *Now go and tell everyone.*

"When he comes in next, we should all go out."

"Sure." I smile. There is no way I am sharing my time with Henry with Jenny or the other two, which is the only reason they'd want to hang out with me. "I've gotta go. Lots to do on the farm."

"Of course. See you around."

I make my way through the parking lot to my old truck, a thirdhand hand-me-down from my dad that I've been driving since I was seventeen.

And I count down the hours until I'm with Henry again, even if it's just on a screen.

# CHAPTER 3

"Seriously, I don't know what we'd do without you guys," I holler over the roar of the farm truck's engine.

"No worries, Abigail. We'll help wherever we can while Roger's getting back on his feet. I wish we could do more but…." Bart Milner shrugs and gives me an apologetic smile.

"You've got your own farm. We get it." Bart has left his son to run the morning routine with their cows three times a week to come over here and help take care of ours, along with the sheep and the pigs, freeing me up to take care of the million and one other things needing attention. He's been a godsend.

"How's Roger doing, anyway? I heard something about a head injury?"

I fight the urge to roll my eyes. Mama screamed and yelled at the doctors until they put him through the scanning machines again, only to come back with the same conclusion—his head is fine, save for a few scrapes and bumps. "Going stir-crazy, but the doctor will be releasing him any day now. You'll have to come to the welcome home party." It's been three weeks since his accident. I've driven down to Pittsburgh on Saturdays and Wednesdays to spend the morning with him and Mama, playing cards and catching up on farm stuff. I haven't had much time with him, though, what with Mama hovering over him constantly, interrupting our conversation with her two cents' worth, which feels more like a bag full of coins dropped on my head sometimes.

"Send them my best when you see them next."

I give his door a good farewell pat. "I'll see you at Sunday service?"

Bart winks, revving his engine. "You betcha."

The big truck bumps along the driveway, kicking up more dust as it hits the countless potholes. I stare longingly after it, nostalgia stirring inside my stomach. It reminds me of driving down the old road into the Wolf family cottage in Alaska.

It's been almost three weeks since I was in Henry's arms last.

It feels like it's been years.

I miss him so much I want to scream.

Sure, he texts me a few times every day—usually in the morning and then again at night. Mainly to say good morning and good night. He's never been the biggest communicator and especially not by text.

And then there are the nights that we're able to connect and video call, when I haven't fallen asleep from exhaustion and he isn't tied up in meetings, or the time zone isn't working too hard against us.

Those nights are thrilling, but they're also torturous. I can see him, but I can't touch him. Can't be touched by him. I don't want to use my imagination anymore. I want the real thing.

I want him to fly back to New York and stay there until I'm free of Greenbank. It's only a five-hour drive. I will do that drive every week, gladly.

But he hasn't come back yet. At first it was this ski hill he wants to put in, to make Wolf Cove a year-round luxury resort. Then last week he had to fly to Prague because of a major issue with the new Wolf they're opening there. Who knows what's going to happen next week. I'm beginning to think that those few weeks having him in Alaska were an anomaly, never to be repeated.

What if that's the case? What if this is what he means about leading such different lives? What if it has nothing to do with his money and power, and everything to do with simply not ever being around?

Never settling?

Maybe Henry isn't the type of man to ever settle down.

I keep myself busy here, collecting eggs and caring for the animals, cutting the grass, paying the bills and answering calls for grain and hay, tending to the gardens until I fall asleep with my phone in my hand and drool dripping down my chin. Then I get up to do it all over again. It's a big job, trying to keep the farm going.

Still, I live for those messages and calls from Henry.

Sliding my phone from my back pocket, I check for anything new. No response to my "good morning" text yet, though. It's six hours ahead in Prague so I probably won't hear from him again until around four my time. Whatever the crisis is over there, it sounds like it's costing the company a fortune. He's been grouchy over the phone.

And a lot more demanding.

Trying to shrug off my disappointment, I tuck my phone away and wander over to where Jed, Thomas, and Ben—two sixteen-year-olds from our parish who Daddy hired for harvest—stack the bales of hay. Jean's out in the fields with the baler.

"What time is Randy's guy gonna be here?" Jed calls out.

"He said eleven, but Daddy says he's always late." Randy

Sohm owns a fancy horse farm about ten miles up the road and he stocks his barn with hay from us every year. The deal's always the same—if we take care of loading our wagons up, they'll unload on the other end. It's always gone smooth, up until this morning when an axle on one of the wagons busted on the driveway. Now we're stuck moving all the bales to another wagon before we can fix it. Sure, I could call up Randy and tell him it'll be another few days before we can deliver, but Mama said Randy's an old bugger who might turn around and buy from someone else, just out of spite.

Jed pauses to wipe his forearm across his brow, pushing his hair off his forehead. He lets out a low curse, his eyes rolling over the bales still needing to be moved. He's already cast his shirt off in an attempt to cool down, showing off his golden, muscular body.

"So we have to assume he'll be here at eleven. Let's hustle," he mutters to the other guys.

They respond with low grunts. It's hard work what they're doing. Sometimes I don't think we're paying them enough. Well, technically Jed isn't getting paid at all.

Of course Daddy will insist on handing over an envelope stuffed with cash, and Jed'll make a big deal of leaving it on the kitchen table, and Mama will coo and say, "Oh, Abigail! See what an honorable man he is!" and I'll hide my eye roll, because only six months ago I caught him being very dishonorable with another girl.

But, I have to admit… Jed's really stepped up and helped out around here. I couldn't have managed on my own without him. It's definitely helped me put aside my anger for his cheating ways, and that's saying a lot, seeing as he obliterated my heart.

I fish three bottles of cold water from the cooler and hand them out to the guys, reminding them, "I think today's a good day for a swim as soon as this is done." Jed and I used to spend our summers swimming laps around our pond. I haven't so much as stuck a toe in it since being home.

"Great idea, Abigail."

"Uh-huh."

My phone vibrates in my pocket and I don't miss a beat, reaching for it, holding my breath. Only to feel the disappointment when I see that it's not from Henry but from Mama. I taught her how to text so she could send me daily updates on Daddy, or I could ask quick questions that she'd relay to him. As handy as it's been these past three weeks, I'm sure I'm going to regret it once things are back to normal and she has nothing better to do than meddle in my life again.

My dismay vanishes quickly, though. "The doctor's cleared him! Daddy's coming home this afternoon!" I exclaim, feeling my face split open in a huge grin. He should be six feet in the ground, by all rights, but he's coming home! He'll be stuck in a wheelchair for the time being but, with help from Jed's parents and the other church families, we now have a hospital bed in our den for him until he can walk.

Jed drops down from the wagon and before I can stop him, scoops me up into his arms and twirls me around.

"Put me down! You're all sweaty!" Even so, I can't help but laugh.

After two full circles, he finally complies, but not without a mischievous look on his face. "Told you everything would be back to normal soon."

I fight the urge to roll my eyes at him. Three weeks haven't helped break him of this delusion that I'm going to "smarten up" sooner or later and realize that we're "meant to be." In reality, the fact that I haven't seen Henry in three weeks is only encouraging him.

And now he's standing too close. I take two steps back

and then turn to busy myself with fetching another water from the cooler.

He hops back up on the wagon, whistling. "You better call the hens. They'll want as much time as possible to set up."

"Right." The hens. The five ladies from our church who basically run all social events. Roger Mitchell coming home from the hospital after nearly dying is an event they'll want to celebrate. Reverend Enderbey already put a call out for food at the service on Sunday in preparation, and one of the husbands dropped off a bunch of folding tables and chairs. They'll be full of casseroles and homemade burgers by four o'clock.

With a sigh, I pull out my phone. Today is going to be a *long* day.

---

I EMERGE from the refreshing water in time to see Jed go sailing through the air. I can't help but chuckle. He still acts like a ten-year-old every time he's in here, launching himself off the tire swing that hangs from a giant oak tree near the embankment.

The pond sits in the middle of the field, almost halfway between our properties, and is just big enough to tire me out when I swim across. None of us are in a rush to do more than just float today, though. Thomas and Ben have found the floating dock that Jed built when we were sixteen and are sprawled out on its surface, soaking up the sun. Mama wouldn't approve of this paid swim break, but she's not here yet to complain about it. Besides, it's after noon and the boys are done with their farm jobs for the day. They spent the last hour cutting grass and cleaning up around the barn for the party.

Jed swims over to where I'm treading water. "A couple of

us were thinking of trying out Billy Bob's this weekend. You wanna come?"

"*Billy Bob's?* Are you serious?" The roadside bar twenty miles outside of town has been a community nightmare for years. I've never been, but I've heard the stories of "lewd acts" and brawls. Apparently, it's run by a biker and crawling with gang members any given day of the week. According to Mama, anyway. Whether any of that is true or not, I don't know. There was a petition going around town some years back to shut it down because of the loud music and drunkenness. My parents and the Enderbeys signed it, along with the entire congregation.

The Reverend would not approve of his son going, but I'm guessing he's not going to find out about it.

Jed shrugs. "Could be fun."

"You should call up Cammie and take her then."

He rolls his eyes. His fingers slide over my skin to grip either side of my waist. "Don't be like that. It's not like you were completely innocent up in Alaska."

If Jed only knew the kinds of things I was up to in Alaska. That kind of gossip would be hot enough to set wet grass on fire in this town.

I twist my body and stroke away from him, but he follows closely behind.

"Come on, Abigail. I've put my life on hold for you. What else do I need to do to prove to you that I'm sorry?"

"It's *Abbi,* and it's not about you being sorry."

"It's about your boss, isn't it?"

"He's not my boss anymore."

"You haven't seen him since he dropped you off. When are you going to admit to yourself that it's over?"

"We still talk *every* day!"

"Yeah, when it's convenient for him."

"He *owns* Wolf Hotels. He's a busy guy."

"Please. Those rich guys golf and party all day long."

"Not Henry."

"Stop being so gullible. When are you finally going to admit that it can't last between you two? Everyone else around here sees it."

"You have no idea what you're talking about." His words stab at me though, because deep down, I'm afraid they could be true. Is there really any chance of Henry and me lasting? That his interest won't stray elsewhere in the weeks—and maybe months—I'm stuck here, running a farm while Daddy heals. The man's sexual appetite is his only weakness and the occasional video masturbation session isn't going to cut it forever. He has beautiful, sophisticated women throwing themselves at him wherever he goes. And he hasn't actually made any big declaration to me, any ironclad commitments. Just, "we'll see where things go."

But he also starts and ends each day with a message to me. I have to believe that means something, given the man he is, right?

He wouldn't bother if he didn't care.

Right?

"Have fun at Billy Bob's. I don't want to go there. Besides, Mama's gonna need me," I say, changing the subject from me and Henry.

"My mom will be over here, helpin' her. Think about it." Jed swims back for the oak tree, climbing it deftly. Once up, he peers across the field toward our driveway. "Finally! Looks like Randy's guy is here. And only two hours late." He snorts. "Guess it's back to work."

"You boys stay here. I have to get out anyway. They'll be comin' in to set up the food and drinks soon." I climb up the embankment, adjusting my bikini bottoms before I reach for my towel.

"Eyes elsewhere. That's not yours," Jed mutters in warning behind me, his voice unnaturally sharp.

I roll my eyes at his possessiveness. *It's not yours, either.*

It's funny, before Alaska I would have been very aware of the two teenage boys in the lake with us. I'd feel their eyes on my body and I'd be scurrying into the water and out for my towel as fast as possible.

I didn't worry about having their eyes on me today. I wouldn't say I'm entirely confident in my skin—what twenty-one-year-old woman is, I guess—but I don't mind the attention so much. Still, I'd rather have Henry's. He has a way of setting fire to my skin with just a look.

I sigh as I wrap my towel around my body ever so slowly, thinking about how badly I want to leap into his arms.

"I'll be right behind you," Jed calls out, a moment before his body hits the water with a splash.

I pick my way along the path toward the house, both sides lined with knee-high grass. There's a matching cut path on the other side of the pond, leading all the way to the Enderbeys', wide enough to drive with a farm truck. It's been there as long as I can remember, Daddy running his tractor over it once a week to keep the grass nice and short, the way clear for Jed and me to run back and forth almost every day of our childhood.

It's only about a hundred yards to our house, but the sun's heating my shoulders through the thin cotton of my t-shirt by the time I'm halfway there.

I squint at the shiny black pickup truck that sits in our driveway, silently cursing myself for forgetting my sunglasses and my hat. It can't possibly be strong enough to pull the hay wagon. There's no way that's Randy's guy. They know better. So maybe it's someone else looking to buy grain or hay from us. We haven't had a new customer in a while.

I'm running through all the prices in my head when a tall,

dark-haired man in a well-fitted t-shirt and dark-wash jeans steps out of the truck, his muscular body and confident movements impossible to mistake.

My heart skips two beats and then starts pounding against my breastbone.

"Henry!" I shriek, unable to keep any level of composure thanks to my excitement. I take off, running as fast as I can in flip-flops, ignoring the pain in my chest that comes with running in a bikini with crappy support.

He leans back against the side of the truck with his legs crossed at the ankles and his hands tucked into his pockets, and watches me approach with that sexy smirk curling his lip. One he has perfected and should outright trademark.

I may look like a childish idiot, but I don't care, the gravel crunching under my feet as I tear across the driveway and throw myself at his hard body, my arms snaking around his neck to lock in a tight squeeze.

He slips his hands from his pockets to scoop me up with ease, his deep chuckle vibrating throughout my body. "I don't think I've ever had a welcome quite like that," he murmurs, setting me on the ground after a long moment.

I take a moment to catch my breath as I admire his marvelous face, committing his crystal-blue eyes and long dark lashes to a fresh memory. And those lips…. I miss the feel of them on me so much. "What are you doing here? I thought you were in Prague?" I ask through pants.

His gaze drops to my mouth and my thighs clench instantly in anticipation. "I was, but I had to be in New York tonight for a meeting. I figured I'd stop here first. I can't stay too long, though." He leans forward and I close my eyes, waiting eagerly for his kiss. But he pauses. "Why are you all wet?"

"Oh." I giggle. "I was just in the pond."

"Hard at work, I see." He gives me a mock frown but I know he's teasing.

"We've been busting our butts all morning actually. Just took a break to cool off, it's so hot."

"Yeah, I'm missing the Alaska temperatures right now." There's a pause. "Who's *we*?"

"Just my two summer workers. And Jed, of course."

If my arms hadn't been around Henry's neck, I probably wouldn't have noticed the sudden tension that stiffens him. "Fuckface?"

"Yeah. He's been helping around here, a lot. I told you that."

"Right." He frowns. "How often is that, again?"

"He's here every day."

"*Every* day."

"You know I can't do this on my own, Henry."

"Which is why I offered to arrange for help."

"And you know exactly why I couldn't take you up on that." Mama outright refused to accept his offer. It's not for pride, because she's had no trouble accepting help from every last member of our church.

"I've been told that she hasn't stayed at the hotel, either."

"The Enderbeys have a cousin in Pittsburgh she's staying with." In a spare bedroom with no air conditioning that requires Mama—all 370 pounds of her—to climb three flights of stairs every day. Even Jed's dad tried to persuade her to take Henry's offer of a luxury suite at the Wolf, but she won't willingly accept a dime from "the wolf who's preying on her daughter's innocence."

He shakes his head. "Stubborn woman."

"I know. There's nothing I can do. I've tried to reason with her." I can't tell anymore if her pigheadedness is borne of her being hung up on having her daughter married to the Reverend's son, or that she simply wants me within arm's reach until the day she dies, and she won't have that if I'm with a man like Henry.

"They're releasing Daddy today, though. Isn't that great?" I lean against his body, letting my fingers slide over all the hard ridges and contours of his beautiful back, his shoulders, and his arms. I stretch onto my tiptoes, wanting to go back to the part where he kisses me.

Henry's attention is not easily swayed though. "Does he know you're not his anymore?"

I sigh. "Yes. He's trying to convince me otherwise, but I've told him many times."

I skate my lips over his. He finally takes the hint, his hands gripping the sides of my waist, sealing his lips over mine and kissing me with a level of skill that I might consider being concerned with, if I wasn't so head-over-heels infatuated with him.

A tiny moan escapes me and he instantly deepens the kiss, forcing my mouth open wide to make room for his tongue. My hands wander over his chest, molding over his curves. "I've been thinking about this moment for weeks," I whisper against his mouth. My daydreams always end with my hands moving south, into his jeans. If we weren't out in the open, it's exactly what I'd be doing already.

"Phone calls aren't enough, then?"

"Not even close."

One of his hands slips beneath my shorts to push my bikini bottoms aside and grip my ass. I can feel myself growing wet, with how close his fingers are. Just an inch to the left and a curl and he'd be inside me, making me feel as good as only he can, whether it's with his fingers or his tongue or his—

"Randy's guy is on his way, Abigail," Jed suddenly announces behind us, the gravel crunching noisily beneath his feet. I break free with a small huff, spinning around to find him standing there, his shirt hanging freely off one shoulder, his shorts still drenched.

A glower on his brow.

He has no right to be upset. I haven't led him on about there being something between us. He's known about Henry since the day I came home.

Sure enough, a tractor is rumbling up our long, winding driveway. Right behind it, I see the baby-blue Parisienne. That's Peggy Sue's, one of the hens. She reveres it, calling it a classic. I think it's just plain old.

I don't know that I would have even noticed anyone coming up the driveway before Henry had me naked and in the back of his pickup, so I guess I have to thank Jed for that, at the very least. "Thanks, Jed. Um... Jed, this is Henry. Henry... Jed." They never did officially meet at the hospital, Henry hanging back to talk to the chief of staff.

Neither man makes a move to greet the other, Jed glaring at Henry in what I'm guessing is supposed to be an intimidating way, and Henry standing a little taller, his face taking on that intimidating stoniness he has mastered.

I have no idea where this will go, but when I spot our two workers trudging back up the path from the pond, I'm relieved for the interruption. "Okay, then. Henry, would you mind moving your truck over there, next to mine, so we have room for these guys to maneuver." I point toward the green Ford. "Jed, if you could help me get Randy's guy sorted out with this wagon—"

"The boys can do that. I've gotta get the rest of the things set up for your dad's welcome home party, remember? They should be home *real* soon, so...." Jed lets his voice drift and folds his arms over his chest, his gaze shifting to Henry. It's obvious what he's trying to say: that Henry should leave. Mama won't be happy if he's here when they roll in after being by Daddy's side for three weeks.

I groan, because as soon as I saw Henry, I forgot about the party. I'm desperate for some more time with him before he has to leave but I'm not going to get it. His timing couldn't be more terrible.

Henry's warm hand slides over the small of my back and then, hooking his fingers around my waist, he pulls me against him. "What still needs to be done, *Abbi*?" he asks me smoothly, ignoring Jed.

"A ton. All the tables and chairs need to be set up, the coolers filled with ice. We've got a banner and balloons. The guests will start arriving within the hour and *Abigail* and I will be greeting them and getting them settled," Jed answers, not taking the hint, insinuating himself into my life. "It's a lot of work, especially in this heat." Again, it's not hard to read between the lines. Jed's making it clear that he doesn't think Henry has lifted a finger in manual labor—ever.

I purse my lips to keep the smile from escaping, thinking back to the sight of Henry swinging an axe, his muscles straining beautifully. This isn't the time to be thinking of that though, because Jed's making it look like there's more going on between us than there is and that's the last thing I want Henry to believe.

"If you could just please take care of Randy's guy, since that's why you're here," I grumble. *And give me at least a few more minutes alone with Henry before he has to leave.*

Jed's jaw hardens with frustration. "Peggy Sue needs help, too. And the others will be following in the next ten minutes. You better go and get ready before you run out of time. We're already behind as it is." His eyes flash to Henry before settling on me, weighing me down. "My mom asked if you'd be wearing that blue dress that she made for you."

I stifle my groan. Last week, Celeste surprised me with a modest cornflower-blue frock, telling me how happy my parents would be to see me in that on my dad's homecoming.

That it would bring out the color in my hair, now that it's finally—thankfully—back to its normal, natural dull ginger.

They're all doing their best to get their pre-Alaska version of Abigail back—the one who smiles and agrees to everything asked of her, who does things to please others, who never yells or argues. Who's going to marry Jed, have a dozen babies, and then die on this land after a long life of caring for her husband while he keeps the Mitchell legacy going.

I sigh, feeling defeated because, while I'd love to throw the dress in the bottom of my closet and deny them even that small, passive level of control over my life, it would be rude to do that to Celeste. She has never been anything but kind and generous to me. It's not her fault her son cheated on me.

Henry steps between us, his giant body blocking out Jed. "Why don't you show me what needs to get done, then go and get ready."

It sounds like he's offering to help. "When do you have to leave?"

He smirks. "The beauty of being the boss is that people work around my schedule. Have you already forgotten how easy it is to reschedule a meeting? Especially the early morning ones with China." Heat flares in his eyes as he reminds me of the morning he canceled his call and stretched me over his desk. It was the first time I'd ever had a man's mouth on me down there.

But he said this New York meeting was important. "You've already done so much to help us." Especially for a woman who is entirely ungrateful.

"Do you need help?"

"Yes, but—"

"Abigail…." My full name sails from his lips smoothly, even with the warning in his tone. His brow raises in that stern way of his and I get a flash of those first few days when

I was just working for him and unable to read him at all, thinking he was two seconds from firing his idiot assistant.

Now I know it just means not to argue with him, because he's going to get his way no matter what.

My stomach flips. "Okay. Well, we were going to set up in the shade between the two barns because that's the coolest spot."

"Can I talk to you for a minute? Alone?" Jed interrupts. I'd forgotten he was there.

I roll my eyes at Henry. I already know the scolding I'm going to get from Jed.

Henry leans in and plants a slow, but modest, kiss on my lips. "I'll go move my truck and then come back and help you deal."

Deal with setting up or with Jed, I can't be sure which he means, but either way I'm grateful. This side of Henry—where he's willing to jump in and get his hands dirty, so to speak, is bizarre.

And a turn-on.

"Okay," I whisper softly. I catch the mischievous flicker in his eye a moment before his hand slides down over my ass to give it a tight squeeze as he's shifting me away from the driver door.

Jed's waiting some ten feet away, glaring at the shiny new truck—a rental, I assume—as the engine roars to life.

"Randy's guy is ready for you." I gesture at the tractor that's backing up toward the trailer hitch.

But Jed's attention can't be broken. "What's he doing here?" he hisses. I don't miss the accusatory tone in his voice, like I've done something wrong.

"He has a meeting in New York tomorrow morning so he had his pilot stop here on the way to surprise me." I've been raised not to covet money, but I can't help feeling proud when I talk about Henry—of his success and his power. Or maybe it's because he's so different from Jed, who's just a boy by comparison.

"Your parents won't be happy about him being here, and it's really selfish of you not to think about them."

"Them? Or you?"

Jed folds his arms over his chest. "*Everyone*. Especially your mama."

Mama certainly won't be happy. I'm honestly not sure if my dad will be bothered too much. He hasn't said much one way or the other in the times I've seen him. "Mama should be thanking Henry for all he's done for our family, including making sure Daddy lived."

"He didn't really do anything," Jed grumbles like a sullen child.

"You know that's not true." So does the whole town now, thanks to Jenny who talked to Lucy at the feed mill, who talked to, well… everyone.

"Still…. You can't have him here. Not with the congregation coming. That's all they'll talk about for the next few weeks."

"Well, how's that any different from the last six months? I'm used to the whole congregation talking about me by now, thanks to you. Remember?"

Jed struggles to hide the sheepish look. "It's just… this is supposed to be a happy day for all of us. It'd be better if he weren't here. He doesn't even have any respect for you, mauling you like that in public."

I could point out that I was doing just as much mauling, but I don't think that would help.

Jed's resorted to acting like a sulky boy, glaring across the way. "See? He's already causing problems." He throws a hand. "Now Peggy Sue feels like she has to go up and talk to him and you know how she is. We don't have time for chitchat."

I turn to where I sent Henry to park and find him

towering over the tiny, hunched-over woman. Peggy Sue looks older and more frail than her seventy years, her white hair pulled back in a wispy bun, her glasses taking up half her face. She's had terrible eyesight for as long as I can remember, those inch-thick lenses giving her rather eerie bug eyes. But she's the sweetest, most giving person I've ever met.

Also, the nosiest. I'm sure she's already grilling him with questions.

Leaving Jed without another word, I skitter over to where they are in time to hear her ask, "So, you're going to stay for the party, right?"

"Hey, Peggy Sue!" I interrupt. "Thank you so much for dropping everything to come and help us with this."

"Oh, heavens." She waves away my words with a wrinkled hand and a chuckle. "I needed a break from crocheting anyway. My fingers were cramping!" Peggy Sue is the town's newborn baby bootie maker. On any given summer day, you'll find her swinging in her porch rocker out front of the small clapboard bungalow that she shares with her middle-aged son—Darcy, the janitor at the elementary school—her hands busy filling orders for all colors of her famous boots.

She peers up at Henry. "Would you be a doll and empty the trunk? There's some water and pop in there, along with a few casseroles and lots of ice. I had Harvey Laker's little boy load it up for me at the grocery store."

I stifle a laugh. Harvey Laker's "little boy" is now sixteen, six foot two, and at least 250 pounds.

Henry flashes that charming smile I've seen on him when he's wanting to impress media people. Still, I know that it's genuine, and the fact that he's treating this sweet old lady to it makes my heart swell. It means he wants her to like him.

"Of course. Where do you want it all, Abbi?"

I should tell him not to worry, that he'll be drenched in

sweat and I've got two able-bodied boys still on the clock to do it. "In the first barn, along the wall closest to where the tables are."

Abruptly, he sets to work, hauling cases of water from the giant trunk, the muscles in his arms cording beautifully. I can't help but stand there and admire them.

"We're expecting close to a hundred people." Peggy Sue interrupts my appreciative gaze.

"That's a lot!"

"It sure is." She frowns at the road. "The other ladies were right behind me in town. Not sure where they got lost on their way here."

Everyone knows that Peggy Sue has a lead foot, made worse by the fact that she drives a tank for a car. Five years ago she rear-ended Mike Bartol, unable to stop in time on slick roads. Luckily, Mike walked away with nothing more than a sore neck. His car wasn't so lucky.

"Thank you so much for everything you're doing."

"It's nothing. We take care of each other, and your daddy would drop everything to help any one of us. I know it because he's done it before, many times."

I smile because she's right, and there's something so satisfying about that. As much as this small town gets on my nerves, there's comfort here in knowing you have a whole army of people to help you when you need it most.

"Everyone's just so happy he pulled through." Her gaze flickers to Henry, who's already halfway to the barn, his arms loaded. "Your old boss is quite something, isn't he? I'd heard from Edith's daughter that he was a looker but…." She waggles her eyebrows.

Edith's daughter, Mary Jane, who has been "kind" enough to follow the Wolf Hotel twitter account and update Mama on all things Wolf Cove over the summer. She's the one who made sure Mama saw that picture of me the night of the grand opening, in the black cocktail dress, my hair and makeup and boobs done by Katie and Rachel.

I laugh, feeling my cheeks burn. "Yes, he is handsome." Handsome doesn't cut it. Henry is basically a specimen of perfection.

"Awful kind of him to stop by. He said he was on his way through for a business meeting?"

"That's right." What else did Henry tell her? I'm guessing not a lot. He's a smart guy and I've already told him what these people can be like. I know telling Peggy Sue anything will inevitably and swiftly steal the focus from Daddy today. They'll be talking about Henry stopping by as it is. There's no point throwing a jug of gasoline on thirsty flames.

Jed's voice catches my attention. He's hollering at the driver of the tractor, flashing a thumbs-up. I guess they're all ready to go, which is good because the giant hay wagon is blocking a lot of valuable space.

"And how is that one taking this surprise visit?"

I shrug noncommittally.

The old woman's face twists up. "Good. Let that boy squirm with jealousy. He deserves every second of it. Heavens, if I had a man like that come callin' on me...." She fans herself with her purse, blatantly staring at Henry, who's on his way back now, his phone pressed to his ear.

*Oh my God.* Even the elderly aren't immune to him.

"I met Bradley when I was about your age. I was head over heels right away. We couldn't keep our hands off each other. My parents didn't approve of him none though. Said he wasn't marrying material and would only hurt me in the end. They pushed and pushed for me to marry their friend's son, this chubby man with bad teeth from three streets down, who I wasn't in the least attracted to. He worked at a cheese factory and smelled of sour milk." She cringes and it makes me laugh.

"So, did they ever accept Bradley?"

She blinks several times, as if processing my question. "Oh, I didn't end up marrying Bradley. I married the cheese man. Marvin. We were together forty-two years before he passed."

"Oh." Not the answer I expected. "What happened with Bradley?" Is this one of those, "it's not all about physical attraction" messages, where she's secretly trying to convince me that, in the end, Jed's the better choice?

She shrugs. "I was stupid. I took the safe route. Don't get me wrong, Marvin turned out to be a good husband, God rest his soul. But Bradley.... Not a day goes by that I don't wonder what my life would have been like had I married him." She clucks. "I respect your mama, but good for you for getting on with your life. I hope that man is teaching you lots. I'll bet he knows a thing or two."

I'm left standing there with my mouth hanging open as the old woman shuffles to her trunk.

# CHAPTER 4

I tug at the collar of my dress. It's too hot to be wearing something like this, even if it *is* cotton. I can't even unfasten the top button, given the style. It would make me look sloppy.

Celeste's broad smile when I came out of the house in it was enough to convince me I'd made the right call. Still, I intentionally skipped the nylons. There's no way I'm wearing those on a day like today.

Henry approaches me now, his brow glistening with sweat from working in the heat. "You look...." His words fade with a twist of his lips.

"Like I could star on *Little House on the Prairie*?" I don't bother hiding the dismay in my voice.

"Something like that." His eyes flicker down my front, where a line of white buttons runs from my neck to my knees.

"She loves buttons."

"I can see that."

"They make it easy to get in and out of the dress."

His blue eyes flare with heat. "I'll have to test that theory out later and let you know."

Flutters stir in my stomach. "I thought you had to leave? Don't you have a meeting tonight?"

"Do you want me to leave, Abbi?"

"No." I emphasize that with a head shake. I don't ever want him to leave.

He takes a step closer. A tiny smirk curls his lips. "The lovely church ladies have begged me to stay. They've sworn up and down that Bernadette Mitchell will want to thank me personally for my part."

"Oh, I'm sure she will." I giggle, my gaze flickering behind us to where Peggy Sue, Edith, and three other women cluster together around a table like, well, clucking hens. Mama would never dare say anything disparaging about Henry to anyone but me. She's smart enough to know how ungrateful that'd make her look and she's all about image.

Jed catches my eye. He's standing next to Celeste, whose wide smile from only moments ago has been replaced with a frown of worry as she watches Henry and me. As lovely as Celeste is, she's as delusional as the Reverend and Mama if she thinks I'd ever get back together with her son.

"They're here!" someone calls out, and I spot the Reverend's green Oldsmobile rolling up the driveway.

"I guess it's too late now, either way," Henry murmurs, stepping back to watch with interest as the crowd of people begin politely cheering.

I reach over to snag his finger within mine, giving it a squeeze. "I'm so glad you're here."

I can feel his eyes on me as I watch the car come to a stop and Reverend Enderbey pop out with a big grin.

Someone runs for Mama's door to open it for her, holding their hand out to help her heave her body out. I was hoping that she'd lose a bit of weight over these past three weeks, stuck in the hospital next to my dad instead of near a kitchen, her focus on him rather than food. I know that's an awful thing to wish for, but it's borne from worry for her health rather than anything else. But if she has lost weight, it's unnoticeable. At least, from here and in her sunny yellow tent dress.

I take a deep breath. How is she going to deal with Henry being here?

"You should probably go over there," he murmurs, ushering me forward with a gentle push against the small of my back.

"I know. I'm just...." It's stupid, but I'm afraid. I want her to accept Henry and love him because, despite how difficult she is, she's still my Mama. It hurts that she wouldn't want me to be happy, and Henry is what makes me happy.

"Go on. I'll wait here." His gaze drifts over the bumper and, more specifically, the duct tape that's holding it in place. I can't imagine what he thinks about that.

I cut my way through the crowd with polite smiles and soft excuse mes. At some point along the way, Jed has intercepted my path and is now beside me. I try to add space between us but each time, he shifts with me, closing the distance, until by the time we reach the car, we may as well be arm in arm. He even ran home to change into a pair of khakis and a blue button-down plaid. Oddly, the same shade of blue as my dress.

I spear him with a glare but quickly wipe it off as some of the church men help Daddy out of the backseat and into his wheel chair. Unlike Mama, he's definitely lost weight. He also looks like he's aged by five years, his skin pale and starting to sag at his jowls.

I gingerly wrap my arms around him in a hug, afraid to squeeze too tight.

"I thought you were running the farm and here you are, throwing parties." He chuckles softly—his voice, his laugh, his demeanor, all of it has always been gentle—and it instantly brings tears to my eyes.

"Just one big one for you, Daddy. Welcome home."

Jed moves to grab the handles of his wheelchair and ease it over the gravel toward the grass. "We've been bustin' our butts but everything's in good working order. Abigail makes a pretty darn good farmer."

Daddy chuckles again, his smile wide as he greets all the people milling around with a small wave. "Oh, I know she does."

Mama is making her way behind him, beads of sweat already running down the side of her cheeks.

"I'll get you a cold water, Mama."

"That'd be lovely. It was a long drive back from the city with all that traffic. God bless livin' in the country." She fans herself with a magazine and smiles as Peggy Sue and Edith meander over. Where Peggy Sue is old, tiny, and sweet, Edith is in her early forties, big-boned, and as opinionated as Mama; at times, bordering on salty.

"Didn't your daughter do an absolutely wonderful job?" Edith preens, waving her thick arm toward where the tables and streamers are set up. We even strung up some Christmas lights from one barn to the other. It'll make a nice canopy once the sun goes down.

"I had a lot of help from everyone," I counter. I can't take credit; everyone chipped in.

"Yes, that man of hers has been helping all afternoon without a single complaint," Peggy Sue adds.

Mama beams. "Yes, I'm so thankful to have our Jedediah in our lives." She only uses his full name when she's exceptionally proud of him.

A mischievous twinkle glints in the old woman's eyes. "Oh, I was talking about that handsome hotel owner over there."

I'll give Mama one thing—she can school her expression with the best of them, and it's obvious that Peggy Sue is fishing for a reaction. "Oh? Is he here?" Her voice has risen at least two octaves in a display of pleasant surprise.

As if Celeste didn't phone and warn her ahead of time.

"Yes, just over there." Edith uses the excuse to look over at Henry, who is surrounded by ladies, all offering something—drinks, plates of food.

Themselves, if they could figure out a way to do it, I'm sure. They're all watching him, some stealing glances, others more blatant in their admiration. I've heard a few asking the standard nosy but harmless questions: *Where do you live? How long will you be here?* I've heard others offer remarks. *I've never stayed at a Wolf before.*

I've caught many giggling in quiet circles, their excited voices tapering off when they see me coming, their eyes rolling over me in various shades of curiosity, envy, and a few in outright jealousy.

"Well, isn't that lovely that he could surprise us with a visit."

"Yes, you'll have to go over and say hello. He really is a lovely man."

Peggy Sue's as bad as a little boy with a stick at a hornet's nest. I have to smother my amusement. Henry's been called a lot of things.

Rich, smart, beautiful, driven....

Arrogant, demanding, condescending....

"Lovely" is a new one.

Mama makes a throaty sound of agreement. "I will certainly do that. Abigail, can I speak with you for a moment?" Her voice is still light and airy.

But I hear the anger behind it.

I sigh. "Of course." Daddy is already in the throng, heading toward the shaded area with tables where Steven

Meyers strums along on his guitar, playing Daddy's favorite Christian songs. He won't notice us missing for a bit.

I follow Mama off to the side. She does a quick glance around to make sure she's not within earshot before that kind tone of hers vanishes. "What on earth is he doing on our farm, Abigail Margaret Mitchell?"

"He surprised me on his way to New York. He had no idea we'd be having this party today." It doesn't matter what I say, really.

"I told you I don't approve of him. Whatever you two did up there in the woods, this isn't Alaska. This is my home, and I won't be disrespected under my own roof."

I open my mouth to argue with her but promptly clamp it shut at her hiss of warning. She plasters on a fake smile as one of the hens passes by on their way to the house, no doubt to pull another casserole out of the oven.

It gives me a moment to think rather than simply blurt out the first thing that comes to my mind: that she's being controlling and unfair and above all else, ridiculous. In those brief moments, I'm able to calm and compose myself somewhat.

"Mama, you are not being disrespected in any way. Henry arrived after lunch and has been busy all afternoon, helping with Daddy's party. He's leaving tonight to go to New York and I, along with all the ladies from the church, asked him to stay and celebrate Daddy coming home."

"Yes, I'll bet they did." She snorts. "Well, don't be thinking he's going to stay here."

"Like I said, he's leaving for New York tonight. He was supposed to be gone already but he rearranged his schedule so he could *help.*"

"And what about poor Jed? You're prancing around here with *that man*. You're hurting him. Maybe enough to turn him away. And then when *he* has gotten his fill of you, it'll be too late to salvage things. Then what will you do, huh?"

I'm not good enough for Henry. That's what she's saying, what they're all saying. I don't know if she realizes how hurtful her words are. She clearly believes she's entitled to say whatever she wants to me because she's my mother.

Now's not the time to address that though. I take a deep breath. "I'm going over there to enjoy the party and the fact that Daddy is home. In large part due to Henry. If you're the Christian that you swear you are, you'll make your way over and thank Henry for all that he's done, because it's the right thing to do regardless of how you feel about him." With that, I move away from her, trying not to stalk because Lord knows, people are watching.

Henry's been circled by the trifecta—Jenny, Beth, and Veronica. I haven't seen them at one of these church functions in years. I'm guessing their presence here now has a lot to do with Jenny's mom, who was helping out with the setup, mentioning that "Abigail's rich boyfriend is here."

"So, are you looking to replace Abigail now that she's stuck here on the farm? Because I'm an excellent executive assistant," Beth says, toying with her wavy blonde hair between her fingers as she peers up at Henry through wide, blue eyes.

"You already *have* a job at John Deere," Veronica mentions next to her. "I thought you loved it."

The look Beth shoots Veronica is nothing short of scathing. "I'm looking to broaden my horizons." The way she bats her eyelashes at Henry there's no doubt what horizons she's looking to broaden. That doesn't surprise me. Of the three of them, Beth is the only one who earned any sort of reputation in high school, after people saw her giving Tommy Chelton a hand job at a party, right out in the open.

A spike of jealousy flares at how openly they're hitting on him, even with me standing right here.

"Abigail!" Jenny throws her arms around my neck, squeezing me like we're best friends. "You remember Beth and Veronica, right?"

"Yes." I offer them polite smiles.

"We were just talking to Henry about his hotels. It'd be so exciting to work somewhere like Alaska."

"Or anywhere, far away from here," Veronica adds. Of the three, she has the most unglamorous future ahead of her, working as the receptionist in her father's mechanic shop. I don't think she ever did well enough in school to go to college, had she wanted to.

"You should apply then. Abigail can tell you how exciting her summer was." There's that playful twinkle in Henry's eye. He's thinking of dirty things, as usual.

I fight my blush and worm my way past them to stand next to him. What I'd like to do is wrap my arms around him in a very bold statement, but out of respect for my parents, I keep my fists balled at my sides and instead ask, "Can I get you anything? The first batch of corn should be ready."

"If you'll excuse us, ladies." He offers them a polite smile before weaving around, unable to avoid bumping into Beth's chest—because she thrusts it out at him—on his way past. "Why did I expect these girls to be shy and reserved," he mutters, low enough for only me to hear as we head toward the shaded area.

"Maybe because I'm shy and reserved?"

"Right. Well, except when you're drunk and hitting on strangers."

I giggle. I'm able to laugh at myself about that horrendous first night now, when I threw myself at him, not knowing who he was.

He glances back at them. "I'd stay away from them if I

were you. They'll be more trouble than your roommates ever were."

"Who, Katie and Rachel?" I can't help but laugh at the thought that they could ever rival those two. "Yeah, whatever."

Daddy is up ahead, talking to Bart. I'm sure he's thanking him for all his help. Jed hasn't left his side, pushing him around like the saintly future son-in-law he's trying to be.

"I'd like to introduce you to my father. He wants to meet you."

"Okay." Henry takes a step toward them.

But I don't follow. "It's just.... He *is* very thankful to you. Please know that. But I don't know how he's feeling about everything *else*." At least Mama's predictable. But what is Daddy going to say?

Henry slides his hand over the small of my back. I want to beg him to keep it there for the rest of the day. "It's fine. I can handle it."

But *I* can't. I desperately want my dad to like Henry. So desperately. My mother's a lost cause, but....

Daddy turns to see us standing there, some twenty feet away. He says something to Jed and points in our direction. By the sour turn of Jed's face, I'm guessing Daddy's asked him to push him over to me.

"I guess we're about to find out," I whisper, nerves churning in my stomach as I move to meet them. Not the fun, flirty kind. The ones laced with a heavy dose of anxiety.

"Don't walk too fast," Henry murmurs beside me.

"But it's hard to push those wheels on the grass."

"Exactly."

I scold Henry with a glare but it's a weak one, softened by my own throaty giggle. "Stop being bad."

"I'm just getting started."

We meet Daddy and Jed halfway, Daddy's eyes flickering between Henry and me, finally settling on him.

"Hello, Mr. Mitchell," Henry offers in a smooth voice, not the least bit nervous. God, I wish I had nerves like he does.

Daddy smiles. "Call me Roger. I'd get up but…." He gestures at his wheelchair.

Henry matches his easy smile with one of his own. "You'll be up again in no time."

"Thanks to you, from what I hear." My dad's face smoothes over with seriousness. "I'm glad you're here today. I didn't have the chance to thank you for all that you did—in getting my daughter back here quickly and in bringing Dr. Eisenhower in. From what all the nurses tell me, I might not be in such good shape had it not been for him."

A tiny bubble of relief bursts in me. Daddy's a man of few words but they're always genuine.

Henry answers with a nod. "It's the least I could do, what with you raising such an incredible woman." He turns to look at me and the veil usually over his eyes is lifted momentarily, showing me a brief glimpse of emotion. The kind that buckles my knees and makes my heart start racing and aching. The kind that makes me have to fight the urge to reach out and touch him. "I can't thank you enough for that."

*Oh my God.*

Everyone's watching.

My cheeks burst with heat. If there were any questions around us being together, I'd say they're extinguished now.

"Enjoy the food. There is more than enough. If you wouldn't mind, I'd like to have a moment alone with my daughter. I feel like I haven't had one in months."

Henry smiles. "I think I hear the corn calling. I'll grab you one, too," he says to me and then briskly moves away.

Daddy turns to look at Jed. "I think the corn's calling to you, too."

A sulky Jed turns and marches away, leaving us together.

"If you're going to tell me that I can't be with—"

"Hush up, now. We don't have much time before your mother hunts us down." As if to emphasize his point, he glances over his shoulder to where she's chatting with someone. Even now, I can see her trying to make her way here. "She's probably over there, telling them about this supposed head injury of mine."

"She probably is."

"Nothin's wrong with my head. In fact, I'm seeing clearer than I ever have. That's what happens when you face death." Daddy's gaze shifts to Henry before moving back to me. "He's a handsome fella."

I grin. "Yes, he is."

"And rich, too. I may not know fashion but those expensive leather shoes are gonna need a good cleaning after walkin' around here."

I giggle. "Yes, probably." He probably has ten more in his closet at home.

"I suppose Jed can't hold a candle to him."

"For so many reasons... no."

He nods, more to himself. "I can see he makes you happy."

"*Very* happy. I know he may not be what you and Mama want, but—"

"I've been doing a lot of thinking since the accident. I know your Mama keeps pushing Jed on you, even after how badly he hurt you." He frowns. "It's not right. Of course we'd love it if you found yourself someone who'd want to run this place, and I gather he ain't it...."

The thought of Henry in coveralls behind the wheel of a tractor flashes through my head.

Nope. He ain't it.

"You should be with whoever you want, and if this billionaire guy treats you well, then... so be it."

"What about Jed?"

"You never would have gone to Alaska had Jed appreciated what he had in the first place."

"Thank you, Daddy. You don't understand what that means to me. Do you think Mama will come around?"

He shrugs, then winces with pain, as if the simple movement hurt. "Don't be expecting her blessin' anytime soon, or ever. But you've got mine. Though that needs to be your and my little secret until my legs work and I can get the hell away from her from time to time. The woman will drive me to drink soon enough." He adds that last part more under his breath, but I hear it loud and clear.

"Yes, I can sympathize." What would I do if I were wheelchair bound and had her hovering over me all day, nattering on and on?

A high-pitched squeal from the church's karaoke machine tells me someone's about to use the microphone. Reverend Enderbey it would seem. Mama, Jed, and Celeste stand on either side of him, Mama with the kind of wide grin on her face that I'd expect the day I hold up a sonogram of her grandbaby.

"Everyone! Hey, everyone!" Reverend Enderbey holds a hand up to get the crowd's attention. He has an easy way about him, and people are used to shushing and listening. "We just wanted to thank you all for coming on such short notice to welcome Roger home from the hospital. Three weeks ago, we almost lost him, but the good Lord prevailed and there he is, put back together and just itching to get back to the farm."

A round of applause goes up and Daddy waves them off with a smile. "I think Abigail and Jed have a new appreciation for all the work you do, Roger. The two of them have been run ragged every single day." As if on cue, Reverend Enderbey passes the microphone to Jed.

"I have been passin' out before my head hits the pillow every single day!" Jed admits with a playful grin, but then it slips off, replaced by a somber mask. "It wasn't even a question that I would quit my job and be here for Abigail and the Mitchells, because they're my family. I'll always be here for them." He nods toward me. "Which is why I've also deferred my last year of college to stay here with you to run this farm. Nothing's more important to me."

Talk about a subtle dig at Henry, who'll be getting on a plane after this to go and run his corporation. I doubt anyone else has picked up on it. Has Henry?

I glance over to see him watching Jed, an unreadable look in his eyes. But that tiny smirk on his lips.... He's smiling. Why?

A round of cheers go up and Jed grins at me. He loves this kind of attention. It's just the kind of pat on the back he's fishing for.

I *do* appreciate the hand around the farm. But oh God, that means he's going to be here all day, every day, thinking he can slowly whittle away my refusal to take him back. He saw me with Henry. He saw how happy I am. Is he completely blind or just clueless?

Or does he see something so obvious that I don't?

Reverend Enderbey takes the microphone back. "Okay, everybody chow down and have fun!"

I heave a sigh.

"That's not a happy sound," my daddy murmurs, low enough for only me to hear.

I force a smile. Even so, it's tight. "It'll be great to have the help. I guess."

"Well, don't expect that boy to give up anytime soon. He's an idiot for what he did, and an even bigger idiot for not seeing that he has no hope as long as that one's in the picture."

"Did you hear that, Abigail?" Mama hollers, her girth shifting with each step as she marches for us. "Jed is putting his whole life on hold for us. That's what a good family man does. He stays put when people need him."

*He does not get on his private jet and fly all over the place, and send workers to take care of things* is what she doesn't say but means.

Daddy and I exchange a glance.

Her eyes narrow with suspicion. "What were you two jabbering on about?"

"Corn," Daddy says, at the same time I say "Hay."

# CHAPTER 5

I settle onto a bale of hay, the rough edges pricking me through the cotton of this dress. "Those are the original beams from a hundred years ago. My great-granddad told me how he watched them haul those up by pulleys when he was just five years old."

As much as I want to throw myself at Henry before he leaves, I guess it's not in the cards. Not unless we leave to go somewhere in his truck, and I can't do that while people are still cleaning up from the party. So, I decided to give him a tour of the farm.

I wasn't sure how interested he'd be, but if there's one thing I'm learning about Henry, it's that he loves architecture.

Henry inhales the everlasting scent of hay, his gaze drifting over the rafters, some fifty feet above us. He looks so out of place in here, the original barn that we now use to store equipment, with his expensive tan dress shoes on the dirt floor, bits of straw scattered here and there. "You need a new roof."

The three gaping holes above us would agree.

"It's really taken a beating the last ten years or so. We had a big storm whip through the valley. Destroyed a lot of crops and buildings. Luckily this was the only major damage we got."

He wanders over to the small workshop, a curious frown on his face. "What's all this stuff?"

"Lye and glycerin, molds… coconut oil. All the stuff I need to make my soaps. Remember that herb garden I walked you through? It's a bit sparse since I haven't been here for it this year, but that's where I grow everything." All that's there now are some lavender and sage bushes, and perennial mints.

He picks up the sheet of labels I printed off last week on our home computer.

"I was thinking of hiring someone to design something a little more professional." I designed those myself with Word Clip Art, something that I'm sure is pretty obvious at first glance.

"What is it you make again? Soaps and…."

"Essential oils, moisturizers…. It's something to keep me busy."

"How long have you been doing this for?"

"A few years. It's just a hobby, but it's mine. I've never made much. It was enough to pay for my flight to Alaska, though."

"It's important to have something that's yours." He adds more softly, "That's what Wolf Cove is to me."

"I love it when people tell me how good their skin feels after using something I've made. I know that probably sounds dumb." Why am I so embarrassed to talk about my little business with him? I guess maybe because running a soap and essential oils production out of a small room in my daddy's barn feels so silly next to his luxury hotel chain.

He looks thoughtfully at the label for another long

moment, his expression unreadable, before setting it back on the table. "You've been busy."

"Definitely trying to keep that way while I'm stuck here." Now that my parents are home, I'm sure Mama will be running me ragged with all kinds of extra errands. And my late-night video calls with Henry… those are basically over.

Will he start looking to satisfy his needs with someone else?

His blue eyes settle on me. "So, what are you going to do with this place when your dad's too old to run it?"

Asked seven months ago, I would have said that I was going to take over. That was the plan all along—marry Jed and run this farm.

Ask me that question now and…. "I don't know. I guess it depends."

"On what?"

*On where you are,* I want to say, but I'm afraid. He's all "let's see where this goes" and I'm over here, all "I'm madly in love with you and want to spend the rest of my life with you." I don't want to scare him away by letting him know how hard and fast I've fallen. How deeply committed I am.

"I'll stick around until Daddy's back on his feet," I say instead.

"Why? Fuckface seems to want to take care of things."

I roll my eyes. "That was a surprise all right, but my family needs the help so I can't say too much."

"You know why he's doing it, right?"

"Yeah. He thinks I'm not good enough to keep you interested. You'll get bored of me and move on soon, and he'll be here to pick up the pieces. Mama thinks that, too." *Are they right about that first part*? Am I too head over heels in love to see any different?

Henry's brow quirks as if he can read my mind, but he doesn't say anything.

"What?"

"Don't start getting insecure on me. You have nothing to be worried about."

He says it so smoothly, so matter-of-factly.... I bite my bottom lip, fighting to keep the nervous smile from escaping.

"What about school?"

"I've deferred until at least January. Next September, if I have to."

"So you're committed to here and Chicago for the next two years then, basically."

"Basically." *Is that too long for you to wait, Henry?* "I could always work at Wolf Cove again, next year."

He chuckles but it's not humorous. "With the outdoor crew? Hell, no. Not a chance." He twists his lips. "Forgot to mention earlier, there was an error in accounting. You'll be getting a check deposited shortly."

I've learned that Henry loves to change topics abruptly. I've gotten used to it. "Really?" I was already netting a lot of money—more than what I could earn at any job around here.

He shrugs casually. "I don't know what happened, but it sounds minor. You'd have to ask Belinda. She manages all of that."

Right. I smile at the mention of the Wolf Cove general manager, a cougar who has slept with Henry and had it out for me for a while. She actually wasn't so bad in the end. We shared a common hatred—Henry's brother, Scott. "How is Belinda doing?"

"Ready to come back to civilization."

"Funny, I would do anything to leave it." Though Belinda would never call Greenbank, Pennsylvania, "civilization." I pause. "And everything else at Wolf Cove? Sounds like it's going well from what I've heard." Ronan and Connor still text me occasionally, but those messages are growing very few and far between.

"Your fuck boys found a new plaything, so they seem to be entertained for now," he answers with an edge to his voice, as if able to read my mind.

I avert my gaze to my feet where I still have hints of red polish left. I'm in bad need of a pedicure, something I didn't even think about pre-Alaska. I blame Katie for that.

"What's wrong? Does hearing that they're with someone else bother you?"

"No! Of course not!" Just as quickly, I meet his gaze. "I wish I could erase what happened."

He strolls slowly toward me, his scrutiny of the barn now shifted fully to me. To my face, and then lower, over the buttons of my dress that run from neck to knee. The dress does very little for my figure, though Celeste did put in darts at the chest to give it at least a bit of shape. "Why? Because you didn't enjoy it?"

I open my mouth to say "yes," but falter because that would be a lie. I *did* enjoy it. "Because I don't want you to be mad at me."

"I let you go. I have no right to be mad at you for what happened."

"So it doesn't bother you?"

"That you were with someone else? I fucking hate it. Every time I think about it, it's like a punch to my gut." He heaves a sigh, reaching up to run his finger along the collar of my dress. "But I'm not angry with you. I'm angry with myself for ever allowing things to go the way they did. Had I been completely open with you, had I put you before myself and Wolf Hotels, we could have avoided it all."

His fingers leave my dress to wipe the tear that slipped from my eye. "I'll try not to bring it up again. Okay?"

My head bobs up and down. I slide off the bale of hay and reach for him, needing to feel his mouth on mine, his body against mine. I press myself against him and rope my arms around his neck, pulling him into my mouth, trying to convey how badly I want him, how much I feel, with each graze of my lip, with each stroke of my tongue.

"You can't start this now, Abbi," he growls between kisses, his arms tightening around me, pulling me closer to him. I feel him growing hard against me.

"Why not?" It comes out in a painful moan.

"Because I have to go if I want to get to New York tonight, and we both know your mother would not be okay with this happening under her roof. Neither would your father. I can't disrespect them like that."

"It's the barn, not the house," I counter with a pout. He's right.

And yet I can't just let him go. I've been watching him all day long, sneaking in touches wherever I can, thinking about kissing him but unable to, imagining him undressed in front of me, remembering what it looks like when he strokes himself for me at night.

I'm completely wound up and no amount of touching myself is going to satisfy me.

Plus, who knows when I'll see him again!

"Hold on a second." I pry myself away from him and dart over to the open doors. It looks like the last of the revelers have left. All the cars are gone, even the Enderbeys'. I can see Mama moving about in the kitchen. No doubt Daddy's in his bed already, exhausted from the day.

My stomach flutters with excitement. "Follow me." I smile at him as I head to the other side, the one that faces the open fields. The sun's just dipping below the horizon, leaving streaks of hazy pink and purple, promising another hot day tomorrow.

"What's out here?" he asks, eyeing the stack of hay that's sitting just outside the door. It's a nice place to sit and rest after a long day.

"No roof." I smile as reach up to unfasten the top button of my dress.

He smirks. "Sex by semantics?"

"It's the only way." I drop my voice to a soft lull. "And I need you."

The humor vanishes from his face in an instant. "Are you sure? Out here?"

"Everyone's gone and Mama's not going to walk all the way out here to check up on us. Not if it means leaving Daddy alone."

I unfasten another button, the one that holds the dress together between my breasts.

Even in the dim light I can make out the heat flaring in his gaze as it rakes over my soft pink bra. "I almost forgot how beautiful your body was, hidden under that ugly thing."

I giggle. "I wish Celeste would stop making me dresses. I look like a ten-year-old girl."

Henry strolls forward with even strides, his hands sliding inside my dress, pushing either side open to uncover my bra. His fingers settle on the outer curve of my breasts, his thumbs stroking the swell back and forth, almost soothingly. "No, you look like a woman to me." With a heavy sigh, he grips either side of the dress and yanks the skirt apart. Buttons pop and scatter all over the ground.

My mouth drops open in shock.

"Just making sure you don't wear this one again." He smirks, pushing either side off my shoulders until the material slides from my arms. He tosses it onto the makeshift hay bench, leaving me in nothing but my bra and panties. Taking several steps back, his eyes travel from my breasts down over my abs and farther, to where my legs are parted, sliding up my thighs to the crotch of my cotton panties. I feel every stroke of his gaze as readily as if it were his fingertips.

"Take off the rest," he demands in that cool, commanding way he has.

Flutters churn in my stomach as I hesitate. I was thinking he'd hike up my skirt. I didn't expect to be completely naked. I should have known better.

"You started this." He folds his arms over his chest, waiting expectantly. "I don't have long. My plane won't be able to take off past a certain time."

It's been three weeks since I've felt him inside me. Three weeks. It could be three more weeks until I see him again.

Holding my breath, I reach back and unfasten my bra. My breasts tumble out, heavy and swollen, my nipples already pebbled with anticipation.

His eyes settle on them immediately, his jaw tensing. He says nothing though and I know he's still waiting.

Setting my bra beside me, I push the sides of my panties from my hips, letting the material fall. I shake my flip-flops off as I slip my feet through the legs.

And now I'm standing stark naked in front of Henry in the great outdoors.

I can just make out the hard ridge of his erection in his pants, so I know he's enjoying this, but he simply stares at me —my breasts, my stomach, the bareness between my legs— for the longest moment, searing my skin. He still fills me with an odd mix of nervousness, exhilaration, and borderline terror.

I fight the urge to cross my arms or legs.

Finally, Henry makes a move, reaching back to peel his t-shirt over his head. "Sit down," he orders, tossing his shirt to the side. I can't help the gasp as I take in his upper body again, so hard and perfectly sculpted. He's religious with his gym regimen and besides the odd Scotch, I never see him consuming anything harmful or of poor quality.

Gingerly, I climb back onto the bale of hay and sit on the

dress Jed's mom made for me, conveniently now serving as a barrier between my naked skin and the scratchy straw.

Henry strolls to me, unfastening his belt and buckle, letting his jeans pop open. The thick, hard ridge of his cock shows through his boxer briefs. I reach for it but he blocks my hands with a smile. And then he pushes my thighs up and so far apart that I'm forced onto my back.

He drops to his knees, settling himself at eye level in front of my wide-open legs.

"Fuck, I've missed this."

Right now I'm wishing I had Katie around to keep me smooth. I've had to resort to shaving because it's not like I can go anywhere in town to get a Brazilian. I don't even know if anyone does them in Greenbank. Discretion or not, I'm afraid somehow Mama would find out and that conversation would be unbearable.

I gasp as Henry takes one long swipe along my slit, the tip of his tongue just skating over my clit.

"Watch," he demands. I struggle to lift my head and meet his eyes, letting a slight whimper out at his intensity, my gaze darting around us. No one can see this, I remind myself.

He seals his mouth over me and I feel his tongue pushing inside with force, making his way deep in me. "Oh my God!" I gasp out, letting my head fall back until I'm staring at the dimming blue sky, his arms hooked around my thighs, holding me still as his mouth works away relentlessly, the buildup coming so fast.

Soon enough, I don't care that I'm out here on a bale of hay, naked and out in the open. All I want to do is come.

Suddenly his tongue disappears. I groan my displeasure and he chuckles, grabbing hold of my hands to pull me up off the bale. "Turn around," he orders, even though his strong hands have already fastened around my slender hips and spun me around. His hand slides up my spine to the middle of my back and then he pushes. His way of telling me he wants me to bend over.

I can hear the rustle of his pants as he pushes them down and pulls himself out. I want to see him—all of him— but he's too fast, his urgent hands finding the insides of my thighs and forcing them farther apart.

I gasp as he rubs the smooth, round head of his cock against my slit once, and then he's pushing in with a single thrust.

I cry out.

"Too much?" There's a hint of humor in his voice but he pauses to let me get used to him.

"You're always too much for me," I tease, even as I'm pushing back against him.

With a sigh, he slips one hand around my waist and between my legs, to rub my clit with slow precision. His fingers slide all over me, I'm so wet. "You don't know how many times I've thought about this these past few weeks." His hips start moving, slowly and methodically.

"Faster," I whisper.

"So you can come too soon? I don't think so." He keeps his leisurely pace. It's both heaven and hell. It can't be just for me, either. If he hasn't had sex since he saw me, then that's three weeks of hand jobs for a man with his appetite.

*Of course* he hasn't had sex since he last saw me. *Get a grip, Abbi!*

A sudden hard thrust makes me yelp.

"Where's your head at?"

"Nowhere." I let my voice fade as he keeps pumping in and out of me.

His hand leaves my clit to slide up and grab hold of my left breast, gripping it to just short of the point of pain. "Knees up."

I do as asked, kneeling on the bale, my ass in the air.

Henry pushes my legs as far apart as they can go, until I'm resting on my elbows, my forehead down on the bale to balance myself, and I feel like I'm about to split open. But Henry, the expert he is, makes me forget the strain quickly, his thrusts growing hard and faster, until I'm fisting the material of my ruined dress in my fingers and trying not to scream. If not for the light breeze, I'd be afraid that our sounds would carry all the way to the house. As it is, all I can hear is his thighs slapping against my ass and the slurping sound of him plunging into my wet core.

"You're dripping," he murmurs between pants.

"I've missed you." And if he keeps up with this pace, I'm going to come very soon.

He slows for just a moment—and I curse myself for acknowledging that because he seems to know what I'm thinking—before speeding up, his hand reaching around to my clit. He's pinching it this time. Gently, but enough to make me hiss because it's already so sensitive.

"Yeah? How much?"

"So much."

"Have you thought of me?"

"Every day and every night."

"And? What do you do at night?"

He wants details. Henry loves dirty details. "Touch myself."

"Until you come?"

"Always. You make me come every single night."

His pace is punishing now. I'm sure my knees will be scratched up from the straw tomorrow, even through the cotton. "Only me?"

"Only you. It'll only ever be you, Henry. I—" I bite down on my tongue to keep from blurting out what I really want to say.

*I am so in love with you.*

Suddenly, he's pulling out and flipping me over onto my back and gripping my thighs tight, lifting my hips clear off the hay. And he's so deep. So impossibly deep, it's borderline painful.

Now I can see all of him—his blue eyes shifting between my face, my bouncing breasts, and where our bodies are joined; his hard chest tensing with exertion; that perfect washboard of muscles; that V that leads down to his beautiful length like an arrow; that cock, plunging in and out of me with abandon, slamming into something deep inside me with each pass.

Blood rushes between my legs, sending my muscles into spasm and my sensibility into an abyss. His name slides from my lips in a breathy cry as I try to keep control. But that's the thing about Henry, about what happens when I'm with him: I lose *all* control.

A second later he lets out that deep, stomach-tightening grumble. I feel him pulsing inside me, filling me with spurts of his hot seed. Just the thought of that has me panting harder, has me stretching my thighs farther apart.

With a sigh, I let my head loll to the side, my hair scattered everywhere, partially draping my face.

Not enough to block my view of Jed, who's standing at the corner of the barn, a stony look on his face.

He's gone in a heartbeat—just long enough for me to blink and open my mouth, but before the shriek actually escapes.

"Oh my God!" Two minutes ago, on the edge of an orgasm, I might not have cared if he and the farmhands all pulled up chairs. But now, I'm horrified.

Henry slides out of me and tucks himself into his boxers, seemingly unfazed.

"Did you see him? How long was he watching?"

He kneels to slip my panties on over my feet and gently

slides them up my thighs. He pulls me off the bale to finish getting them on. "Just long enough to get the message, I hope."

*What?* "You *knew* he was there?" My voice is thick with accusation.

"Yes," he murmurs, leaning forward to run his tongue over my nipple and suck.

It's distracting, but not enough. "Henry…."

"What? You like watching but you don't like being watched?"

"Not by Jed! He saw me completely naked!"

He stands and tugs his shirt over his head. "He's never seen you naked before?"

"No! You were the first!" Well, and Katie, my friendly and promiscuous roommate at Wolf Cove, who took to barging in on me in the shower. But Henry was the first man.

He chuckles. "Even better. Now he knows *exactly* what he lost." He grabs my bra and frowns at it. "How does this one go on?"

"Not an expert at something. Finally," I grumble, tugging it from his grasp to pull on and fasten. "And this isn't funny."

Henry sighs. "I noticed him just before we were coming. It's not like I was going to stop that."

"Great." My cheeks flush. Who knows how long he was standing there, then.

"Hey…." He grasps my chin between his fingers and lifts my eyes to meet his. "He knew damn well he'd be interrupting something when he came back over, looking for you. So what, he saw us fucking. Maybe he'll pack his shit up and go back to college like a good little boy now."

I'm not convinced he'll do that.

"Didn't you walk in on basically the same?"

"Yeah, I did. It hurt!"

"But you don't owe him anything. You guys are done, right?" There's a challenge in his tone.

"Yes, of course we're done."

"So then, do you care that reality might sting for him, after how he's treated you?"

I think about that for a moment. "No, I guess not. It's just… that was such a private moment for us." *Even out here, behind the barn, in the open.* "I don't want to share that with him."

He slides the ruined dress up over my arms and begins fastening the buttons that weren't torn off. "You have nothing to be embarrassed about. He stayed and watched because he wants what I have." He pulls me to my feet to plant a sweet, warm kiss against my lips. "And he can't have it."

Henry's being possessive, but I don't mind. I like it.

The cooler evening air reminds me that my dress is gaping open.

"How am I going to explain this dress to Mama?"

He smirks.

"She's going to figure it out and hate you."

"She already hates me." When I glare at him, he heaves a sigh. "I saw another dress hanging on the clothesline. I assume it's yours. Why don't you throw that on before you go in? She may notice that you changed but at least you won't go in half-naked."

I can't help but smile at his slyness. "Always one step ahead of me. It's like you planned this out."

"You're the one who seduced me back there, remember? I was being perfectly respectable. Though, I've been thinking about tearing that dress off you all day." He curls his arm around my waist and leads me back through the barn. "I do have to go now, though."

I rest my head against his chest, enjoying his warmth for a

little longer. "Thank you for staying. I didn't think you were going to."

"I didn't think I was going to either."

We walk along the cut path, the five hundred yards to the house and his truck is suddenly too close. The evening sky is creeping up and, with it, the hint of many stars. "So, New York and then…?"

"LA, Seattle, Alaska. After that… not sure. You'll have to ask my assistant."

"How's it going with… what's his name again?"

"Miles." He smirks. "Well, I haven't found him on my bed in his underwear yet, so there's that."

"Blame those stupid nylons you make your staff wear," I say with a giggle, thinking back on my first days being Henry's assistant. They were absolute hell. I had no experience and kept screwing up. I was sure he would fire me. Little did I know that he was attracted to me. What I'd do to be back there and his assistant again. Though, that would mean hiding our relationship and I don't ever want to go back to doing that.

I may be stuck on this farm in Pennsylvania, but at least I don't have to hide us.

"Has anyone figured it out yet?"

"Belinda strongly suspects but she hasn't come out and asked, surprisingly. Aside from that… no, not yet. I'm sure they will, soon enough."

"Will it matter to you?"

He heaves a sigh. "I'll catch some flack from my father, no doubt, but the fact that I transferred you to a different department and left Alaska will help. And now… it doesn't matter. You're not a Wolf employee, I own 61 percent. More, when my father passes."

He rarely talks about his father, or the fact that he has three years left to live, at most, before the pancreatic cancer takes him. I open my mouth to ask now, but a gust of wind distracts me, catching my dress, forcing me to fix my grip to keep it from flying open.

He slows as we pass by the vegetable garden, eying the vines of plump red tomatoes. Beyond them are rows of peppers, zucchinis, and cucumbers. The string beans are almost over. "What do you do with all those?"

"Sell them at the Saturday farmers' market on Main Street. We preserve some for sauce, but I don't see that happening this year, with Mama minding Daddy. We'll probably just sell them fresh off the vine. That's what I'll be doing tomorrow. Super exciting, right? Life of a farm girl. Bet you never expected to be with someone like me." As soon as the words leave my mouth, I regret saying them. I just reminded him of how different our lives are.

In case he momentarily forgot.

"I assume that's yours." He nods to the line of clothes—dresses, tops, panties—that runs between two giant oak trees. I should have taken everything down before the party but I had too many other things on my mind, the biggest one being the tall, gorgeous man beside me.

I peek at the house. The lights are all on, but I don't see Mama's scowling face pressed against the windowpane. Daddy must have distracted her with a request. "Yeah. Can you toss it over to me, please?" I ask, shifting to hide behind the truck as best I can as I unfasten the two buttons left and let the dress drop to the ground.

Henry pulls the sundress off the line but takes his time bringing it over, leaving me standing there in my bra and underwear.

"Hurry up!" I hiss with a nervous giggle.

If there's one thing you can't do with Henry, it's rush him when he doesn't want to be hurried. He throws the dress over his shoulder and leans against the trunk, a smirk on his lips as he gazes over my body.

"*Seriously*, Mama is going to look out that window soon and when she sees me standing here in my underwear, she's going to have a heart attack. I know you don't care if she hates you, but I do. It bothers me."

The amusement slips from his face. He passes the dress to me and quietly watches as I slip it over my head. It's a long black-and-white striped figure-fitting cotton dress that I dared buy, knowing Mama wouldn't approve, because I thought it would be cool for the summer.

I smooth my hands over my hips. "Okay, ready."

He's still watching me. "It's not that I don't care if she hates me, Abbi. In fact, I'd be quite happy if she liked me, but I figure that if rushing you across the country and flying in the best trauma surgeon doesn't earn me a chance, then nothing will. I'm not going to kill myself trying to please someone who has very clearly written me off. I've already spent enough time doing that with my own mother." He grits his teeth, as if he didn't mean to say that. With a sigh, he pulls himself from the tree trunk. He begins walking toward his truck.

I speed up to close the distance, slipping my hand into his. "Have you seen her at all lately?" I ask tentatively.

"No." That's all. One single word. Clearly this isn't something he wants to talk about.

I hesitate. "Belinda told me that you aren't close with her?"

His feet slow to a stop and tension begins radiating from him. "Why the fuck were you talking to Belinda about my mother?"

"It just came up, back when Scott and your father were at Wolf Cove."

"My personal life *just came up*?"

*Great.* Now I've pissed him off. Angry Henry has never been easy to talk to. "I asked if she'd be there and she said your mother… hasn't been around in a while." *Had enough of them,* were Belinda's exact words, if I recall correctly, but I'm not about to repeat that.

"She doesn't know the first thing about my family." He makes to keep walking.

I step out in front of him, reaching up to rest my hands on his chest, rubbing as soothingly as I can. "Neither do I. But, I'd like to. Talk to me."

He's not even looking at me, his eyes locked beyond me, on his truck. To escape. "I don't talk about my personal life with women I'm f—" He cuts himself off, his jaw tensing.

I caught the gist of what he was going to say. I back away slightly, unable to hide the hurt from my face.

I'm unable to stop the question from slipping out. "Is that all I am?"

Finally, he settles his steely gaze on me.

And I suck in a breath, terrified of the answer.

"She walked out the door when I was eleven. Said she'd had enough. Sent her lawyers to collect her divorce settlement and that was the end of it. We spent our years in boarding schools and summers in Alaska. I didn't even see my father until I started working at Wolf."

I frown. "And you haven't seen her since?"

"Not in almost twenty years."

I'm trying to wrap my head around this but I just can't. "How does a woman just do that?" I don't even have children, and yet I can't imagine just walking away from them. Granted, Henry and Scott wouldn't have been babies, but still….

They were her children.

"I don't know, Abbi. I guess some women just aren't made for it. That was her excuse, anyway." He clears his throat.

"I've got a plane to catch." Stepping around me, he opens the driver door and tosses his wallet into the console. "I'm glad to see your father doing well."

I want to say something to him about what he just revealed about his mother. I just have no idea what. "So am I."

I can feel the sudden strain between us and I hate it.

He must feel it too because he heaves a sigh. "Come here."

I step forward until I'm within arm's reach. He pulls me into his body, one hand curling around my back, his other brushing the hair from my face. "Thank you for an... interesting day." He leans in to plant a soft, sweet kiss on my lips. "And an amazing fuck."

Despite the tension, my thighs clench with his words. I can still feel him inside me and it's a delicious burn. "I wish you could stay."

He smirks. "And what? Climb up your TV tower and sneak into your room?"

My cheeks flush. I feel like such a child right now. "There's an inn in town, just off Main Street. Maybe next time you come, you could stay there." Will there be a next time?

"What's it called?"

I hesitate. "The Inn."

"That's... original."

"It's an old Victorian house. Small but quaint. Really pretty. People seem to like staying there. I'm sure Mr. and Mrs. Rhodes would go out of their way to make you comfortable." Preferably not in the cat-themed room. "I mean, I know it's not exactly at your level but—"

"I'll consider it for next time. Gotta go. I've got a packed schedule and I'm meeting with a new business partner."

Wolf Hotels is partnering with someone? The curiosity gets the better of me. "For what?"

He smirks. "Stop trying to stall me." He leans in again for another kiss, this one quick and chaste. "Your mother's watching."

I glance over my shoulder. Sure enough, her silhouette fills the den window. She doesn't even try to hide the fact, having pulled the drapes wide open, standing there with her hands on her hips.

Did Jed call and tell her what he saw? No… she'd be on the porch, screaming at Henry to get the hell off the property and never come back.

"Call me when you land."

My heart is heavy with disappointment as I watch Henry drive away until his taillights vanish around a bend in the road. Then I drag my feet into the house.

*Creak…*

*Thump.*

*Creak…*

*Thump.*

*Creak…*

*Thump.*

Mama's in her rocking chair in the den and, judging by the tempo, she is fuming.

She loves me, I remind myself. I have a mother who loves me and would never abandon me because she didn't feel like being my mother anymore. I'm lucky to have that.

"Abigail!"

*Crap.* "Just a minute!" Despite Henry's rationale, I can't go in there wearing a different dress. There is just no good explanation for that. So I scurry up the stairs and into my room to throw on my pajamas as fast as I can.

I head back down and pour myself a glass of water. With great reluctance and trepidation, I take a deep breath and enter the den as if nothing's wrong. I head straight for Daddy, settled into his hospital bed. "I'm going to sleep."

"Not before we have a little talk," Mama demands behind me.

I can feel the daggers boring into my back. "About what?" I ask casually.

"You know exactly what about."

I heave a sigh, peering down at Daddy, who looks exhausted. He's given me and Henry his blessing, I remind myself. So at least I'm only gravely disappointing one of my parents.

He reaches out to take my hand and squeeze it. "Good night, Abigail. Thank you for the lovely welcome home party."

"I'm just so glad you're home." I smile and lean down to lay a kiss on his forehead.

"Don't let her get to you," he whispers, then gives me a secretive wink.

If only it were that easy. Mama has a way of getting under your skin and staying there.

"Why don't you let her get some sleep, Bernadette. She's been worked to the bone these last few weeks."

"You wouldn't be sayin' that if you saw what I just did, out by that man's truck," she retorts. "I will not allow that kind of behavior under my roof!"

"All he did was kiss me!" I avert my guilty gaze, because what happened outside the barn was definitely more than that.

"Don't you raise your voice to me, Abigail Margaret Mitchell. What if Jed had seen that?"

This time, my cheeks *do* flare with heat. I wish that's all he'd seen. And honestly, despite Daddy's kind words, I can't see him being too supportive if Jed blabs.

I finally turn to face her. "Jed and I are not getting back together, Mama. You need to accept that."

She scowls. "You say that now, but when that man stops

comin' by, like he will, you are gonna be upset that you didn't treat Jed better."

"Who says Henry's going to stop coming by?"

"Oh, come now. You're my daughter and I love you, you know that. So I'm only telling you this to help you avoid more pain. You are not the kind of girl that is going to keep that man interested for long."

Again, she doesn't guard her words, delivering them like a knife plunged deep into my insecurities. The ones that have plagued me since I first met him and have caused so many problems.

But I won't let her poison my thoughts. "Maybe I am."

"Don't even say that. The kind of woman he would need…." She cringes. "Well, I won't utter those kinds of words in front of your father, but let's just say she's not the moral kind."

*Is she the kind who just let him fuck her on a bale of hay outside your equipment barn?*

I drop my gaze. I still can't believe I did that, but Henry has a way of making me forget my inhibitions.

"It's time to start remembering your responsibilities to your family and this farm."

Anger flares inside me. "Everything I've been doing for the past three weeks is for this family and the farm! I quit my summer job, I've deferred college… what more do you want?"

"It's not about what *I* want. Look at your father! He's not getting any younger. He's started thinking about retiring."

"No, I haven't," my dad grumbles.

She ignores him. "But he can't until we know the farm will keep going and we can pay our bills. Do you want us livin' on the street in our old age?"

I fight the urge to roll my eyes. "That's not going to happen."

"What do you think we're gonna do, just sell the farm? Four generations of Mitchells have farmed here. Four. That's history. You don't just turn your nose up at that. You and Jed need to sort things out and settle down. Take over the farm just like we planned all along."

I'd love to tell her that was her plan all along, not mine, but that wouldn't be completely true. I'd thought that's what I wanted, too. Until I saw what else there was out in the world. "Things have changed, Mama."

"What does that mean?"

"It means I don't think this is the life for me."

She snorts. "What on earth are you talking about? Of course it is!"

I heave a breath to keep from yelling. "No… it isn't. Why won't you listen to me?"

She stares at me as if I've just told her I'm about to burn the house down. And then she shakes her head. "Mark my words, whatever has gotten into you is gonna move out quickly enough. I knew you going to Alaska was a bad idea. But we allowed you to go so you could—"

"You didn't *allow* me to go. This is my life, not yours, and I was going, regardless," I snap.

Mama's mouth drops open. "See, Roger? See what's happened to our sweet daughter because of that man? You try to reason with her. I give up."

Daddy heaves a sigh. "Abigail, why don't you get some sleep. It's late and you have to be up early."

This is the last thing he needs to be dealing with. I take his dismissal as my excuse to leave, muttering a, "Good night," as I march out the door.

Behind me, Mama is still talking. "That man is not steppin' foot on this property again."

"This is Mitchell land. *My* land. He is welcome here anytime."

"That's your head injury talking. Didn't we both agree to let me make the decisions around here until you're thinkin' straight again?"

"Good God, woman! I don't have a bloody head injury! How many doctors need to confirm that to get it through your thick skull?"

I hear Mama gasp. "Well, you're clearly not yourself!"

"Good night!" I hear the lamp click.

I scurry up the stairs, not wanting to deal with Mama anymore.

I'm not sure what time it is exactly when I fall asleep, but it's well after two. Late enough for Henry to message to say that he's landed safely.

But he doesn't.

# CHAPTER 6

Jed frowns as a truck turns into our driveway. "I thought he was gone," he mutters, more to himself, as he lifts a bushel of tomatoes onto the trailer we'll be taking to the market. He's barely spoken to me all morning, only wiping his scowl off when Mama pokes her head out the door to see if we need a drink.

I ignore him now, my heart beats wildly in my chest as I watch the silver truck approach. I did get a text from Henry this morning, just to say that he'd arrived late and that he'd be tied up for most of the next two days.

So I know it's not him, but still I can't help but wish it was.

A car soon turns in to follow the truck up the driveway and now my frown matches Jed's.

We watch as a middle-aged man in jeans and a button-down steps out of the shiny silver Dodge Ram. It looks like it was just driven off the lot. "Is there an Abbi Mitchell here?"

I raise my hand.

He smiles and ambles over, pulling out the clipboard that's tucked under his arm. "Would you mind just signing here, here, and here."

"Uh… and what am I signing for?"

"Your new vehicle."

"My new…." The green Toyota pulls up behind the truck but the driver remains where he is, busy talking on his phone. "What?"

"Yeah. Paid for in cash this morning. I'll tell ya, I need a fairy godmother like that. Even if he was a bit demanding." He chuckles, tapping on the paperwork.

I scribble my name down without really thinking. *Henry bought me a new truck?*

"Keys are in the console. Do you need me to walk you through it?"

"No, I'll figure it out."

"Well, then. Enjoy. She's a beaut. Limited edition, fully loaded." With that he climbs into the passenger seat of the car. The Toyota turns and is gone in seconds.

The gravel crunches behind me. "Are you kidding me, Abigail? He treated you like a whore and you're going to accept that? That's, like, a sixty-thousand-dollar truck!"

My mouth drops open and I turn to face him dead-on for the first time this morning.

He does a lightning quick glance at my chest, and I instinctively cross my arms, knowing what he's probably picturing. I can't help but be embarrassed by what he saw. I wish I could be as cavalier about it as Henry is. "Henry has never treated me like *that*."

Jed purses his lips tight. "He doesn't even have enough respect for you to rent a hotel room. I would never do that to you, out behind the barn where anyone could walk in."

"We used to make out in that barn all the time." Hiding in the loft, amongst the hay.

"Well… that's different. And I found buttons, too. Scattered all over the ground. What did he do, tear apart the dress my mother made for you like some kind of animal?"

I bite my tongue. Yes, actually, he did. And I liked it. "Stop sulking, Jed. You have no right. You broke up with me, remember?"

He purses his lips. "If you're going to carry on with him like that, I'm going back to Chicago." He says it like a threat, a smug expression on his face as if he's holding something over me.

"Go ahead. I never asked you to stay."

"No, but your mother did."

I roll my eyes, but I believe him. That's exactly something she'd do.

"You're not stupid, Abigail. Don't you see what he's doing? He's buying you. He'll throw money at you, here and there. Then, every few weeks, when it's convenient for him, he'll come through to use you, and then he'll leave."

"*Convenient* for him?" I start to laugh. "You think coming here is *convenient* for him?"

"Until he's gotten what he wants, yeah. And when it's too much, when you're no longer this sweet little farm girl... you'll never see him again. He's not even faithful to you, I promise you that."

First Mama, now Jed. They just keep attacking my weak points. I won't let them. "Your promises don't hold a lot of water, Jed."

He throws his hands in the air. "Oh, come on! I made a mistake, but I'm here now. When did you become so cruel?"

I burst out in laughter. "When will you learn to take ownership for your fuckups?"

He winces. "Really classy. I can see he brings out the best in you."

"No, Jed. You just bring out the worst in me." We're going to stand here, throwing words back and forth, saying the same things over and over. I'm done. "Do whatever you want to do, stay here or go back to Chicago. I don't care." I spin on my heels and march over to my new truck, taking deep breaths to try to calm myself down. No one has the ability to make my blood boil like Jed.

The dealer wasn't kidding, I note, sitting behind the wheel. It has all the bells and whistles—leather seats, push start, alarm system, navigation screen, power roof window.

And it's a stick.

Shaking my head, I pull my phone out.

**Abbi:** *Are you crazy?*

Henry responds almost immediately, like he was waiting for my text.

**Henry:** *Me? No. Crazy people drive around with duct tape on their bumpers.*

I roll my eyes.

**Abbi:** *You can't just buy me a new truck.*

**Henry:** *I can do whatever I want.*

**Abbi:** *My old truck works fine.*

**Henry:** *It's a hazard on the road. What if you hurt an innocent bystander when that bumper finally falls off?*

**Abbi:** *Then you could have bought me a new bumper.*

**Henry:** *It's only a matter of time before you're left stranded on an old dirt road in the middle of the night.*

**Abbi:** *I don't go out in the middle of the night.*

**Henry:** *I don't have time to argue with you, Abigail. Take the damn truck.*

I roll my eyes. I can hear the serious tone in his message, and the fact that he's used my full name means he is serious.

**Abbi:** *This is too extravagant.*

**Henry:** *Then you won't like what you see in your bank account.*

I glare at my screen. Last night he said there was an accounting error and Belinda would be depositing the difference.

**Henry:** *Can't talk now. Heading into a lunch meeting. Enjoy* *the truck, buy your father a new roof for his barn, and hire help so fuckface can go back to Chicago.*

It's followed by a winky face.

"What have you done, Henry?" I mutter, opening my bank account app on my phone to see how much has been deposited.

My mouth drops open at the digits.

"Abigail!" Mama comes stomping down the stairs, glaring at me. "Whose truck are you sitting in?" She's already figured it out. That's why she's so mad.

I need to message Henry back. No, I need to call him and tell him that he can't be depositing money into my account, that he needs to take it back. Accounting error, my ass. This is ten times what I made for the entire summer!

But first, I have to deal with Mama.

"Abigail, don't you ignore me!"

"It's hers, apparently," Jed answers for me.

I shoot him a glare.

"What do you mean, it's hers? This is a brand-new truck! We don't have money for a new truck. Did *that man* buy it for you?"

I let my head fall back against the nice, contoured head-rest. This is going to be a nightmare.

"Oh, no. Absolutely not. You are not accepting these kinds of gifts from him."

I just said as much to Henry, but now that Mama is telling me what I can and can't do, I'm suddenly much less interested in returning it. "What am I supposed to do?"

"Take it back."

"I can't. It's already been driven off the lot." I don't know a ton about cars but I know the value drops significantly as soon as a brand-new car has been driven off the dealership lot.

"And you can drive it right back. Jed will follow you to the dealer and bring you home."

My hands curl around the steering wheel. This is his gift to *me*, not her.

"Jed, go and grab the keys to Abigail's truck. They should be on the ring by the door."

He starts heading inside.

"You can't tell me what to do. You don't own this truck. I do."

Her hands settle on her hips. "And I can only imagine the kinds of things he will expect from you in exchange." I feel Jed's knowing gaze on me but I ignore it, watching Mama's nostrils flare instead, my own anger ready to boil over. "I want that thing off my property right this instant, you hear me?"

"No problem!" I hit the engine button and it comes to life with a quiet but powerful rumble that only a brand-new truck can manage. Throwing it into first gear, I pop the clutch and take off down the driveway with a roar, checking my rearview mirror once to see through a cloud of dust, Mama and Jed standing side by side, shocked looks on both their faces.

---

LUCY HORNBACK PUNCHES the buttons on the old-school cash register. Her father, Lloyd, who owns the feed mill, doesn't believe in computerizing the store. He only brought in debit and credit machines five years ago, and he makes you spend at least twenty-five dollars before he allows you to use it.

"Can you just add it to our tab? I'll come settle it tomorrow. Silly me, I forgot my wallet at home." *In my mad rush to get away from Mama.*

"Of course." She furrows her thick, dark brows as she

scribbles down the amount in her book. I can't help but imagine how Katie would react to those caterpillars. "So, I heard you got a new truck?"

*Two hours.* That's how long it's been since I left Mama and Jed in a cloud of dust. People are already talking about it. I've done a few laps around town, just getting used to it and trying to cool my temper. Plenty of people saw me, so it's quite possible that someone casually mentioned it to Lucy while stopping in to pick up feed. Or maybe it was someone from the dealership, talking too loudly in the coffee shop about the truck that was bought and paid for in cash and driven out to the Mitchell farm.

"Just got it today."

"Jed called, wanting to know if you'd been by yet. He told me," she says, confirming her source without me needing to ask. She rounds the corner to peer out the window. "Wow! That's, like, *brand* new."

"Yup."

"You didn't make *that* much money in Alaska, did you?" There's a curious glint in her eye. "Did your boss buy you that?"

I guess Jed didn't tell her that part. I can't see him wanting people talking about how rich my new boyfriend is. He wants them talking about how he's staying back from college to help us, and how it's only a matter of time before the two of us get back together.

I've known Lucy since grade school. Maybe that's why she thinks it's appropriate to outright ask me. Whatever I tell her will make its way around town, that's for sure. Do I want everyone talking about this? I'm sure most people will assume that's how I got it anyway, but will they judge me for it?

Will everyone assume he's buying *me,* like Jed and Mama seem to believe?

Thank God Lloyd appears from the back just then, scratching his hard belly and adjusting his baseball cap. "Abigail Mitchell. How are you doin'? How's Roger? I hear he came home yesterday."

"He did. He's on the mend." Every time I come in here, without fail, Lloyd asks about Daddy. They've known each other since they were in diapers. When Lloyd's wife—Lucy's mother—died three years ago from cancer, me and Daddy helped run the feed store for a few days to give them time to grieve.

"You in for chicken pellets again?"

"Four bags."

He fishes his work gloves out of his back pocket. "Pull around back and I'll toss them in for you."

"Great, thanks." They're heavy bags and, while I can manage, I'd prefer the help. "See you later, Lucy."

"For sure!"

I duck out before she can continue her interrogation.

---

"WHY CAN'T she just let me live my life?" I quietly complain over a slice of peach cobbler. It's three o'clock in the afternoon and the Pearl is dead save for a man in the corner by the window, reading his newspaper. It'll pick up again in an hour when people come in to take advantage of the two-for-one dinner discount while they gossip.

"She will, as long as it fits with how she wants you to live it." Aunt May sticks her tongue out at me.

"Did she do this to you when you were growing up?"

"When we were growing up?" Aunt May snorts, taking a sip of her coffee. "Just last week she told me that it's time for Lloyd Hornback to find himself a new wife, and I need to let him know that I'm interested." She leans in. "I like Lloyd

Hornback. He's a nice man. But I ain't interested in him, and I doubt he's lookin' for a new wife. He just likes my spaghetti sauce."

We share a laugh. Poor Aunt May. She works so many hours, she doesn't have time to date. More than a few men have come around sniffing over the years. It's not hard to see why—she's an attractive, curvy lady with a loud laugh and a fun sense of humor. But she has never married, much to Mama's dismay.

"She still thinks she can live my life better than I can. The good thing is I don't have to listen to her. She's not my mother."

I groan. "I can't let her run my life anymore."

Aunt May sighs. "Bernadette loves you. Really, she does, so don't ever doubt that. And everything she does and says, she does because she loves you and thinks that her way is the best way. She got it from *our* mother."

"She still thinks I'm going to get back together with Jed and run the farm. I am not getting back together with him!"

"And the farm? You've definitely changed your mind about that, too?"

"Yes. I mean, I think so. I don't know. I'm twenty-one, Aunt May! What the heck do I know about what I want to do with the rest of my life? But I just don't see myself here for the rest of my life. Not anymore."

She studies me pensively. "Of course you don't. You had a taste of the outside world and you saw what else was out there, which is a whole lot. There's nothing worse than being trapped somewhere by guilt. Look at me." Her olive-green eyes roll over the wallpapered floral walls of the Pearl, the restaurant opened by my great-grandmother, Pearl. It was passed down to my grandma. Aunt May took over when Grandma died from a heart attack. I was nine years old and my mother was already firmly ingrained in the life of farming.

"You don't hate it that much, do you?"

"Not anymore. And if I did, it wouldn't matter because I'm too old to pick up and start a new life. I wouldn't know where to start."

"You're not *that* old." Actually, she's only four years older than Henry.

*Oh my God.* I never did the math before.

Her head tips back and that deep chortle of hers that can be heard anywhere in the restaurant fills the dining room. "My point is, this may not have been for me when I took it over, but it kind of feels like mine now. That's what you need, something that's yours. That you do for yourself, because *you* choose to do it. Not because it was forced on you." Her face turns serious. "Let me ask you this: if you weren't with this man—"

"His name is Henry," I correct her. He has a name and it is not "this man" or "that man" or "the wolf" or any other name Mama has taken to calling him.

"Right, *Henry.* If you weren't with Henry, would you still be so desperate to get away from Greenbank and the farming life?"

I open my mouth to answer, but no words come out. I don't know. Would I?

The sad thing is, had I come back to Greenbank for the summer and suffered in silence as Jed paraded Cammie around, never having met Henry or Ronan and Connor, never got onto that plane for Alaska, I would have gladly taken Jed back, not knowing any better.

She holds her hand up. "Don't answer. Just think on that. I have to go check on the Bolognese sauce. I'll be back in a second." Aunt May makes most things from scratch for the menu and she's known for her exceptional cooking skills.

My phone starts ringing.

"If that's her, you ought to answer," she calls over her shoulder. "As difficult as she can be, she's still your Mama."

With a groan—because she's right—I reach for my phone. Only it's not Mama. It's not even a number I recognize.

"Hello?"

"Yes, is this Abbi Mitchell?"

"Yes?" I frown. "Who's calling?" The woman said Abbi, which means she's tied to Wolf Cove. No one else calls me by that name.

"I'm Zaheera Khan from Nailed It Branding. I've been assigned to your account and I'd like to go over a few things with you."

I frown. "My account?"

"Yes, for your business."

"For… excuse me, who are you again?" I must sound like an idiot.

"Zaheera Khan for Nailed It Branding. We're based in New Jersey. We specialize in consumer goods product branding and launching. We've been hired to help you design your packaging and platform for your products."

*My products?*

My soap. That must be what this is about.

"Who hired you?" Why do I bother asking? This has Henry written all over it.

"Um… I'm not sure, honestly. But I've reviewed the initial specs and I'm excited to come up with some design plans with you."

*Initial specs?*

There's a long pause. "Can we schedule a time for a week Monday?"

"Yeah… Sure. Okay."

After I've agreed to a phone call with her, I hang up and immediately text Henry.

**Abbi:** *Nailed It Branding?*

He answers almost immediately.

**Henry:** *Is there a question?*

I roll my eyes. He's in business mode.

**Abbi:** *Why are they calling me?*

**Henry:** *You said you wanted to hire someone to design packaging for you.*

**Abbi:** *So you went and hired them the very next day?*

**Henry:** *I don't waste time. You know that.*

I shake my head and sigh.

**Abbi:** *It's just a hobby.*

**Henry:** *Then make it a well-packaged hobby.*

**Abbi:** *Why are you doing all this for me?*

**Henry:** *Just talk to them. Gotta go. In a meeting.*

"You're always 'in a meeting,'" I mutter. I don't know what kinds of important business meetings he's in if he keeps answering me immediately.

Aunt May slides back into the booth. "What'd Bernadette say?"

"That wasn't her. That was… nobody." As much as I love my aunt and I trust her more than anyone else in my family, I can't completely trust that she won't tell Mama about this next "extravagance" that Henry's bought for me, something Mama would also not approve of. What do these kinds of companies even cost?

"I heard the party last night was a big hit. Wish I didn't have to miss it, but I couldn't get anyone into the kitchen on such short notice and I can't afford to close down for dinner."

"It was really great. So many people came out. I think Daddy was happy."

"I hear this man… sorry, *Henry—*" She smiles her apology. "—was there until late last night?"

"Where'd you hear that?"

She gives me a "where do you think?" look.

"And what did she say about him?"

"Nothin' I'm gonna repeat. But he was quite the talk of the town around here. So are you officially an item?"

"We're 'seeing where it goes.' Honestly? I don't know."

She glances out the front window at my new Dodge parked out front. "Sure seems like it's going somewhere."

I sigh. "I told him it was too much but he won't take it back. I don't know what to do."

"So he likes spending money on you. I don't know when that became such a bad thing!" She adds quickly, "Tell your mother I said that and I'll deny deny deny."

"Thanks for always having my back."

She winks. "So when am I gonna get to meet this handsome billionaire? You need to bring him in for a meal."

My gaze shifts over the quaint interior. It's small, enough room for only twelve tables, each dressed in red-and-white-checkered tablecloths and balanced with coasters to even them out. I've never figured out if it's the floor or the tables that are the issue. I try to picture Henry, in one of his five-thousand-dollar suits, sitting in here with a bowl of spaghetti but I'm having a hard time. Even though he wouldn't show up dressed like that, I remind myself. He has a casual side too. Even so, he'd stick out like a gazelle at a dog race.

"I don't know when I'll see him again. He's so busy with work and travelling all over the place."

"I'm sure he'd be more than willing to buy a ticket so you can meet him somewhere."

Or send his private jet. I don't think normal people can comprehend what being a billionaire looks like. I'm terrible with math, but I'm sure the interest he made on his assets today more than paid for that truck.

"Yeah, but what about the farm and Daddy? Mama can't do all that on her own."

"Bern could stand to lose a few pounds, but she's still able to take care of your father. Plus, I can help her, if I have some notice. And there are plenty of farmhands around to help with the farm for a day or two. Let Jed do it, he wants to run that farm so bad."

"I don't know."

She slides out of the booth. "Well, the offer stands. Just give me some notice and I'll see what I can swing."

"Thanks, Aunt May." Why couldn't Mama be more like her?

"Okay, I gotta get ready for the rush."

"Do you need any help?" It's been a while since I took orders and ran plates at the Pearl, but it's not hard.

"Hoping to avoid her for a while longer?"

I grin sheepishly. "Maybe."

She nods toward the kitchen. "Fresh aprons are on the hook."

---

IT'S a quarter after ten when I pull up to the house again. The Reverend's green Oldsmobile is parked next to my old truck, which means that Jed's parents are inside. They hardly ever travel alone.

Aunt May sent me home with the rest of her Bolognese sauce in a plastic take-out container, along with an entire loaf of garlic bread and her homemade Caesar salad dressing.

Dinner made for tomorrow, minus the pasta—my peace offering for storming out of here earlier today and not answering a single phone call.

Hushed voices buzz from the den when I step into the kitchen. Moments later, heavy footfalls that I recognize creak down the hallway. Jed's here, too.

"Where have you been? We've been worried sick!"

I sigh. "I was at the Pearl, and you know I was at the Pearl because Aunt May called here to tell Mama so she wouldn't worry." I shoot a glare his way. A "nice try with the guilt trip" glare.

He chews on the inside of his cheek. "You were there all day?"

"I went to the feed store, too. Got four bags of chicken pellets."

"Guess I had better go put it away before we have another bear problem," he mutters, marching out the door.

We used to keep our chicken feed in metal cans outside the chicken coop. They had little latches that kept the raccoons out, so we figured we were fine. We'd never had issues. Then five years ago, a black bear wandered here from the mountains. He got into the entire supply one night, ripping the cans apart and making a horrible mess.

Worse, he kept coming back, because when you feed a bear once, they're as good as your best friend, only with teeth and claws that they'll use on you. We called Forestry a dozen times but they didn't come. It turned into such a destructive nuisance, Daddy had to go out with his gun and shoot it.

Thinking back on it now, it was a scrawny, sad-looking thing, its black fur patchy with bones lacking muscle and meat. At the time, I was terrified.

But it was nothing like the grizzly bear that tore apart my jacket in Alaska, that day I went out with Henry to chop wood.

I smile. All thoughts somehow lead back to Henry Wolf. I swear, I'm obsessed with the man. It's almost painful, being trapped here when I want to be out there with him.

With his hands gripping me and his mouth on me.

With him inside me.

Hushed voices from the den break my reverie. "We're all just going to have to let this play out, Bernadette," the

Reverend whispers. "She's being tested, that's all. Power and greed, and bodily temptations. But in the end, she'll see the light. She'll come back to us, stronger for it. I know she will."

"How on earth am I supposed to just sit by and allow that man to prey on her innocence?"

*Not so innocent anymore, Mama.*

"It's in God's hands now. We can't force it. We've guided her as best we can, but now she must learn how to fight temptation and win."

"And we will pray for her," Celeste adds. "We will pray that in the end, she'll see that he's no good for her, just like our Jed came to his own conclusion. She'll see that she belongs here with us, with Jed, living a humble, honest life."

"And until then, Roger and I are supposed to just idly watch our daughter turn into some sort of materialistic heathen?"

*What?*

I clench my jaw with frustration as tears prick my eyes, and I listen to them talk about me and condemn Henry for being wealthy. Even though it's his wealth and connections that saved Daddy. But they're so narrow-minded, so judgmental, they won't ever admit to seeing that.

At least Daddy hasn't joined in on their witch hunt, I note. That brings me some small level of comfort. It likely means that he doesn't agree with them, but he won't say anything because he won't ever argue with the Reverend, no matter what he thinks.

"If you push too hard, you'll lose her to him. We just need to try and guide her gently."

"You heard what Jed saw last night. The unspeakable things he was doing to her back behind our barn! Tore her dress right off her!" Mama hisses.

My mouth drops open as my cheeks flare. Oh my God. He actually told them? That sniveling little....

The porch door creaks open. I spin around in time to see Jed stroll in, dusting his hands on his thighs. "There was still some feed left so I—"

The sound of my hand hitting hard across Jed's cheek carries through the kitchen and, I'm sure, down to the den. "I hate you!" I hiss.

He reaches up to cover his face with his hand, an angry red welt forming quickly. "What did I do to deserve that?" His eyes are filled with genuine shock. He actually has no idea.

I'm a split second away from slapping him again. Before that happens, I march out of the kitchen and upstairs. I grab pajamas and head for the shower to clean the day's sweat off my body, the one and only place where I won't be bothered while I try to calm myself.

---

I'M FRESHLY SHOWERED and in my pajamas, and there's no other way to avoid this. So I bite the bullet and head for the den. The Enderbeys left at some point—thank God. Mama's in her rocking chair watching some British soap opera and Daddy has the latest John Grisham out, his brow furrowed deeply at the page.

I try not to flinch as they both turn to look at me. Daddy, with a look of resignation in his eyes. Mama, with a mixture of disappointment and hurt in hers, as if I've done something to personally offend her.

I guess I have. I've become my own person and it's not the person she wants me to be.

"Just wanted to say good night. I'm going to sleep." I turn to leave.

"Abigail, wait." Daddy sets his book down and slides his

glasses off. "Come in here and talk to us for a moment, please. Let's not go to bed angry."

He doesn't sound angry, at least. I veer around Mama to sit down in the wooden kitchen chair next to his bed.

No one says anything, but Mama's lips are pressed firmly together like it's taking everything in her power not to speak. Her face is literally turning red from the challenge.

He sighs. "That's some truck you're driving."

I sigh. "It is. Henry thought I'd appreciate it and he was worried about me driving my old truck. It's not in the best shape. He thought this would be a lot safer."

"No, it's not. You're right. And I like that he's worried about your safety."

"If he were worried about her safety, he wouldn't be—"

"Bernadette!" Daddy's voice booms in the old house.

She clamps her mouth immediately.

*Creak.*

*Thump.*

*Creak.*

*Thump.*

*Creak.*

*Thump.*

Back and forth on the rocking chair she goes, at a furious tempo.

"We all want you to be happy. But it's also important that you don't lose sight of who you are. Sometimes things like money can make you say and do things that aren't… things you'd normally do. You could end up not being proud of who you are one day, and it's our job to try to not let that happen."

Is this his way of saying that I should be ashamed of having sex behind the barn with Henry?

I sigh. "I know, Daddy. But I have to make my own mistakes and figure my own life out. And I can tell you now that no matter if Henry is in my life or not tomorrow, I'm not the same girl I was when I left for Alaska, and I'm happy for that. That girl would have taken Jed back. I never will. I'm too good for that."

Mama opens her mouth to speak but Daddy spears her with another glare.

"We've heard you loud and clear, haven't we, Bernadette?"

Finally, she offers a nod, swallowing a few times until whatever opinion is burning a hole in her tongue dissipates. "You hit Jed. Hard enough to leave a welt."

"I know. I'm sorry. It's just that he...."

She arches a brow in warning and my excuses fade.

"You're right. There's no reason good enough. I'm sorry."

Her gaze wanders to the TV, though she's not paying attention to that. "Don't say sorry to me."

I sigh. "I'll call him."

She nods, and I can almost see her checking off a box in her list of "Things Abigail Must Do."

"The Enderbeys and I had a fine idea. We have that BBQ coming up and we're fundraising to fix up the hall. We're short on raffle prizes, so we figure if we sell tickets at fifty dollars apiece, that truck will fetch more than enough in no time. The phone's already been ringing off the hook all day, with people who've seen you drivin' it around town, asking about it."

My mouth drops open. They've been discussing raffling off my truck. A gift from Henry, to me. My truck?

"No way!"

Mama's brows raise. "Are you sayin' you won't share your good fortune with the church and your community?"

This isn't about sharing my good fortune. This is about Mama getting her way, one way or another. Now she's playing the charity card because she knows it's a strong one. "This isn't fair! Besides, the Milners are already donating a full cow. And I know Aunt May put in a hundred-dollar gift card. There are already plenty of prizes up for grabs."

Mama shakes her head. "It's already startin'. The materialism. The selfishness."

Selfish? She's calling me selfish now?

Daddy reaches out and grasps my hand, pulling my attention away before I start screaming at her. "The Enderbeys were simply trying to give you options, in case you didn't feel right giving the truck back but didn't feel right keepin' it. No one's gonna make you do something you don't want to do. If you want to keep the truck...." He sighs. "Then that's your choice."

My lips twist. While I'm relieved to hear him support me, I can't help feel that it's all for show. That I'd be wrong to keep it. After all, the church could use it. Our entire community could use it. Is Mama right? Am I being selfish?

"What would you do?" I ask softly, pleading with him to give me his honest opinion, regardless of what it is.

His mouth wavers. "They'll have no problem raising money another way. I'd rather see my daughter safe on the road and happy."

The rocking chair comes to a jarring halt. Mama skewers him with her gaze. He's just earned himself a few days of browbeating, unable to get away from her while she natters on about how he's working against everything she and the Enderbeys are trying to achieve. She'll just keep going and going and going, thinking that if she talks *at* him long enough, she'll break him down and get her way.

I give him a pitying smile.

Finding his page in his book once again, he slides his glasses over his eyes and grumbles, "But what do I know? I have that head injury, remember?"

I lean down and plant a kiss on his forehead before

ducking out and heading upstairs to crawl into bed. Two messages from Henry are waiting to cheer me up.

If you're still awake... Good Night.

And ten minutes later a second one:

And if not... Good Morning.

I smile.

Just going to sleep now. Rough day. Miss you.

I decide to message Jed while I wait for a response.

You shouldn't have told them about me and Henry behind the barn. But I'm sorry I hit you.

He responds a few minutes later.

I only told them because I love you.

As much as I want to tell him to go to hell and to move on, I can't bring myself to do it.

See you at the market.

I fall asleep waiting for Henry's message back.

# CHAPTER 7

"We had some for dinner last night. It's extra sweet this year." Mama says that about our corn *every* year. I usually can't tell one year from another, except for that one time we didn't have enough rain. The cobs were half the size and tasteless.

"You always do have the best corn around." Peggy Sue counts out two dollars and seventy-five cents' worth from her little change purse, eying each quarter and dime carefully. I'd love to just give her the corn for free because she's so kind and has helped us out a ton, but by that thought process, I'd be giving everyone corn for free. It's just an unwritten rule that we support each other's businesses where we can and today, that business for us is our stand at the farmers' market.

With it being August, everyone's having corn roasts. Jed's already topped up the wagon once and it's only noon.

"I saw you driving through town in your shiny new truck," Peggy remarks, accepting the bag of cobs I handpicked for her. "Charlie down at the dealership said that Henry had that delivered to your house?"

I knew it wouldn't take long for that to come out, even if

Mama is trying her best to hide the fact that her heathen daughter is accepting a sixty-thousand-dollar gift from the devil himself.

The fan muffles whatever Mama grumbles under her breath, but I can imagine it isn't in the least pleasant. We exchanged nothing but light civilities this morning over breakfast, something I'm relieved for. While she won't come out and say anything negative about the man who helped save Daddy's life to anyone besides the Enderbeys, I'm sure everyone has already figured out that she doesn't approve.

I ignore her, but say loud enough for her to hear, "At least now I don't have to worry about breaking down somewhere, or losing my bumper and hurting an innocent person. Henry wanted me to be safe." *Good luck disparaging him for that, Mama.*

"That's so kind of him. And how's Roger doing, Bernadette?"

"Oh, he's settlin' in just fine. May is over there right now, fetching him water and food, so I could help sell some of these tomatoes."

I could have sold the tomatoes fine on my own. Mama's just in gossip withdrawal. Next to church, the market is the best place to catch up on who's cheating on who and who's pregnant. Mama likes to show up at Sunday service already in the know, so she can add her two cents' worth with some conviction.

Peggy tucks her half dozen corn cobs into her trolley, a sly smile curling her wrinkled face. "So, Abigail, when will we be seeing your handsome friend again?"

She just loves getting under Mama's skin apparently.

"I'm not sure, honestly. Not any time soon, likely. He travels a lot."

"Not exactly family man material, is he?" Mama makes a

small chortle of satisfaction and I don't bother hiding my eye roll.

"Well, I hope you get to join him on some of those trips. What an adventure that would be."

I smile at the old woman. "I hope I do, too. See you at church tomorrow."

"Yes, dear. And do you think you're going to make any more of that chamomile soap? It does wonders for my skin."

"I'm just waiting on the avocado oil I ordered. As soon as it gets in, I'll make a batch and let you know." Which reminds me, I have that call with the branding person in just over a week. I'm beginning to grow curious about what she could possibly suggest. I have to trust Henry's judgement about this. He *is* good at what he does.

"That'd be just wonderful. Good day, Bernadette."

"Uh-huh." As soon as Peggy Sue's out of earshot, she adds, "That old coot drove her husband to drink with all her meddling. It's not a wonder he died so early."

*Really charitable, Mama.* "I like her," I murmur, smiling as the next customer approaches the table.

For such a small town, our market is one of the biggest around. It brings in tourists from all over the State. I sold out of whatever soap I brought within the first hour. If I had time to make more, I could have made a pretty penny. Not that I need any money right now, anyway.

It's three o'clock and we're almost through our stock of corn when Edith's daughter, Mary Jane, trots up. "Hey, Abigail! Long time, no see!"

"I know. How are you?" She hasn't changed much since I saw her last, her long straight blonde hair pulled back in a ponytail, her eyebrows natural and in need of some grooming. She's put on a bit of weight around her already sturdy bottom half. Kids in middle school used to call her Thunder Thighs, on account of her thick legs.

She's always been nothing but kind to me, even with her secret crush on Jed that everyone, including Jed, knows about.

"Have you heard? I'm running the Sunday school program for the kids. Temporarily, for now, but I'm hoping it'll turn into something more permanent."

Temporarily because Reverend Enderbey still hasn't given up the hope that I'll run it once I'm done with college. I guess he's hoping that, if he gets me firmly ingrained back into the church, I'll change my mind about Jed.

"That's great. Congratulations."

She beams with pride. "It's what I've always wanted to do."

I smile at her as I quietly wonder if she'd still say that had she left Greenbank. Truly left. Sure, she went to college, but it was an hour away and she commuted each day. Does she really know what she wants to do with the rest of her life, or is she simply choosing from the options she's aware of, like I was?

But that's up to her, I remind myself. If she's happy, then... good for her.

"Hi, Mrs. Mitchell!" She waves at Mama, who's off her feet and helping another customer buy a few jars of jams and such.

Mama gives her a warm smile back. "Be with you in a sec, hon." Mama *loves* Mary Jane for many reasons, one being that Mary Jane is a social media junkie and has taken a personal interest in Wolf Hotels.

"I'm so sorry I missed your daddy's welcome home party. I heard it was fantastic." There's a twinkle in Mary Jane's eye. "So Henry was in New York last night?"

"He was." I stifle my eye roll. So she's on first-name basis now?

"I don't know how you do it, Abigail. I'd be insane with

jealousy every time I saw pictures of him with another woman."

Her words are like a punch to my gut, but I keep my smile plastered on my face. "He has a lot of business meetings. And the media likes to take pictures of him." Another woman? What is she talking about?

I sense Mama listening.

"Oh, I know." She waves that away like she does actually know. "But still, I'd go crazy! Especially with Margo Lauren!"

*Margo Lauren?*

The supermodel?

That's who Henry had an important business meeting with?

He had to so urgently fly to New York to meet with a supermodel in person?

"I trust him."

*I trust him.*

*I trust him.*

*I trust him.*

How many times do I have to repeat that in my head before I'm confident that I do? *We're not going down this road again, Abbi.*

"Mary Jane!"

She glances over her shoulder to the honey stand across the way, where Edith waits for her. "Gotta go. See you later!" Mary Jane offers a little wave and trots off, leaving me to feel ill.

What did Mary Jane see? And where?

I need to find it.

"Didn't I tell you?" Mama's voice is higher than normal. She's trying to hide the fact that she's gloating inside.

"I need to use the restroom." I grab my purse from beneath the table.

"Okay. Jed's here. Jed, you'll take over for Abigail, right?"

He drops the cooler of jams and jellies under the table and then turns to face me, letting me get a good look at the red bruise across his cheek. "Sure thing." He's all sugar and pie today. No talk of whores.

I head to the nearby coffee shop, counting out enough money to buy a cold drink. That's the only way Ms. Delyn will let people use her restrooms. She watches like a hawk and will embarrass you in front of everyone if you dare sneak in.

"A peach smoothie please, Ms. Delyn!" I wave the bills up on my way past her.

As soon as I'm safely in the stall, I check my search feeds. One of my roommates, Autumn the concierge, got me following Wolf Hotels on social media and I still do it religiously. I don't see anything about Henry and Margo Lauren in them. Where would Mary Jane have seen it? After a bit more sleuthing, I find it on Margo Lauren's Instagram account.

It's a picture from behind, of the two of them walking up to a restaurant with a bright marquee and globe lights lining a red carpet. They're smartly dressed, her in a sexy backless black dress, him in a suit.

His hand is splayed over the small of her back as he escorts her toward the doors.

I would recognize Henry even if she hadn't specifically called him out in her caption:

*A lady and a wolf. Henry Wolf, that is.* Followed by a series of heart emoticons.

My stomach rolls with jealousy. Why didn't he tell me he was having dinner with a beautiful and glamorous French supermodel? If he didn't tell me, does that mean he's hiding her from me? It's clear she isn't hiding this dinner from anyone. And that she has a thing for him. Of course she does. Any female would.

*Stop it, Abbi!*

*He didn't cheat on you before and he's not cheating on you now!*

*I* was the one who cheated on *him*, I remind myself.

But he didn't know exactly what had happened with Ronan and Connor before. Now he does. What if learning that turns out to be too much for him? What if he feels like he should get a free pass?

Or two.

The restroom door squeaks open, reminding me that I've been sitting here for far too long. I'm sure my drink is sitting on the counter and beginning to separate by now.

But what do I do?

Should I say something to him? Ask him why he didn't tell me?

Say nothing and pretend I don't know and continue on in ignorant bliss?

Too late....

This is going to drive me insane!

After three seconds of gritting my teeth, I quickly punch out,

**Abbi:** *Had dinner with any gorgeous supermodels lately?*

And then I hit Send before I can change my mind, collect my drink, and head back into the hot tent.

---

IT TAKES NEARLY an hour for Henry's response to arrive, and when it does, it doesn't set my mind at ease.

**Henry:** *I have, actually. Why do you ask?*

**Abbi:** *Just thought it would be something you would mention.*

"Abigail, put your phone away. If he wants to waste his breath lyin', he'll have to do it when we're not servin' customers." Mama smiles, as if that balances out her sharp words.

It's ten minutes before I catch a break and can check my phone again.

**Henry:** *I didn't realize I had to give you details about every business meeting I'm in.*

*A business meeting?*

**Abbi:** *Is that what I saw?*

**Henry:** *Are you jealous?*

**Abbi:** *Maybe.*

There's no point lying. Henry sees right through my lies as it is.

**Henry:** *We can't do this every time you see my name attached to an attractive female. I thought you trusted me.*

It's a text, and tone in texts is hard to get right. Yet, I sense his anger coming through.

It's happening again. I'm assuming he's screwing around on me.

**Abbi:** *You're right. I'm sorry. I can't help it. It's this place, and everyone around here. They keep filling my head with doubt. I don't know how much longer I can take this.*

"Abigail!"

I slide my phone into my pocket. This really isn't the right time or way to be having this conversation—via text in the middle of a corn stand, me trying not to worry and failing miserably.

Twenty seconds later, my phone rings.

I immediately reach for it.

"We have customers," Mama says, adjusting the speed on the fan.

Henry's name and picture fills my screen and my heart automatically skips a beat.

I answer it under her scathing eye. "Give me a sec?" I round the stand.

"Abigail!"

I come out from under the canopy, smiling an apology at

the two people waiting to buy corn as I pass them. Mama and Jed can handle two customers.

"Hey, I'm just at the market," I explain, cutting through the crowd, heading for the small park across the street.

"What's going on?" His deep voice vibrates inside me. There's a hint of something there... worry?

I close my eyes and sigh, and wish that he were right here with me. "A lot." I tell him all about yesterday with the truck and the Enderbeys, and Jed. "And then Mary Jane tells me about Margo Lauren and, I don't know... I just panicked. I thought maybe.... Why didn't you just tell me you were going out with her after your business meetings?"

"She *was* my business meeting, Abbi. She has a proposition for a property in France. It's an old castle that's been in her family for generations. She wants to turn it into a hotel under the Wolf name."

"A castle? Seriously?" My relief is momentarily overshadowed by curiosity. "That would be really cool."

His deep chuckle tickles my ear. "Yeah, I thought so, too. It's all very preliminary and confidential at this point. In fact, no one knows about it but me. And now you."

I sigh. "I'm so sorry. I just.... I need to get away from my mother. Even for a night. She wants what she wants and she doesn't care if she's hurting me trying to get it."

"I've already told you, I'll hire help to run the farm while your dad recovers so you don't have to stay there."

"No, I can't. Thank you, but I can't." Accepting the truck is one thing, but abandoning my family when they need me to travel around and have endless, fantastic sex with Henry is wrong. I don't even know if that's an option. He hasn't exactly offered it up.

"Fine. Come to New York when you're done for the day."

My heart flutters. "What?"

"You heard me."

"*Today*?" I quickly do the math. "That means I wouldn't get there until ten, *at least*."

"Can you be ready for six?"

"Uh…." I frown. "I guess. Why?"

"I'll come get you."

"Wait! I don't know if I can get away." Aunt May said she'd help out if I gave her notice. This would be… four hours' notice. Not great. But my parents will be at the Enderbeys' for Saturday dinner, so she can come after her dinner shift. And we don't have to do any baling tomorrow. Jed can handle the animals without me.

"Do you remember saying that you'd drop everything and come running if I demanded you come to me?"

"Yes."

"I'm demanding it. Be ready and waiting outside for me at six."

"Okay?" I cringe. "What should I bring?"

"Yourself."

He hangs up before I can respond. I'm left staring at my phone, a mixture of shock, confusion, and excitement overwhelming me. I'm going to see Henry again, tonight?

I'm going to see Henry tonight.

I glance back at our stand. A few people rifle through the stack, searching for the best cobs from what's left. Is it wrong for me to leave for the night?

I quickly dial the Pearl and cross my fingers that Aunt May isn't too busy to answer.

"The Pearl, what can I do for you?"

"Hey."

"Abigail?"

"Yeah." I hesitate. "I have a favor to ask."

The phone fills with her sigh. "When are you leaving?"

"At six?" How did she know?

"Okay. I can wrap up the busy stretch and get Chrissy to

close up." Chrissy and my aunt have been best friends for years. She's at the Pearl almost as much as May is. "I'll have to leave early in the morning though, what with the after-church rush."

Sunday church. "Shit!" I totally forgot.

"Gesundheit." That's Aunt May's way of responding to a cuss word. It's her gentle way of scolding me.

"Sorry, it's just, I forgot tomorrow was Sunday. It's Daddy's first service back. Mama's gonna have a meltdown if I'm not there." I'm on the verge of tears as reality sets in. I knew this wasn't going to happen.

I'm not going to see Henry. I had better call him back before he gets on his plane.

"Abigail?"

I sigh, my disappointment overwhelming. "Yeah?"

"Would you rather go to church or see Henry?"

"See Henry." I don't miss a beat.

"Then that's what you should do. You can talk to God anywhere. You can be a good person anywhere. You don't need four walls and a reverend telling you right from wrong to be a good person or to talk to God."

"But Mama—"

"Will survive. Just maybe don't mention that you're going until your bag is in the car. Save yourself the headache. But remember…."

"You'll deny deny deny." I smile. "Thanks, Aunt May."

"I'll be there for around eight. I'll even bring leftovers. What time will you be back?"

"I don't know, exactly. Afternoon? Evening?"

"Okay. We'll plan for evening. You go and have fun."

I hang up. And smile.

A night with Henry in a hotel. My first night staying with Henry. No Mama, no hiding from employees. It sounds like heaven. I just have to pass through hell first to get there.

Mama must mistake my dread over telling her for heartache, because the second I return to the corn stand, she's reaching for me, rubbing my back soothingly. "Now, now. It'll hurt for a while, but you'll get over it soon enough and you'll be so thankful." She clucks her tongue. "I'm just glad that man found someone else. You don't need the likes of him. You've got exactly what you need right over there." She nods toward Jed, who's tossing the last few cobs left—picked over and good for nothing but the animals now—into a box.

She's the Terminator.

She won't ever stop.

"We'll get home and clean up, then head over to the Enderbeys' for dinner. And after that, the Baldwins are coming over. You can take your Daddy's spot if he's not up to playin' bridge."

I cringe. Bridge with the Baldwins almost always results in Mrs. Baldwin asking me about my menstruation cycle and Mr. Baldwin staring at my breasts without shame. Those two are plain fucking weird.

I don't say a word. I simply collect the money box and head for my truck, trying to hide the slight bounce in my step.

# CHAPTER 8

"Abigail! Time to head over!"

I smooth the cute cream-colored lace dress over my hips one more time, studying my reflection in my mirror. It was an impulse purchase, on my way home from visiting my dad in the hospital. I saw it on a mannequin in a window display and had to get it. It's much shorter than anything I've ever worn, but it makes my legs look long, especially in the strappy sandals I bought to go with it. And with the faded denim jacket that the sales girl convinced me to buy?

I actually look stylish.

Is it enough for New York City and Henry, though?

I tried to mimic what Rachel and Katie did with my makeup that night of the grand opening. While it's nowhere near as good, I think I look decent.

Grabbing the small duffel bag that I stuffed with a change of clothes and my toiletries, I take a deep breath and head down the stairs.

"We're a few minutes late but I'm sure they'll understand, what with your father—" Her words die on her tongue as she sizes me up from head to toe. "You can't go anywhere dressed like that."

"I'm going to New York for the night. Aunt May will be here around eight to help you with Daddy if you need it, and again tomorrow." I don't wait for her response. I keep walking toward the door, my bag slung over my shoulder.

She can move fast when she wants to, practically on my heels all the way out the door. "You are not going to *New York City*!"

Jed is helping my dad into the back of the Enderbeys' Oldsmobile. They both turn to see the commotion.

"No... you're not! Your daddy just got out of the hospital two days ago! You need to be here to help take care of him!" She reaches for my duffel bag.

"Stop it, Mama!" I step out of her reach. "Like I said, Aunt May is coming to help. You'll be fine. I just need to get away for a night."

Her head is shaking before words even come out. "I will not have my daughter comin' and goin' as she pleases and shackin' up with a grown man. We did not raise you to sin like this!"

"I'm not 'shackin' up' with anyone!"

"Oh? And where exactly do you think you're going to be sleeping?"

She knows exactly where I'm going to stay and I really don't want to have this conversation with her at all, but especially not in front of Daddy. "I'll be back tomorrow night."

Her mouth drops open in shock. What did she expect me to say? *Okay, Mama! I'll stay.* "Roger! Tell her she can't go!"

"She's a grown woman. I can't tell her that."

She shoots him with a glare before turning her wrath back on me. "You need to be at church tomorrow. It's your father's first day back. Roger, she's going to miss your first day back! Say something!"

He heaves a sigh of exasperation. "So, she'll be there *next* Sunday."

Her hand flies to her chest, over her heart, as if she's in pain. "You're just going to let your daughter drive five hours to New York City on a Saturday night?" To me, she glares. "I thought you said he cared about your safety."

"I'm not driving. He's picking me up." Every argument she lobs out, I have a counter to it. But it doesn't matter. It'll never matter with her. "I'm going, Mama. I'm going and there's nothing you can say or do to stop me."

She huffs and puffs, but can't find her words.

"Stop it! You're going to give yourself a heart attack."

"No! My daughter is going to give me a heart attack, dressed like that. You look absolutely ridiculous! Your dress barely covers your behind! Did he buy that for you, too?"

I self-consciously tug at the bottom of it, suddenly not feeling so stylish. "No, I bought this myself."

"This isn't you!" The pain on her face is genuine. "Next thing we know, you'll be collecting money on the corner."

"Bernadette!" my dad roars.

My mouth drops open. "Now *you* are being ridiculous, Mama."

"How are you getting to New York?" Jed interrupts, squinting up at the sky.

"In his plane." At least, I assume we are. He wouldn't be arriving until eleven otherwise. I squint to see what Jed's focused on. Is that…?

"Are you fucking kidding me!" Jed exclaims, his tone full of annoyance.

"Jed!" Mama scolds, but he doesn't even attempt an apology, his expression turning sour as the sleek black helicopter approaches, the whirl of its blades growing louder.

Good God. We're going in a *helicopter*?

It's coming down on a flat grassy field to our right, its

descent slow. Dust kicks up in a cloud around it. We're standing too far to be caught up in it, but the wind reaches us, catching the bottom of my dress. I have to hold it down until the helicopter has landed and the propeller cuts off.

I stare at the Wolf company logo spanning the side of it in disbelief. Of course he owns a helicopter, too.

The door pops open and Henry climbs out, catching my breath with the easy, sleek way he moves.

"You get in that thing and you'll be choosin' him over your own family," Mama warns, the scorn in her tone cutting.

He begins walking toward me. He means to come here.

I can't have him coming here, not with Mama behaving the way she is.

"Bye, Mama. Bye, Daddy! Jed!" I sling my bag over my shoulder and start running, the grass tickling my bare toes through my sandals. Henry's in dress pants and a charcoal button-down shirt, the collar unfastened. He must have come straight from whatever Saturday meetings he had, and he looks delicious.

And he's all mine tonight.

I smile as I accept that, closing in on the helicopter. His gaze roams over me, lingering over my chest with that look I'm beginning to recognize. He's picturing my breasts when they're bare and bouncing under him.

I plow right into his hard body and his arms as they wrap around me. Just the smell of his cologne brings me such comfort right now.

"Should we go over and say hello?"

"Let's just go." I plead with my eyes. *Please don't ask questions.*

His gaze flickers over to my parents, to my mother, standing there with her fists resting on her hips, a scowl reserved for the devil himself furrowing her brow. "You got it." With a polite wave their way—I turn back in time to see that my dad actually waves back—he takes my bag from my hand and helps me climb into the helicopter's small interior. I'm not sure that I'm ready for this. And my dress is definitely too short for this, I note, feeling the breeze behind me.

Crawling into my seat—one of four—I give the pilot a nervous smile. Had anyone told me in May that by August I'd be flying around in a helicopter, I would have laughed.

Had they told me that I'd be in love with another man, I wouldn't have believed them.

But I am. Madly.

"Good to go?" The pilot asks Henry.

"Abbi?" Henry's questioning gaze is on me.

With one last glance at my parents and Jed, who looks like he just found his dog dead at his feet, his face a mask of sadness and resignation, I nod.

And whisper, "No, Mama. I'm choosing me."

---

THE PILOT BRINGS the helicopter down on the rooftop of the Wolf Tower just two hours later, the sky orange with a spectacular sunset.

At least, I think it's been two hours. I haven't actually been paying attention, too mesmerized by the view below us, a smile on my face the entire time.

I've spent three years in Chicago, so I can say that I've lived in "a big city." And yet New York is something altogether different, a looming, overwhelming force, a sea of architecture stretching out in every direction. High rises are a dime a dozen here, blocks and blocks of them lining streets filled with an army of yellow cabs.

This is Henry's world.

It's completely different side from the one I saw in Alaska

—a vast expanse of wilderness and peace, a link to his childhood. A place where he was still rich and powerful, and yet it felt somehow removed from the world. A place where we found a connection.

Here, some eighty stories in the air of a sleek building he *owns*, stepping off a helicopter and heading for the two-level glass penthouse I saw on our approach, nothing about him seems subdued or understated. Even the air around him feels suddenly different here.

Can I ever possibly fit into this world?

I watch Henry shake the pilot's hand with more than a hint of awe, unable to stop from asking myself what he's doing with a twenty-one-year-old farm girl from Pennsylvania.

"What time will you need me tomorrow?" the pilot asks.

"Around seven tomorrow night. Thank you."

My stomach does a small flip. I get him for an entire day, too.

The pilot gives us a small salute and then continues on his task of flicking switches and checking things on the dashboard.

"Come." Henry slips his hand through mine and leads me toward a door. He uses a key card to get us in, and then it's a series of steps and a narrow hall, until we're walking through another door. Cameras watch our moves from above, I note, as he uses his key again to get us through another set of doors and into a bright and spacious foyer of cool gray marble and white walls. My mouth can't help but drop open as I take in the sprawling place with awe. The exterior walls are all glass. *All* of them, giving me a spectacular panoramic view of Manhattan's skyline. The penthouse itself is sleek and modern, mostly black and white in décor, with a few hints of color—a bronzed lamp base, crimson cushions, a thin strip of silver along the bottoms of the sheer drapes—to give it some personality.

So completely opposite to my family's farm.

"So this is your penthouse." In Wolf Tower, the tallest mixed residential and hotel building in the city.

"It is." He tosses his keys and wallet onto a heavy-footed round table.

The table he had sex with his ex-assistant on, I realize. I look up at the ceiling, searching for the camera that captured it all, that provided him with leverage when she was blackmailing him for money and accusing him of assaulting her.

"It's to the left, behind the molding." There's definite humor in Henry's voice. He's not the least bit ashamed of anything he's done in the past. I wish I could be the same.

I can't help but look at that table and flinch, picturing Henry stepping out of that elevator right there to find a naked woman sprawled out across it. Him, with heat sparking in his cold blue eyes, tossing his things as he just did, unbuckling his dress pants, and diving right into her without so much as a kiss. Women don't need foreplay with Henry.

Just looking at him is foreplay.

"Are there any more in here?" I trail him in, feeling completely out of my element as I scope out the all-white kitchen to the left and the large outdoor patio to the right.

"No. Not unless you would like there to be. That can easily be arranged."

I know he's not talking about security cameras now.

He heads for the tall crystal decanter of amber liquid, pouring himself what I'm assuming is Scotch. But he leaves it there to sit and goes to the kitchen. "Red or white?" When he turns to see my confused look, he adds, "Wine. Red or white wine?"

"Um…." I swallow, admitting with some embarrassment, "I've never had either."

With a deep sigh, he pulls a bottle from a narrow fridge below the counter. "Let's go with a Pinot Grigio. It's probably safer for that dress."

I watch with fascination as he uncorks the bottle and pours into a tall, sleek glass. Swirling the yellowish liquid around in the bowl a few times, he then slides it forward to me. "Try that. See if you like it."

"It's…." I smack my lips with the first taste, the cool, crisp flavor reminding me of fruit. "It tastes like apples."

He smirks. "You thought all wine would taste like grape juice, didn't you?"

"No." *Yes.*

He replaces the bottle in the fridge. "We should talk."

The sudden seriousness in his voice makes my stomach tighten. Those three words sound ominous. They sound like they're going to end with me heartbroken.

I take a deep, calming breath. *Get it together, Abbi.*

He retrieves his glass of Scotch and then comes over to lean across the island, his fingertip tracing the grain in the marble countertop. "I don't want to be the cause of issues with your parents."

"You're not."

Henry's dark brow arches.

"It's just my mother. My father wants me to be happy."

"I'm sure your mother does, too."

"In her own way. But that's the thing. I'll never be happy trying to please her. I'm not the same person I was before, and I don't want the life she wants for me. She's gonna have to accept that, or…." I shrug. "I don't know what. But she's gonna have to accept it."

He hesitates. "So if I wasn't in your life, you wouldn't be back with fuckface and taking over the farm?"

I shake my head, even as inside that voice is screaming at him not to even suggest things like him not being in my life.

He takes a long sip of his drink, his face thoughtful. "I know what it's like to not have a mother in my life. I don't want to be the cause of that for you."

I slide my hand over his, the raw truth in his words painful. "You're not going to be. She's not going anywhere, trust me. She may keep fighting, trying to get what she wants, but she's not going to pack her bags and leave." Where would she even go?

"But is that what you want to be doing? Years from now? Fighting with her, still? I don't think it is, Abbi."

"If it's not over you, it'll be someone else. Anyone who isn't Jed."

*What is this?* Is he starting to reconsider *us* because of Mama? Maybe he doesn't want to deal with it. Maybe it's not worth it to him.

God, I'm going to drive myself crazy if I assume he's breaking up with me every time we have a conversation. This is the kind of insecurity he doesn't like.

"Come." He takes my hand and leads me through the main floor, showing me the various rooms—the private, fully equipped gym, the twenty-seat theatre room, a double-story library attached to his own personal office. He doesn't highlight all the specific details, like the Brazilian rosewood and travertine marble halls, but I notice all the delectable, rich details.

Upstairs are three massive bedrooms, his being the largest. All feel airy, the furniture not too bulky, the fabrics subtle and soft.

"You have a *pool* up here?" I stare in astonishment at the rectangular swimming pool just outside the patio doors of his bedroom, the crystal-blue waters looking so inviting in this hot, sticky air, even at this hour.

"You can go in if you want."

"I didn't bring my suit."

That deep, throaty chuckle of his vibrates right down to my very core. "Do you honestly think I'd let you wear a suit?"

I glance around at the buildings surrounding us. There are plenty of them at near eye level in the distance. Would they be able to see me naked up here?

Henry's phone rings then. While he answers, I walk over and, slipping off my sandals, I dip my toes in. It's even warmer than I expected. I'm definitely going swimming later, after dark.

"Abbi, come." He stands at the patio door, waiting for me. It's not in a "come here because we're going to have sex right now" way.

"What are we doing?"

He starts unbuttoning his shirt. "We're meeting Margo and her boyfriend at nine for dinner. We don't have a lot of time to get ready."

*Margo Lauren?* "Where?"

"Some French place. It's supposed to be the best in the city. And then out after, I'm sure. I don't know where. I let her make the plans. She's into the nightlife."

I look down at my dress. "I didn't really come prepared for clubbing." Not that I'd have anything to choose from.

"Her people are on their way. They'll get you ready." He peels his t-shirt off and tosses it to the bed next to his dress shirt and then moves to his buckle, all while I just stand there and stare at his golden body, thinking about two nights ago when it was straining and coated with a sheen of sweat.

That's mine.

And just the sight of it makes my blood race through my veins.

I find myself moving for him as his pants come down. He's not even aware of what he's doing to me, his mind on the nine o'clock deadline. He doesn't like to be late, especially if it's for a business meeting.

"Abbi, they're going to be—" His protest cuts off with a soft groan as I slip my hand into his boxer briefs to take hold of his dick. He instantly begins to grow within my grasp.

I smile, sitting down on the bed's edge in front of him. I push his underwear off his hips and let them tumble to the hardwood. And then I lean forward and run the flat of my tongue all the way up his length.

"I'm going to make you finish," he warns.

I wrap my lips around the end of his cock and slide down, taking him all in. I've been dreaming of doing this for weeks.

There's a wicked smirk on his lips. "Okay.... You asked for it." He adjusts his legs apart and then, gripping the back of my head, he starts gently thrusting in and out of my mouth, holding my hair off my face so he can see his length disappearing into me, hitting the back of my throat.

"Hello?" A woman's voice echoes through the vast space.

I make to pull away but Henry's hand tightens around the back of my head.

"Set up in the first bedroom at the top of the stairs. She'll be there in a minute!" Henry calls out, his eyes still on me, that wicked gleam in his eyes. In a softer voice, he adds, "Keep sucking my dick, Abbi. The sooner I finish, the less likely it is that we'll get caught."

The door's wide open and, while Henry's room is far enough down the hall that no one coming up the stairs or standing in the first bedroom will see this, if they should happen to wander down to ask a question, or for anything else, they're going to walk in on this. As it is, I'm afraid they'll hear it soon enough.

Henry doesn't seem at all concerned. In fact, he's swelling inside my mouth. "It's this or I bend you over the bed and finish off that way. Which one do you want?"

Would that be preferable to this?

No, I don't think so.

He sighs, grazing my cheek with the backs of his fingers. "Come on, baby. I have to come now."

I want him to come and not by himself in the shower. So I try to ignore the sound of more than one set of feet climbing the steps up to the second floor. They seem to have found the right bedroom at least.

"What size is she again?" a woman calls out.

"Size four. Shoes are a six. Breasts are 36D," Henry answers for me, a waver in his voice now as he begins plunging into my mouth. How he knows all this, I can't say.

"And Margo said you wanted a black dress?"

Henry's lips part, his eyes dark with lust as he stares down at me. "Yes," he manages to get out, and then his hand is gripping the back of my head tightly. A grimace takes over his handsome face but not a sound comes out of him as warm, salty fluid explodes into my mouth and I feel his length pulsing. This is the fastest he's ever come. It's like the risk of getting caught turned him on even more.

I suck hard as I slide off him, earning a low growl of discomfort—he's sensitive—and then swallow what's remaining of him in my mouth.

He brushes across my bottom lip with the pad of his thumb, a glaze of adoration in his eyes as he peers down at me, his chest heaving in and out. "You are...." His words fade.

I'm what?

Taking my hand, he pulls me up. Planting a kiss on my temple, he slaps my ass to usher me from the door. "Hurry. We don't have a lot of time."

---

I TAKE my time descending the steps a half hour later, the heels that Bonnie and Morgan dressed me in higher than anything I have ever worn. Not treacherously high, but still, I foresee being sprawled out face-first on a floor in my future if I'm not careful.

The team of twentysomething-year-olds worked on me fast, Bonnie on makeup, Morgan on hair, both on dressing me. They work in the modeling industry, dressing models for runway shows, so they're apparently used to tight timelines and seeing lots of flesh. That's why they didn't think anything of peeling my dress down and unfastening my bra so they could tape my breasts in place. I felt like a Barbie doll being dressed, their cool fingers touching me where only men have before. But I sucked it up and just stood there, allowing them to do what they needed to do, knowing the end result would be worth it.

Henry's standing at the bottom of the stairs, his back to me, talking to someone on his phone. He looks striking in head-to-toe black, his tailored dress pants hugging his ass so deliciously.

My heels click against the travertine, pulling his head my way.

I do a twirl for him, showing off the sexy black strapless dress they put me in. It's loose enough not to cling to my flesh, and it's short. I thought my legs looked long earlier, but with these heels on, I feel like I'm five foot ten.

Combined with the smoky eye makeup and the loose curls in my hair, I actually feel like I might belong on Henry's arm tonight. Or at least look the part.

"Yeah, okay. Gotta go. We'll talk more on the way tomorrow." He sets his empty glass down on the counter, his gaze roaming my entire body. "Are they gone?"

"Yeah, a couple minutes ago. Do I look okay?"

Stalking forward to close the distance in seconds, his

hands go straight for the hem of my dress. He lifts my dress up to my waist. He holds the material there, and simply stares at my lower half for a long moment, clad in black panties that came in the girls' suitcase of things. My thighs squeeze together in anticipation of everything he's going to do to me down there.

Finally, with a heavy sigh, he lets go and steps back. My dress falls back in place. "We need to go right now or we won't be going anywhere tonight."

He locks eyes with me and I can see that he's not joking.

Not even a little.

# CHAPTER 9

Our driver weaves around traffic, jolting to avoid the countless cabs cutting him off. It's a sea of honking horns and red lights here. I don't know how anyone drives in this city.

"So, what's she like?"

"Who, Margo? She's nice." His gaze drifts out the window.

"And this boyfriend of hers?"

"Never met him."

"How long have you known her for?"

"What's with all the questions?" He turns to look at me. "Are you still worried that there's something going on?"

"No." *Maybe.*

He gives me a flat look, like he can read my mind. But his hand settles in the crack between my legs, his thumb grazing over my smooth skin. "You have nothing to worry about, I promise. This is strictly business."

"Going out to clubs is for business?"

"Sometimes it is. Tonight it's for fun. We *have* become friends, too."

It's odd to hear Henry discuss friends. One might think

he has none. But apparently he does. Gorgeous French supermodel friends.

"Relax. You'll like her." His lip twitches in the hint of a smile. "And I think she'll like you."

---

"ABIGAIL! It is nice to meet you, finally," she croons, the greeting so pleasant on her French tongue. She rounds the dining table, her willowy, delicate body swaying seductively with each step, her cream-colored dress flowing with her movements. It's such a contrast to her poker-straight hair, the color of ravens' wings and somehow glossy even in the dim candlelit restaurant. It frames her angular face in a shoulder-length bob so beautifully.

I thought my legs looked long but I was only fooling myself. She stands a good five inches taller than me and all I see are legs and perky breasts.

She grasps my shoulders and leans in to air kiss my left cheek, before swinging her head to the other side to do the same with the right. Her hair smells delicious. She steps back, her sharp green eyes studying my face closely.

The warm, friendly greeting is so unexpected, I find myself at a loss for words.

She makes it sound like she's been waiting to meet me.

When did Henry tell her about me?

Finally, I manage a "hello." Because I'm smooth like that.

"Henry. Two nights in a row. This is a treat." She does the air kiss with him too, though he matches it with the grace of a sophisticated man who knows how to deal with the French.

He steps away and she smiles adoringly up at him.

Like she wants him.

*Stop it, Abbi. Don't be jealous.*

It's hard not to be, even more so now that I'm standing in

front of her. I don't know much about her, except for what I read in that hour between me seeing the picture and Henry responding to my text message. She's twenty-five years old and comes from what might be considered French royalty; her father's ancestors were kings and queens. She began modeling at fourteen and walked every major catwalk the world has, several times over. Now she graces Times Square billboards and bus shelters, storefronts and magazine covers.

She's perfect, and exotic, and glamorous.

She would fit well on Henry's arm, much more so than me.

*Stop it, Abbi. Henry is with you.*

"This is Joel. Joel, Henry and Abigail."

The way she says Henry's name, dropping the *H* altogether, is so charming. And I don't even care that she's using my full name; it sounds glamorous rolling off her tongue.

Her boyfriend, Joel, a tall, handsome, blond man with dimples and a mischievous glint in his eyes, stands to first shake Henry's hand and then plant a soft kiss on my cheek, his spicy cologne tickling my nostrils, his equally appealing French accent caressing my eardrums. I'd put him in his late twenties, likely.

"Have you eaten here before, Abigail?" she asks, ushering me to the stately wing chair directly beside her. Everything about this restaurant is elaborate—from the candelabras hanging above, to the damask wallpaper, to the waiters serving champagne in tuxedos. I'm not sure I even want to see what the plates cost.

"I've never been to New York City," I admit.

"What?" Her beautiful eyes widen in exaggerated shock as she suddenly rambles off a string of French words. "Joel, help me convince Henry to make sure his Abigail sees everything there is to see here. I don't think he appreciates this city as he should."

*His Abigail.*

Henry was wrong, I don't *like* her.

I freaking love Margo Lauren.

---

MARGO MAKES A CUTE, playful sound as she pats her perfectly flat belly through her dress. "Well, it is official. I have eaten and drank too much here, as usual. I need to go and work it off."

I glance at my phone. It's midnight. We've been eating food I can't pronounce and drinking red wine that I adore for three hours. The time passed quickly, with Margo telling funny stories about runway catastrophes, and Joel, a photographer with pieces now hanging in art museums all over the world, sharing horror stories of the horrendous models he's had to deal with in his career.

Henry glances back to grab the waiter's attention. He comes running and Henry hands him his card.

"No, Henry! You picked up last night as well," Margo admonishes, reaching across the table to place her hand over his. It's such an intimate move and directly in front of me. I glance to Joel. He must have noticed, but he doesn't seem in the least bit fazed by it.

I really need to calm down. She's done nothing overt to make me suspect that she's after him.

Henry rambles something in French—because, yes, I just found out that Henry is fluent in French from his years in boarding school, along with German and Spanish—and she squeezes his hand tight before pulling away.

"Fine. But when you come to my chateau for a visit, it will be my treat." She turns to me. "You will come too, Abigail. *Oui?*"

"Uh… *oui?*" I steal a glance Henry's way to see him studying Margo carefully.

He spouts off something else to her in French. I can't read his tone, but it doesn't sound all that relaxed.

Margo merely shrugs, and then winks at me.

What was that about?

I need to learn French.

Joel taps the table with his hands. "We are ready?"

Margo eases out of her chair with the grace of a feline. I wonder if all models move like that, or just Margo. It's impossible not to appreciate her as she and Joel walk ahead of us, leading us out of the restaurant, her back naked, her slender but curvy hips swaying with each step, the material hugging her round ass just snugly enough that I find myself picturing what it looks like bare. Something I don't think I've ever done before. She has this appeal to her that I can't quite figure out.

"You're attracted to her."

I startle at Henry's words, low and against my ear. "No, I'm not!"

He chuckles. "Don't be embarrassed by it. She has a draw to her that very few can ignore, even entirely straight women. Which, by the way, are few and far between."

"So you *are* attracted to her?"

His hand settles on my lower back, his fingers hot against my bare skin as they push under the material of my dress, his pinky toying with the very top of my ass crack. "I want you."

I stretch to my tiptoes to plant a quick kiss on his jaw. But I can't completely shake the conversation. "Has she hit on you?"

He hesitates, as if to choose his words carefully. "Margo is an intensely sexual person. She's hitting on you, even when she's not."

I frown, trying to understand what he means by that. I'm

still trying to figure it out as we climb into a waiting black SUV.

---

"WHAT'S THIS PLACE CALLED?" I yell over the music. My eyes struggle to adjust to the lighting. It's dimmer than the restaurant we just left, but the darkness is broken up by strobes and other flashing spotlights over the dance floor.

Henry doesn't answer—or maybe he does and I can't hear him. His arm hangs loose but protectively around my back as we make our way deeper into the club, past the throng of dancers, the heavy bass music pounding in my chest and in my throat.

Margo flashes a smile at the bouncer guarding the staircase and he lifts the rope, allowing us up the stairs and to the second floor, where a woman in a black leather bra and the shortest black shorts I've ever seen greets Margo with the two-cheek-kiss thing and tells her that her room is ready. She leads us down a hallway to a small private room overlooking the dance floor through a floor-to-ceiling window. The room is just large enough for a round table and the four leather chairs surrounding it.

Margo sighs. "There. That's much better. I can hear myself think!"

The music is still booming, vibrating through my body, but it's muffled now. We don't have to yell to talk.

I wander over to the window to watch the crowd of people gyrate to the music. It's a mess of scantily clad women and tangled limbs and swaying hips, some dancing in their own worlds, others in groups of three to four, pressed tight against each other, their drinks sloshing this way and that as they laugh and grind. I'm assuming a lot of them are drunk.

I sense someone sidling up behind me a second before

hands deftly slip under the sides of my dress to fill with my bare breasts.

"Henry!" My face burns as I grab his hands and yank them away. I look up to find him grinning.

"It's a one-way."

"What?"

"The window," Henry says, tapping on the glass. "We can see them, but they can't see us."

I allow myself a chance to breathe, though my heart's still racing. "That's not funny! You should have warned me. And besides...." I give him a knowing glare, then nod toward Margo and Joel, busy pouring drinks behind us.

"Trust me, they don't care." He leans down to treat my mouth to those full lips of his, his finger covertly dipping into my top to skate across my nipple. "I'm sorry, don't be mad."

I roll my eyes, but smile. Like I could ever be mad at him for touching me.

"Vodka or tequila!" Margo calls out. "Abigail, you choose." Behind us, she's lining up four shot glasses.

"My vote is neither. I've seen her drunk before and I don't think I want to be carrying her home." He softens his words with a playful slap across my ass, his hand lingering afterward.

"You are a frigid old woman tonight, Henry!" Margo teases, earning Joel's laughter. "Pick one!"

"Tequila, I guess?"

Henry shakes his head. He sits, pulling me into his lap, murmuring, "You're going to regret this."

She winks at me as she hands me my glass, her fingertips dancing over mine. "Bottoms up!"

I manage to get the shot down under Henry's watchful eye, my face twisting in disgust. "That's horrible."

"Yeah, especially after you two shared three bottles of wine."

"No we didn't," I deny, though I'm pretty sure we did because I'm feeling pretty damn relaxed right now.

"I paid the five-hundred-dollar-a-bottle bill, so I think I'd know."

My mouth drops open. The menu didn't even have prices listed on it, so I have no idea what that dinner might have cost.

"Here, have one more. It will taste better." Margo shoves another shot into my hand, watching expectantly.

I pour it back. And cringe. "You lied." If nothing, it might be worse. Though, I can already feel the burn coursing through my body, warming me from the inside.

Henry chuckles, cracking open a bottle of water. "Drink this or you'll be puking tonight, and I can think of other reasons for holding your hair."

Margo and Joel have turned their attention to the dance floor, their backs to us, so I take the opportunity to lean in and nuzzle my nose against Henry's ear. "Like what?" I whisper, letting my teeth graze against his lobe.

"You don't want to start this here, Abbi, trust me." He hands me the water with a look of warning. "Drink it."

I settle against his chest, my body relaxed from the wine and shots of tequila and humming from the music, and I drink my water as I watch Joel and Margo spy on the crowd below. My eyes are on Margo especially, her hips rolling to the music, her fingertips toying with the hem of her dress as if she might lift it off at any moment, her legs apart in an almost suggestive way. God, she's even more seductive when she dances. That's what it is, she oozes seductiveness. I'm sitting here on Henry's lap, mesmerized, wondering what she'd look like naked.

At some point in the song, Joel shifts behind her and

starts dancing with her, his hips grinding against her like the people below are doing.

"We should get going," Henry whispers in my ear, chasing it with a lingering kiss against my neck, his hand smoothing over my thigh in a slow draw, back and forth. It's an automatic move, my need to turn and meet his lips with mine. I think the alcohol and music and the touches he's stolen all night—his very presence, really—have finally come to a head because suddenly I can't wait to get home.

"Okay."

I turn back in time to see Joel slip Margo's dress up over her hips.

She's not even wearing panties.

My mouth drops open as she pulls the top of her dress down, exposing her full breasts. She rests her hands on the metal bar that runs across the length of the window in front of her, adjusting her stance to spread her legs.

"Oh my God. Are they going to—"

With his back to us, Joel fumbles with his belt buckle, unzipping his pants. They loosen around his hips as he positions himself behind her. She cries out as he thrusts into her.

They're going to fuck right in front of us, overlooking the busy club.

I turn to look Henry. "We should *definitely* go."

He doesn't seem to hear me, his eyes—hooded and heated—locked on them, skating over Margo's naked flesh, his hand tightening around my hip.

He may have said that he doesn't want her, but I can feel the bulge growing in his pants, straining against the material.

Margo murmurs something in French and Joel turns her around to face us. Settling her ass on the metal bar, she hikes her legs. He slides back into her.

"Henry...," she purrs, her seductive eyes locked on his as

she says something to him in French, a "please" slipping through her lips with a slight moan at the end.

He doesn't respond but he doesn't break eye contact with her—her eyes, her breasts, where Joel is joined with her—his jaw tensing. His entire body tensing, his fingers tightening on me almost to the point of pain.

I feel like I'm not even here.

And suddenly I don't *want* to be here, to watch them eye fuck each other.

I climb off Henry's lap, a sharp ball swelling in my throat as I grab my purse and head for the door.

"Abigail…," he calls out in that low, warning tone of his.

"I'll meet you outside when you're done," I snap, throwing the door open. The hall sways a little as I rush along it. Or I sway, which is more likely the case, the tequila hitting me hard.

I get all the way to the stairs before a hand seizes my elbow. "Where are you going?" He actually has the nerve to sound angry with me.

"Figured I'd give you two some privacy." I tug my arm away and begin taking the steps down.

Too fast in these heels, when I'm more drunk than I first thought. How'd that happen so fast?

My ankle folds, followed by my knee buckling. My body crumples forward.

Henry is somehow suddenly there, his arm roping around my waist, his shoulder stopping me from tumbling. He swiftly carries me down the rest of the way.

"Put me down! I can walk."

"You broke your heel," he mutters, moving through the crowd.

In seconds he's sliding me into the back of an SUV. "Next time I tell you to stop drinking, please listen."

"You're not even going to apologize?"

The severe glare I get in return makes me second-guess myself and my anger for a moment. "For what?" He says it so coolly.

"For lying to me."

His jaw tenses. "Even a gay man would be attracted to her, Abbi. You're drunk and acting ridiculous. Stop talking right now, before you say something you're going to regret."

"You want to fuck her, admit it!" I hiss. I should be embarrassed, having this conversation in front of the driver, but whether it's my emotions or the alcohol—probably both —I can't control the words spewing from my mouth.

A condescending smirk twists his lips.

The realization is like a punch to my stomach. "You already have." Of course he has.

He doesn't deny it.

I'm so stupid.

We're silent until the driver pulls up to the front of the building. I jump out and start rushing for the front door, desperate to get away from him. I get all of ten steps before I'm off the ground and in Henry's arms again. It's not nearly as romantic as the time he carried me from the dock to my cabin. This time I just want to get away from him. "Put me down!"

"You're not walking into my building drunk and in bare feet. Have more class than that, Abigail."

"Because Margo fucking her boyfriend in front of you is *so* classy," I snap.

His stony blue eyes dart to the security guards manning the door. "Good night, gentlemen." He doesn't set me down until we're in his private elevator. It's a smooth ride up and yet I'm still feeling queasy, my nerves shot. "How could you lie to me and bring me out with her tonight?"

"I've never lied."

I let out a small scream of frustration as the elevator

doors open. I barrel through his foyer, bumping into the table on my way. "Whatever."

"I've never lied!" Henry yells. It's so rare to hear him raise his voice. Normally his words are ice, his tone cutting. But to hear him yell...

I freeze at the bottom of the stairs.

"You never asked."

"Bullshit, I didn't! You told me this was just a business relationship."

"It is."

"Do you sleep with every woman you have a business relationship with? Hell, do you sleep with every woman you meet? Because it's sure starting to feel like it!"

"Watch it, Abbi," he growls.

*Oh God, I don't feel good. The room is starting to spin.* "Why didn't you tell me? When you don't tell me these things, it makes me think you're hiding something."

"Because it happened a year ago. And you didn't ask if I fucked her in the past. If you had, I would have told you. You asked if there is something going on between us and there isn't."

Somehow he's turning this on me, like it's my fault he wasn't forthright. "So you slept with her, she clearly still wants to sleep with you—don't deny it!" I yell when he opens his mouth. "And now you're partnering with her for this hotel. How am I supposed to just deal with that?"

He levels me with a gaze. "The same way I'm dealing with you still talking to the grounds crew guy you fucked. Who is *still* employed by me, along with the guy you did everything with *but* fuck, because I promised you I wouldn't fire their asses even though I *really* want to."

That reminder takes a bit of the hot air from my argument. "I was completely honest. I told you exactly what happened with Ronan and Connor. You could at least have done the same."

"You want to know *exactly* what happened?" He begins stalking toward me in that intimidating way of his. "Okay, Abbi. Twelve months ago I met Margo and she made her proposal about the place in France. I flew out to see it. I watched her and her boyfriend at the time fuck. Then she asked me to join them, so I did." He stops just in front of me, his massive body hovering over me. "I've had my dick in her mouth and in her ass. Is that specific enough? Do you want *more* details?"

I bolt for the bathroom just in time, the vomit sailing up my throat.

# CHAPTER 10

I come to with the morning sun streaming in my eye and a hand on my hip, gently shaking me awake.

"Abbi? It's time to get up."

I groan, squinting against the light as I check the clock. Eight a.m. "I thought we had all day." He's the insane early bird, not me. The acrid taste in my mouth is making me wince. "Can I have some water?"

"Right here." The mattress beside me sinks and a cold glass is set into my hand, along with two Tylenol. I struggle to sit up and swallow the pills. "God, why did you let me drink so much!" Braving the sunlight, I look up to see Henry's flat glare and I immediately drop my gaze. I'm naked.

"Your dress is hanging in the bathroom. It'll need to be dry cleaned," he says as if reading my thoughts.

"Why.... Oh, God." I cringe as memories of vomiting into a toilet flood my thoughts. My first night together with Henry and I spend it drunk and puking. Those memories quickly give way to more horrific ones—of Margo and Joel at the bar, of Margo's eyes locked on Henry, of Henry entranced by her.

Of Henry admitting he's already slept with her.

"Oh my God." I curl up into a ball, feeling ready to vomit again.

"Yeah." He sighs, his gaze drifting off toward the window. He's already showered and dressed. "Come on. If you want a shower before the plane, you'd better get it now."

My eyes begin to sting with tears. I'm not nearly as upset about him sleeping with Margo as I was last night. Now I'm feeling more stupid than anything, especially given it happened so long ago. And panicked, that I have permanently screwed up things between us. "So that's it? We have a fight and you throw me on a plane and send me home first thing in the morning?"

"That wasn't a fight, Abbi. That was you acting like an unconfident little girl. You know how unappealing that is to me."

"I'm sorry, I just...." Why did I have to drink so much? I would have been fine, had I stayed away from those shots. "You were watching them. Watching *her*. I got upset."

He heaves a sigh. "Look, I should have told you. I thought about it, but you are so goddamn insecure about us as it is, I didn't want to make a big deal of something that meant nothing to me."

"How can I not be insecure about you? I don't know a woman who doesn't want you, Henry. And I can't compete with a woman like *that*." She's up to bat in a stadium and I'm still on the playground.

And she was calling his name, so seductively.

"You already know how I feel about you."

"No I don't!" I exclaim. "When have you ever told me how you feel?"

"I *show* you, Abbi. Every time I'm with you."

"Like you showed Margo?"

He glares at me, annoyed. "I haven't touched her since

that night. I haven't touched another woman since the day I met you. You can't say the same."

I flinch at the reminder.

"Look." He sighs, hangs his head. "Nothing good will come of talking about any of them, so let's stop that right now."

"Okay." He doesn't sound like he's ending things, at least. Though I can still sense his mood and it's sour. So, I peel myself up again to crawl toward him, curling my head into his lap because I can't punish him with my breath right now. "Let me make it up to you." After I brush my teeth a thousand times and shower in scalding water.

Henry's chuckle is soft but I sigh all the same, because he's laughing. His fingers stroke through my hair. "I wish we could, but we really do have to leave."

"Why?"

He slides me off his lap and moves for his closet. That's when I notice the two suitcases sitting next to the doorway that weren't there yesterday. "We just got our annual projections in and two of my Wolf hotels are underperforming. The one in Barcelona is on the verge of shutting down. That'll be the first Wolf Hotel in history to be forced to close because of economic problems. I need to be on the ground over there to try and fix this. Fire some fucking people and rebuild my teams."

"How long will you be gone?"

"Don't know. I'm flying to LA today, and then to Wolf Cove to meet with the engineers about the ski hill. After that, I'm guessing I'll be overseas for five or six weeks. Could be longer."

Five to six weeks? Maybe more?

Do we have any chance of lasting that long without seeing each other?

"I'll meet you downstairs." He grabs the handles on his

suitcases and disappears out the door, now in full Henry business mode.

Dragging myself out of bed, I head for the shower, my heart heavy.

---

"Give us a minute, Miles."

I smile at Miles before ducking out the door of Henry's jet, though inside I'm insanely jealous of Henry's assistant for the fact that he's traveling with Henry. I want my job back. I want to travel around the world with him.

Henry leads me to a black sedan waiting at the edge of the tarmac for the forty-minute drive back to Greenbank. "I'm sorry that I had to cut this trip short."

"It's okay. I understand." That's all I've been since I woke up: understanding. Trying to soften the damage I might have caused with my tantrum last night, even though I hate this. Hate the fact that he's leaving—again. Hate how we're leaving things, feeling strained.

I took longer than I needed to in the shower, hoping Henry would join me and allow me to apologize for my behavior.

He did step into the bathroom, but only to tell me to hurry up.

Then I hoped for a chance to reconcile on the hour-long plane ride.

But Miles was there.

Now I'm considering pulling him into this sedan, but the windows aren't tinted.

"I'll call you," he murmurs, handing my bag to the driver to slide into the trunk.

I take a deep breath and, pressing myself against the contours of his body, I stretch to my tiptoes to kiss his mouth, dragging my tongue against the seam of his lips the way he likes it.

He groans. "Abbi...." I inhale the smell of his cologne, and it brings me back to those first days at Wolf Cove. "I miss Alaska. I want to go back so badly."

He stares down at me, an unreadable look in his eyes. "So then come."

I smile. "Funny."

"I'm serious. Fly to Seattle on Wednesday. I'll meet you there and we'll go up together."

"Seriously?" My heart swells with relief. If he's inviting me out, he's still in this. He's still willing to try "us."

"I leave for Beijing on Friday morning, so it'll be a short trip."

Two days with Henry. Two days in my favorite place.

"Okay."

His brow spikes. "Okay?"

"I think so. I'll have to check." I already took off on Jed and Mama for a night. This might be pushing it.

He tucks my still-damp hair off my face. "Let me know. Miles will book your flights."

Leaning down, he plants one more, deeper kiss on my lips. "Gotta go."

I watch him jog back to his plane, a smile on my face.

I'm going back to Alaska.

And I don't care what Mama says.

# CHAPTER 11

Just one more hour until I leave for the airport.

Seven hours until I land in Seattle.

Eight hours until I see Henry.

I pause my last-minute packing to peer at my flight reservations for the hundredth time, my chest filled with only excitement by the prospect of being back there. Miles put me in first class to Seattle. Henry will pick me up in his jet and we'll fly to the private airstrip. From there, it's just a quick ferry ride and I'll be at Wolf Cove again.

It's going to be weird. I'm no longer an employee there and that means that *everyone's* going to know about Henry and me.

Jed trudged around like a sour child all day yesterday, but he hasn't said a word in protest. Neither has Mama, oddly enough. She sniffed a little at dinner last night, acting hurt, waiting for me to console her. When I didn't fall for it, she reluctantly agreed with Daddy that I deserved to get away for a few days. That I'd been working hard and I had every right to go.

It was rather odd, but I'm guessing Reverend Enderbey had a hand in that because I heard her on the phone with him. He's still trying to convince her that time will change things. That I'll break up with Henry like Jed broke up with Cammie, and we'll find ourselves back together. I don't know when they'll finally accept that—

A loud crash sounds downstairs.

I take the steps two at a time. "Mama? Daddy?" When I get to the kitchen, I let out a scream. Mama is sprawled out in the middle of the kitchen floor, gasping for air, her hand on her chest over her heart.

"I need an ambulance!" My dad demands into the phone receiver. He was sitting in his wheelchair having his breakfast. Luckily, the phone was within reach.

"Mama!" I dive to the floor.

"It hurts!" she manages to get out through gasps.

"Daddy, I think she's having a heart attack!" It wouldn't be surprising. Both Great-Grandma Pearl and Grandma Maggie died of heart attacks, though Mama's young yet.

"Does your left arm hurt?"

Her eyes widen. "Yes!" She grabs her arm and moans.

Oh my God. I can't believe this is happening. She's only thirty-nine years old. "Okay, hold on, Mama! The ambulance is coming!"

She paws for my hand, grasping it tightly until the paramedics arrive. "Stay with me, Abigail. I'm scared."

"Of course!" Tears sting my eyes. "I would never leave you."

Celeste Enderbey arrives just as they're wheeling Mama into the ambulance. She must have heard the sirens wailing. "What do they think it is?"

"They don't know. Her heart rate is all over the place."

Celeste squeezes my arm. "You go ahead, I'll stay here with Roger."

I wedge myself in the corner as the paramedics hook

Mama up to all kinds of machines, managing to keep hold of her hand the entire time.

The ambulance races toward the hospital and I pray.

Everything else is forgotten.

---

"INDIGESTION?"

I stare at the doctor, waiting for him to correct what I thought he just said, because I must have heard wrong.

"Honestly? I don't know what else could have caused the pain. I've gone through the tests several times. Everything has come back clean. Even her heart is fine. Surprising, to be blunt. All I could see was some irritation in her esophagus, common to acid reflux."

"I've been sitting in this hospital for twenty-eight hours because of *gas*? I missed my flight to Seattle because my mother ate pizza?"

He gives me a sympathetic smile. "With her family history and her weight, we had to run the tests to make sure. And her heart rate was irregular when she came in."

"Yes, of course. I'm glad you did. I'm sorry, I don't mean to sound...." Ungrateful, selfish, horrible. I shake my head, still surprised. "Is it normal that gas would knock you on your back like that?" Mama was literally lying on the floor, clutching her chest.

"Well... people's pain thresholds are different. Combine that with the high levels of anxiety your mother says she's been experiencing and *maybe*?" His expression isn't convincing. "I'm going to talk to her about making some serious changes to her diet while we finish up with the paperwork, and then I can release her. You're welcome to go in and see her."

"Thanks." I watch him stroll away.

And wonder, would Mama have faked a heart attack just to keep me from going to Alaska to see Henry?

No. She's stubborn and resourceful, but that's downright crazy.

Still....

I eye her door for a long moment, deciding if it's smart that I go in there right now, with this doubt brewing.

I walk past it toward the cafeteria.

---

"WELL, that's just great that it turned out to be nothing. Isn't that just great?" Celeste turns in her seat to smile wide at me.

"Yes. Great." My voice lacks enthusiasm, but I can't help it. I turn to watch the roads drift by, quietly playing out the whole thing again. Her face didn't turn red, she wasn't sweating. And.... I frown as it all comes back to me. Her arm didn't seem to hurt until after I mentioned it, and then it was suddenly *so* painful.

Seriously, did Mama just fake a heart attack to keep me from seeing Henry?

No. I'm horrible for thinking that.

Horrible.

"Thank goodness my Abigail was here to take care of me." Mama reaches over. "The doctor seems very concerned about my heart. He said I need to be extra careful for the next few months, to make sure I don't aggravate it any more, what with my family history. Gosh, between me and Roger, I don't think this poor girl is going to get a moment's rest."

I replay the conversation in my head. I'm pretty sure the doctor said her heart looked fine and that she needed to lose weight and not eat pizza.

She babbles on with Celeste and the Reverend, her gaze shifting to me every once in a while, just long enough to smile and pat my knee. Though each time, those smiles grow more wary.

Reverend Enderbey pulls into the gas station just outside of town. "I just need to top us up. I'm afraid we won't make it back."

"I'll do it!" I hop out of the car before he even has time to unfasten his seat belt, struggling to unclench my jaw as I jam the gas nozzle into the Oldsmobile. If she was trying to keep me from seeing Henry, she has succeeded. Even if I fly to Seattle now, by the time I get to Alaska, it'll be night, and Henry is leaving for Beijing in the morning. Honestly, I considered it. I even went as far as to try and book another flight while I sat in the cafeteria, waiting for Mama to be discharged and the Enderbeys to pick us up. But nothing was available.

I won't see Henry for weeks. Months, possibly.

I'm fighting tears when a car pulls up beside us.

"Hey, Abigail!"

I look over to see Jenny climbing out of the driver side, adjusting her skirt. Veronica and Beth are also with her, surprise, surprise. "Hey, Jenny." I can't keep the melancholy from my voice.

Veronica nods to Jenny once, a silent communication.

Jenny turns back to me. "We're going out tonight. Do you want to come?"

I've never gone out with any of them. It doesn't take a genius to see what's going on here. They figure they can get close to me and then have an in with Henry. And right now, all I want to do is curl up in my bed and cry anyway.

From inside the car, Mama clears her throat loudly. She doesn't approve of me going anywhere. Of course.

"My mother just got out of the hospital. I should probably stay home."

Jenny's eyes flitter to the back window. "I hope she's okay."

My defiant streak flares. "Yeah, she's fine. Just bad gas," I say, loudly enough for Mama to hear.

"Oh." Jenny presses her lips together, trying not to laugh. She lowers her voice to say, "If you change your mind, we're leaving out from my place at nine."

"Okay, thanks." I glance at my watch. It's two o'clock. I should be tangled in Henry's sheets right now. Instead, I'm pumping gas and letting Mama win. How long will I last at home before I make my suspicions known?

With each passing minute, going out with three girls I don't even like is sounding better and better.

---

"Why would you say such a thing!"

I push through the screen door and into the kitchen. Daddy and Jed are sitting at the table, bewildered looks on their faces.

"What in heaven's name is going on now?" Daddy's spoonful of soup is halfway to his mouth.

"I'm fresh off the heels of a heart attack and she's mocking me!" Mama cries, huffing and puffing as she tries to catch up.

"You didn't have a heart attack. You had *gas*!"

"Well… I *thought* it was a heart attack," she mutters with indignation.

"Did you? Did you *really*?"

Her mouth drops open. "You heard the paramedics. My heart was going haywire. What are you insinuating?"

"Abigail!"

I turn to see the harsh disappointment in my dad's eyes and

mine immediately begin to burn with tears. I take the stairs two at a time, running all the way to the bathroom, slamming the door shut behind me, somehow managing to kick the trash can over in the process as I crumple to the floor in a fit of sobs.

Guilt weighs heavily on me.

I can't believe I've actually convinced myself that Mama would fake a heart attack. What is happening to me? I never would have done that before. I just wanted to see Henry so badly. Is this what Daddy was talking about, when he said he didn't want me to turn into someone I couldn't be proud of?

I need to apologize to them.

Pulling a tissue from the box, I blow my nose a few times, then set to cleaning up the mess I just made.

Five small foil wrappers catch my attention. I pick one up to read the small writing on one side. And frown. Caffeine pills?

Who's been taking caffeine pills? And five of them. I emptied the trash for collection yesterday morning, so someone took five caffeine pills between yesterday morning and—

Realization dawns on me. I march downstairs, wiping my tears from my cheeks with the back of my hands, an odd sense of vindication taking over.

I hold up the pill packaging in front of Jed but I'm looking at Mama. "Do you know anything about this?"

"What are those? Caffeine pills? Heck, no," Jed says.

But I'm not even listening to him because the look on Mama's face says it all. She tries to smooth it over, but it's not fast enough for me. Not even for Daddy.

He frowns as he looks from Mama to me, to the pill packaging, and back again.

"Someone took five of these yesterday morning after I emptied the trash. Do you know something about that, Mama?"

Mama's eyes dart to the freshly brewed cup of coffee in her hand, that the doctor specifically asked her to cut out. "No. I like my caffeine in a cup. Must have been… someone else."

"The only other person here was Celeste, Bernadette. Why would she take those? And why would she do it in our upstairs bathroom?" Daddy's been married to her a long time. Long enough to see through her bullshit, too.

She swallows, feigning indifference. Something she's not good at doing, because there isn't anything she doesn't have a strong opinion on and, if she suspected Celeste was popping pills like this, she'd already be on the phone. "I couldn't tell you."

"You took them yesterday morning to spike your heart rate, just so you could keep me from going to Alaska to see Henry."

She opens her mouth and I know denial is coming.

"That wasn't a question." I toss the wrappers onto the table. "If you ever try to interfere with me seeing Henry again, I will tell every last person in this town what you did."

"Good Lord, Bernadette. If anyone needs their head examined, it's you! Do you know how dangerous this is? You could have killed yourself!"

I leave them to argue because I'm done. I march right back upstairs, intent on getting out of here. Maybe not to Alaska, but at least to wherever Jenny is planning on going. Anything is better than staying here.

# CHAPTER 12

"Are you guys sure about this?"

My stomach does another flip as I pull my truck into the parking lot of Billy Bob's, a white clapboard building with no neighbors in sight, twenty miles outside of Greenbank, near the highway. It looks like it might have been a large ranch house at one point, its second story built into a high-peaked attic. The sides haven't seen a coat of paint in a few years.

Music blares through the gaping windows, where neon lights flash, advertising various liquor and beer brands.

"My friend is meeting us here tonight." Veronica eyes the row of bikes parked along the curb, leather-clad men and women alike hanging off each other, bottles of beer in hand, laughing boisterously.

What the hell am I doing here?

We pile out of my truck. I can't help but do a double take at all of them. When we pulled away from Jenny's house, waving at her mom, they were in regular t-shirts and summer skirts. As soon as we rounded the corner, they started stripping, revealing tank tops and jean shorts that barely cover their asses. They traded sandals for heels hiding in someone's backpack, and spent the last fifteen minutes testing out the lights on my visor mirrors to cake on their makeup.

I do a quick glance at my clothes. Having no idea what we were doing and not having many options, I settled on jeans and a black tank top that I had borrowed from Katie and forgot to return. It's far from fancy, but it's tight and low-cut and has a slogan across the front that says, "If it feels good, do it." The scathing look on Mama's face when she saw me come down in it made it all worth it.

But Jenny made me pull over and take my jeans off right in the driver side, swapping them for this black skirt that's loose but short. *Really* short.

A man in his midtwenties is leaning against the thick post on the front porch, his smirk growing more lascivious as his eyes pass each of us. He's one of the bikers, I gather by his heavy black boots and leather cut. His chin-length blond hair is pushed back off his forehead, allowing me a good glimpse of his handsome face.

When his eyes land on me, they settle on my chest for a good five seconds.

I can't help but cross my arms.

He chuckles. "Sounds like you and I are a lot alike."

Doubt that.

Reaching a hand out, he scoops Veronica up with one tattooed arm, his fingers sliding up her shorts to grasp her ass. And squeeze. In front of everyone.

"Hey, baby. Missed you," he murmurs, burying his face in her neck for a second.

I can't help but widen my eyes.

Veronica is with a biker?

Oh boy. Between simply wearing cut-off jean shorts and dating a biker, I think her mother, who leads the choir at the church and wears a dress 365 days of the year, would gladly take the shorts.

I'm guessing she has no idea about him, though.

"That's Declan. She met him at her dad's shop. He brought his car in for fixing."

"Oh." I guess that would make sense. How else would their two worlds ever collide?

Veronica pulls away to give him a pouty look. "Where have you been?"

He shrugs, releasing her but not without running her body down the front of his in a very deliberate move. "Here and there." His gaze shifts to me again. "Who's the new girl?"

"That's our DD. Come on, I want a drink." She grabs hold of his hand and tugs him inside. He follows with a playful grin on his face.

It stinks of beer inside. Not freshly poured beer either. Stale beer, as if it's been spilled and left to soak into the worn wood floors and tables for decades, and it's never coming out.

To the left is a simple bar with a weathered-looking bleach-blonde woman about twenty-five pounds too heavy behind it, gabbing and smiling as she pours drinks, breasts to rival mine in size spilling out of a loose top. Everywhere else are people of every age, most of them people I don't recognize. Which is odd, being only twenty miles away from Greenbank, where it's like I know everyone.

"Band plays over there on Friday nights." Jenny points to a stage on the right.

"How often do you come here?"

"This will be our third time." Her eyes graze the crowd. "There are so many hot guys here."

Clearly I have misjudged the debate team captain and mathlete Jenny in a major way.

I let my eyes wander, too, to the source of music—a jukebox beside the stage. A muscular man with sandy-brown hair flips through the catalogue of songs while an exotic brunette woman in a spandex tight-fitting dress grinds into his side, running her long, hot-pink nails back and forth over his back intimately.

I wanted to get out of the house and forget the fact that I'm not with Henry, but this isn't where I want to be. The staff lodge at Wolf Cove, sharing drinks and stories with Ronan and Katie and my other friends… that's more what I was thinking.

This place feels… off.

Beth thrusts a bottle of beer in my hand.

I try to give it back to her. "I can't. I'm driving." After Saturday night, I'm definitely not ever drinking again.

She rolls her eyes at me. "It's one drink, and we're not leaving for a few hours."

A few hours. Great.

I take the bottle for the sake of holding something, and then trail them toward the back.

---

"WHEN ARE you going to see Henry again?" Jenny leans in to glance at my phone.

I pull it against my chest, protectively. *So you're on a first-name basis with him, too?* "Not for a while. He's leaving for Beijing in the morning."

She sighs. "Wow, that's so cool. Too bad you can't go with him."

"Yeah, too bad." Though, after what Mama pulled, I want to just pick up and leave. But I can't do that to Daddy.

"Jenny!" A blonde girl waves at Jenny from the other side of the table.

"Sherri!" Jenny squeals. "I'll come around and give you a squeeze in a bit, okay?"

"Okay!"

The blonde gets herded along the path by a broad-chested guy who's holding her hand. He glances once our way before continuing on.

Jenny leans in. "She has no idea that I fucked him out back about a month ago."

It takes me a few seconds to recover from that bit of naked truth. "Were they together then?"

She snorts. "Yeah. For, like, a year now. And she thinks he's so in love with her." The smug smile on her face as she watches them talk to someone else tells me she doesn't feel the least bit guilty about it.

"Wow. That's…." I'm not sure exactly what I want to say.

*I really don't think I like you?*

One of Declan's friends hollers at Jenny and she immediately abandons me to climb over the table, flipping her hair over her shoulder. They've been flirting all night and I'm pretty sure they're going to hook up soon.

Declan and Veronica disappeared for a while, but they're back and standing at the next table over, her hand settled on the buckle of his jeans possessively. She's had at least two shots of something amber since she's been back, so I'm guessing she's drunk.

Where Beth is, I have no idea. I haven't seen her in a while.

Everyone at that table is drunk, I'm sure. They're all smiling and laughing hysterically, shouting over each other, their hands all over the place. And the one guy has this intense expression on his face like….

My eyes widen as I catch a glimpse of a head in his lap. I'm guessing it's a woman. She must be crouched under the table, her body mixed among the tangle of feet because I can't see the rest of her. All I can see is that head, bobbing up and down to the beat of the music, her brunette hair spilled on either side.

Is this what they do at bars like this?

I avert my gaze and shrink into my corner, where I've been holed up for the past two hours, watching everyone chug back pitchers of beer.

My phone vibrates in my hand.

Tell them they can get a ride with you now or they'll have to find their own way home.

I can't just abandon them.

I didn't hear from Henry until about an hour ago, after I told him where I was and how much I'd rather be anywhere than here. I haven't told him what my mother did. Partly because I'm embarrassed, but mostly because I don't want him looking at this as proof that maybe we shouldn't be together. He suggested that once already, and it nearly ripped my heart out.

Honestly, I don't even think it's about Mama hating Henry. Mama just has a plan for her life, and her life involves my life, and she may be the most narrowly focused human being on the face of the earth.

A commotion starts at the table right next to us. Declan is standing chest to chest with a guy who looks a lot like him—blond hair, scruffy face, leather, handsome. They're staring each other down as they exchange low words. Veronica has been pushed off to the side, replaced by three or four guys, their hands flexing.

Readying for a fight, it would seem.

Where the hell are the bouncers? I glance around, but don't see any. I do, however, see the bartender pulling a baseball bat out from beneath the bar and tossing it to a big burly man with a long beard and a bandana over his head.

He cuts his way through the crowd and taps Declan's

shoulder with the end of it. "Am I gonna have to send you home with a cracked skull?"

I note that he doesn't address the other guy. Either he has ties to him, or Declan is the real threat here.

After a painfully long moment, Declan's body visibly relaxes and that wide, leisurely grin stretches across his face. "No issues at all, Dad. Just making sure he knows she's mine."

Several eyes flicker over to Veronica, clearly the root of this confrontation.

"She's with you. Got it." The other guy's Adam's apple bobs with a hard swallow.

"Well, all right then." Declan ropes his arm around the guy's neck playfully, ruffling his hair once. "Glad I didn't have to beat your ass. Mom wouldn't have liked it."

Oh my God. They're brothers.

Who were going to start a brawl over Veronica.

I've got to get out of here.

"Take your dick fight outside next time," the bearded man—their father, apparently—mutters, sauntering back toward the bar, tossing the bat toward the bartender. She catches it with one hand, her other hand keeping a pitcher held up to a tap with deft precision.

Veronica shifts back into Declan's side with a nervous smile, her eyes flickering to his brother's face a few times. The second Declan looks away, his brother winks at her.

I have a feeling these two are going to fight before the end of the night, and I really don't want to be here for that.

I squeeze out of my corner and weave through the crowd toward the narrow hallway in the back. It's unmarked, but I've seen enough people milling in and out of there to guess that this is where the restrooms must be.

It's lined with people, leaning against either wall in small groups of two and three, beers in hand. None of them look like they're actually waiting in line, so I slip around them, looking for the sign for women's. I find it on the left. But the door is locked, occupied, forcing me to wait.

"Abigail!" Jenny calls out. I turn to see her pointing to a door I just passed. "Meet us in here, after."

"Actually, I really think I want to…." My voice drifts as she disappears into the room. "Leave."

With a sigh, I settle against the wall and wait.

Ten minutes later, there's a line behind me and I'm crossing my legs. I'd even consider using the men's bathroom, if it wasn't occupied too.

"Come on! Hurry up!" A guy pounds on the men's room door, turning to shake his head at me. "Ridiculous that they don't have stalls, isn't it?" he mutters with a slur.

I nod in agreement, because it is. There must be two hundred people packed into this bar. This has to be some sort of code violation. Among many, I'm sure.

He holds up the half-empty pitcher of beer. "You need a drink."

"I've got one back at the table. Thanks," I lie, trying not to cringe. I watched the busser dumping the ends of several pitchers into one and then topping it up with draft beer when they thought no one was looking. I guess they don't like waste.

The door to the men's washroom opens.

"Finally!" he hollers, watching as, of all people, Beth stumbles out, drunk.

And trailing behind her… Jed.

I'm not sure who's more shocked.

His eyes widen when they take me in. "Abigail? What are you doing here?"

"If you're gonna fuck, next time go outside so people can piss," the drunk guy with the pitcher complains before slamming the door shut.

"It's not what it looks like." His eyes dart to Beth, whose

smooth, sleek hair is all mussed and her bright pink lipstick has been smeared.

Some of it, on his lips.

He couldn't possibly look more guilty than if I had actually walked in on them doing it.

I do the only thing I can. I start to laugh. "It's exactly what it looks like, Jed. And I don't care. I'm glad you're moving on." Even if it is with Beth.

"I'm not, though! I swear. I'm still waiting for you!"

The women's bathroom door opens and two women walk out, smiling and brushing their hands against their noses. I try to step in but he grabs my arm.

"I swear, I'm not moving on. I just needed…." He frowns. "I have needs!"

I tug my arm away. "And you should go fill them with Beth, or whoever else you want. Because I seriously don't care!"

He flinches as if I slapped him. "You don't mean that."

"Actually, I do. And I have to pee."

Beth sways into Jed, falling against his chest, her eyes closing.

"Be a good person and drive her home now. She's too drunk to be here." With that, I lock myself in the bathroom.

*One down, two to go.*

Something tells me getting Jenny and Veronica out of here won't be nearly so easy.

---

The door to the room is pushed shut, and there's a sign hanging off the nail that says Private.

I knock on it once, rather gingerly.

"Just go in, doll!" someone hollers, chuckling at me as they pass by.

*Okay….*

I turn the knob and step into a narrow hall that leads into a dimly lit room.

"Who is it!" a deep male voice hollers.

"Abbi."

"Close the door."

I comply, pushing it shut softly behind me. Ahead of me, balls skate across the green felt surface of a pool table as someone takes a turn, and a red-striped ball sinks into the side pocket.

A round of male cheers goes up.

"Better catch up soon, ladies," Declan teases.

They're playing pool. Okay. This, I can handle. More than what's going on out there.

I step into the room just as Jenny's shorts hits the floor. On the other side of the table, Veronica is stumbling out of hers, too.

"What took you so long?" Declan smiles down at me in that mischievous way of his. "Your friends are losing and losing fast."

And they're clearly playing for clothes.

The girls are down to nothing but their bras and panties, everything else, including shoes, cast to the floor.

Meanwhile Declan and the guy Jenny was flirting with are only missing their shirts.

"We're just warming up." Veronica chalks her stick and puckers her lips to blow on it, sending blue powder into the air.

"Beth just got a ride home with Jed. I'm going to head out too, so if you want a ride now…."

"Let us just finish this game." Declan's big hands fall on my shoulders to massage them, a touch too rough. "Okay?"

"Okay," I hear myself squeak. Because what else do I say

to this big, burly guy, no doubt anxious to see these girls naked?

"Here, we'll even let them take the next shot, even though it's ours." He guides me over to a black leather couch that has probably seen a lot of asses and, by what's going on in here, maybe other things too. There's actually a small sign above it that reads, "No cum on the felt —Management."

*Oh my God.*

"Why don't you just sit your pretty little self next to my brother and watch. Gunner, this is DD. DD, this is Gunner."

"Hey, Double D."

I turn to offer Gunner a polite smile, and find his eyes locked to my chest.

"Maybe you two can play each other next," Declan suggests, slapping Veronica's bare ass as she leans over the table to take her shot, her pink thong leaving nothing to the imagination.

I avert my gaze, feeling my cheeks blush.

"What's wrong? Never seen this before?"

I've seen this and a lot more, I could say, but I have a feeling that admitting that won't help me in this situation.

Veronica misses the shot. "Damn it!" She giggles.

"This isn't fair!" Jenny moans.

"Top or bottom, top or bottom…. What do you think, bro?" Declan calls out.

Gunner seems to ponder it for a moment. "Let Double D pick." He nudges my leg with his.

I shrink away from him, earning his laugh. "No. It's okay."

"Come on. You gotta pick!" Declan booms, and they all stare at me, expectantly.

"Whatever ends this game faster so I can go home," I finally mutter.

Declan grins. "You heard her. Bottoms, ladies."

They look at each other with a hint of nervousness and then, with matching giggles, they slide their panties off.

"Damn...." Jenny's guy—Mutt, I heard Declan call him a minute ago—murmurs, his eyes locked on the thin strip of hair between Jenny's legs.

"Take your shot." Declan slams the end of his pool cue against his thigh, making him flinch.

He does, quickly and with seemingly little effort, sinking two balls at once.

Declan grins, his eyes shifting between Veronica and Jenny, watching expectantly as the two of them reach for their bra clasps. Beside me, Gunner shifts in his seat, his legs falling farther apart.

I'm beginning to grasp the rules, and they don't seem very fair. So, if they miss a shot, they have to strip, and if their opponents sink a ball, they have to strip. The guys have only lost their shirts, which means they've only missed once.

Did Jenny and Veronica realize they'd be naked long before the game was even finished?

Because that's what they are now: buck naked in a pool room in Billy Bob's, with three guys staring at them, looking ready to bend them over the table any second.

And somehow I've been caught in the middle of this.

"I can wait in my truck for you guys." I reach for my purse but Gunner's faster, grabbing it and moving it to the other side of him, out of my reach.

"You're the only sober one here. You've got to make sure your friends make it home safe." He says that with a dark look in his eye. He's toying with my guilty conscience. Because, yes, I'm the DD and yes, I can't just leave them in here. Especially not now.

"So, what now?" Jenny asks shyly, tucking a strand of hair behind her ear as her eyes dart from Mutt to Declan to Veronica, dropping to take in her friend's naked frame.

They're quite similar, though Veronica's breasts are bigger and perkier.

I wonder if they've done this together before? Jenny seems nervous enough to make me think not.

Mutt takes a step back and gestures at the table. "How about we let you take a shot."

She bites her bottom lip as she searches the table, settling on the solid yellow ball in front of him.

She leans down to ready her stick.

And Mutt moans at his view of her from behind, inciting a round of laughter from his friends. "This just isn't fair," he grumbles.

She sinks the ball into the hole with a squeal and a jump, her perky breasts bouncing.

The guys kick off their boots.

She misses her next shot.

*What now? There's nothing left to remove.*

"Rony, why don't you take a turn?" Declan nods toward the table.

Veronica shrugs, seemingly more comfortable right now than Jenny. Or Mutt, who's had to adjust his groin area twice in the past thirty seconds.

She faces us this time as she gets ready, leaning over the table, her brow furrowed as she eyes the solid green ball.

"Hey!" She jumps a little, enough for me to see the wide end of the pool stick just barely sticking out between her legs.

Declan doesn't stop though, coming up closer behind her, nudging one of her legs farther apart, sliding it back and forth against her clit.

"You're distracting me!" she complains, but it's through a soft pant. Beside me, I hear "fuck" slide out between Gunner's lips and his own breathing grows ragged. He climbs off the couch and comes around to stand next to

Declan, his arms flexed and folded over his chest, his eyes sharing the same view as his brother.

My purse still within his grip.

Declan smiles, adjusting the angle of his wrist slightly. The tip of the pool cue sinks into her.

Her eyes close and her lips part. The moan that escapes her lips isn't one of pain.

"Take the shot."

She does, finally, and somehow manages to sink the ball.

Declan yanks on his belt, unfastening it, letting his jeans drop to the floor. His hard cock juts out inside his boxers, waiting. "One more ball, baby. That's all you need to get."

*Until what?*

Wariness grows inside me. I really don't want to be here.

Jenny cries out. My head snaps to the far right corner to find her sprawled out on an old wooden rectangular table with her legs thrown over Mutt's shoulders. Mutt, with his pants pooled down around his ankles, and his hands gripping her thighs, is thrusting in and out of her with abandon. I was so distracted by the others, I didn't even notice those two sneak off.

Jenny's drunk. Am I supposed to stop this? She may have been nervous to strip in front of everyone, but it doesn't seem like she cares who's watching Mutt fuck her now. I know that stage. I've been there a few times and it's heaven.

Despite how uncomfortable this whole situation is, I find myself squeezing my thighs tight with anticipation for that feeling.

"Purple, in the corner pocket," Declan demands. "From over there, on Double D's side."

Veronica's eyes flicker to me once and then she's rounding the table until she's on the side closest to me, twisting and turning her body, trying to figure out the right angle. Finally, she perches herself on the edge of the table and lifts one thigh up, opening her legs up wide. She stretches the stick behind her back, pushing her chest out. It's an odd, very revealing position, and I'm sure Declan knew that when he chose the ball.

As she tries to get a handle on the angle, Declan comes around to continue sliding the slick, fat end of his pool cue over her clit. "What do you think, Double D? You want to play a round with my brother, after?"

Over to the right, the table bangs repeatedly against the wall. Mutt has flipped Jenny over onto her stomach and is driving into her. It reminds me of the way Henry fucked me in the barn.

God, what will Henry say when I tell him what happened? Will he be pissed that I stayed and watched instead of leaving them here? Or would he be more pissed that I left two drunk girls with these guys?

Two drunk girls who don't seem nearly as innocent as I thought they were.

"No. I can't. I'm sorry." I stand and begin moving away from the couch and the table.

Gunner's suddenly there, blocking my view of the exit. "Where are you going?"

"Just over there." To the doorway, to hide.

Veronica takes the shot, putting the ball into the pocket. She flops on the table with a laugh. But it doesn't last long before Declan's dragging her off the table by her thighs. "You know the rules about the felt." He gives her a gentle push into the couch, and yanks his boxers down.

And then he turns to look at me, his rigid cock in his hand as he languidly strokes it.

I avert my gaze but not nearly fast enough to avoid the sight.

He grins and grabs the back of Veronica's head, pushing himself into her mouth.

She opens wide, accepting him hungrily. "So, Double D? You gonna play or what?"

All I can do is shake my head.

"Too bad." He juts his chin toward Gunner. Some sort of silent signal passes between the two of them.

Gunner thrusts my purse into my hand on his way past me. "Stay and watch, or wait in your truck for them. Up to you. We'll be a bit." He unbuckles his pants and pushes them down as he settles back onto the couch, giving me a glimpse of his rigid cock. It's even bigger than his brother's. "Ready, Rony?"

Declan pulls out of Veronica's mouth just long enough for his brother to hoist her up and onto his lap. She cries out as he sinks into her, only to have the sound muffled by Declan's thick cock sliding back into her mouth.

For a brother who was going to start a brawl earlier over her, he certainly shares well.

And I think both girls are fine. Drunk, but fully aware of what's going on. I'm the poor sucker here.

"I'll be waiting in my truck for you guys." I doubt that anyone's listening to me. Hugging my purse to my chest, I run for the door.

Someone—likely Declan—pulled the latch across the top, locking people out.

I yank on it now and throw open the door.

And plow into a hard body.

I look up into familiar and devastating crystal-blue eyes.

# CHAPTER 13

"Henry?"

His chest heaves with a sigh. "Why didn't you answer your phone?"

"I didn't hear it. I thought you were leaving for Beijing in the morning?"

"I am, but…." His gaze skates over my lips. "I needed to see you."

I don't care that we're in the middle of Billy Bob's and it smells like beer and, because we're near the restrooms, faintly of urine. I throw myself against his body, tears threatening. "Why wouldn't you just tell me? Why do you keep doing this?"

His brows spike with amusement. "What? *Surprising* you? I thought that was a good thing."

From inside the pool room, someone lets out a guttural cry.

Henry's eyes narrow. "What the hell is going on in there?"

"I'll explain. In my truck. Outside." Far away from here. I push against his chest, urging him on. "Please. I don't want to be here."

He's as easy to move as a concrete block. "Did someone hurt you?"

"No. It wasn't like that."

He hesitates. "Did someone touch you?" There's an edge of danger in his voice.

"No! Please. I'll explain, but not here. Just please, trust me." I'm not sure who'll be in bigger trouble—me or Declan and Gunner. If it's the latter, then it'll inevitably mean Henry getting hurt, because as strong as he is, he can't take on a horde of guys.

Henry takes a deep breath.

And then he barges in.

I hold my breath as he turns to where the couch is. He simply stands there for a few seconds, watching.

"Get the fuck outta here!" Declan roars.

I rush forward, to stand next to Henry, averting my eyes from yet another full frontal view of Declan. "He's with me."

Declan grins. "Oh hey, Double D. Does that mean you're gonna join us now?"

"Can we please just go?" I plead to Henry.

He turns to glare at me through hard eyes, then shifts his gaze to Veronica. "You have ten minutes to finish up and get outside."

"Can you make it twenty?" Veronica leans forward and runs her tongue up Declan's shaft, all while her eyes sit on Henry.

He doesn't turn away. He doesn't flinch. He watches her swirl her tongue around Declan's tip for a good five seconds.

"Twenty minutes, or you find your own way home." He ushers me out of the room, pulling the door shut behind him. Grabbing me by the arm, he leads me out of the bar, shouldering aside anyone in his way. Several turn to say something to him, but one look at his face and they back away, glancing at me with pity.

"That wasn't what it looked like, Henry. I promise."

"It looked like you were sitting in a pool room watching a group fuck."

I cringe. Okay, maybe it was what it looked like. "I wanted to leave!"

He disarms the black Suburban parked right beside my truck. "Get in, *Abigail*."

I scramble into the passenger side, my fists balled tightly with anxiety.

He slams his door shut and tosses his keys to the console. His broad chest heaving up and down.

The front row has a middle seat, allowing me to shimmy closer to him. I open my mouth to start explaining.

"Stop."

Tears begins to spark. "You're mad at me."

He turns to glare at me. "Furious."

"I didn't—"

My explanation dies at my lips as I watch him unbuckle and unzip his jeans and push his briefs down, seizing his rigid cock in his hand. He may be furious with me, but he's also turned on.

He hooks his hand around the back of my head and pulls my head down, into his lap. I open just in time, as he thrusts himself in past my teeth and fills my mouth. What turned him on like this? Was it that pool room back there? Was it Veronica, teasing him?

Whatever it was, he's now fucking my mouth with abandon, slamming into the back of my throat each time, his fist wrapped around my hair at the back, using it as leverage. His zipper is irritating my neck. I tug at his jeans and he finally relents, lifting his hips just enough to let me push them down.

He comes without warning and without making more than a grunt, shooting into my mouth with warm streams of cum. Not until he's done pulsing does he release my hair. I pull away to swallow and wipe my mouth with a tissue. When I turn back, he's already tucking himself back into his pants, his eyes on the darkness beyond the window.

Finally, he heaves a sigh. "You asked me to trust you, and let you explain. So here I am, trusting you. Now please, explain." There's iciness in his voice, but also something else.

Hurt.

I force down the painful knot growing in my throat.

And then I tell him exactly what happened.

Every last detail, delivered in a rambling, incoherent mess of words, right down to the pool cue.

"I was afraid to leave them at first, but as soon as I realized they were going to be fine, I ran out. That's when you got there. Nothing happened."

Some of the tension seems to have eased out of his body. "I warned you to stay away from those girls, didn't I?"

"I know! I should have listened. I was just so upset, I couldn't stay home. But then the second I got here, I wanted to leave."

"And yet you ended up in the private room of a dirty biker bar, watching people fuck on a couch."

I roll my eyes at myself. "I don't know how these things happen to me."

Finally, Henry chuckles.

And I can breathe again.

"If you enjoy watching, I'll take you somewhere much better than Billy Bob's."

"I don't want that!" I deny, feeling my cheeks burn.

In the darkness of the parking lot, I can just barely make out his knowing smirk. Suddenly he's grabbing one of my thighs and pulling, until I'm sliding across the seat toward him. He reaches between my legs and without ceremony hooks his fingers around the crotch of my panties. With a swift tug, he yanks them off until they're halfway down my thighs.

Blood instantly rushes to my exposed core.

"These are soaked, Abbi," he murmurs.

"Because of you."

He coaxes my legs up so he can slide them off the rest of the way. "You've been scared shitless since you saw me. These?" He holds them up to his nose and inhales deeply. I feel my cheeks heat. "They've been wet for awhile."

"I...." How do I explain that? I guess I must have been a little turned on by what I saw? All it would have taken was imagining Henry doing those things to me while I watched. "I don't want anyone but you." I slide the rest of the way forward, pressing myself up to his side, my arms wrapping around his shoulders. I reach up to touch the hard lines of his jaw with my fingertips first, then my mouth.

He doesn't make a move for me, but he also doesn't pull away. "I believe you. You were angry with me when I got hard watching Joel and Margo."

"I know. I'm sorry."

"I got hard watching them for the same reason you got wet watching tonight. Same reason you stayed and watched your roommates with Ronan for almost two minutes before you ran out that night. I know because I've seen the surveillance videos. Same reason you were turned on listening to that couple having sex next to you when you were with Michael. There's nothing wrong with it, Abbi. Not if we're doing it together."

I frown. "What are you saying?"

"I'm saying that all you have to do is ask. We need to talk about these things, openly."

I hesitate. "Do you enjoy it? Watching, I mean?" Or was it just Margo he enjoyed?

"Watching, being watched...." He chuckles, his gaze

drifting over to the drunken crowd lingering on the porch. "There's *a lot* that I enjoy, Abbi. And there's not a lot that I haven't done at least once."

The few times I've tried to talk to him about women and his past, he's shut me down. He said he won't talk about previous women with me. Now here he is, divulging details. Not many, but some.

Somehow his words reach down and slide right into me. My thighs tighten. "Veronica was teasing you tonight."

"She was."

"Did you enjoy it?"

"Yes."

Jealousy flares in my stomach. "Do you want her?"

"No. I want you. I want you doing that to me."

*Okay, I understand that.* That's what I'm inevitably always thinking about—what it would feel like to have Henry touch me like that, kiss me like that.

Push himself into me like that.

I swallow my nervousness. "What else do you want?"

A ghost of a smile passes over Henry's lips. "You really want to know?"

I take a deep breath. "Yes."

He runs his tongue along his bottom teeth, his gaze locked in the distance. Sliding out of the driver seat to the middle, he shifts my body onto his lap with ease—my back to his chest, my legs splayed on either side of his thighs. I instinctively grind my ass back against him and moan at the press of his erection against me.

But then he adjusts my body forward, out of reach of his dick. He holds me firmly in place, his warm hands running up and down my thighs, never quite reaching all the way up.

A soothing gesture.

And also torturous.

"The two walking out now."

I frown, spotting the couple from the jukebox earlier walking down the steps, the guy's arm hanging languidly over her shoulders. "What about them?"

"They're going to fuck beside that rig." He points to the transport truck parked across from us. "And you're going to watch them."

"No, they're not." I shouldn't be surprised if they do, considering what else I've seen inside tonight, and yet there's no way he could know that.

Henry chuckles. "Care to place a bet?"

"Sure. It's your money, either way."

He slaps my bare thigh playfully. "How about something other than money."

"Like what?"

"I don't know, but you'll have to agree when I come to collect."

The vagueness of that makes me a touch nervous. There's no doubt in my mind it's something sexual. But this is Henry, I remind myself. I've never not enjoyed anything he's pushed me to do. "*If* you win."

He chuckles again. "You in?"

"Sure."

"Good. Now sit back and enjoy the show," he whispers, leaning forward to catch my ear with his mouth. Unable to resist, I turn and press my lips against his. He relents, giving me a single kiss before breaking free. "*Watch.*"

The couple doesn't seem to be in any rush, their pace slow, their steps a little staggered. She's laughing at something he said, her hand pressed against his chest, those hot pink nails visible from here as they keep walking and walking... walking.

Around the back of the truck and up along the side. They stop halfway up, his arm falling from her shoulder to wrap around her waist and pull her into him for a kiss. The woman breaks free long enough to glance around her, scanning the cars across from her, including ours. She slows over ours.

I'm already still but now I freeze. "She can see us."

"No, she can't. It's pitch black over here."

The woman turns back to kiss the man some more, only this time she's also fumbling with his belt.

"What will I make you do...," Henry teases, and it's like a deep purr, rumbling deep in my belly.

The woman drops to her knees. I can just barely make out the guy's dick before she takes him in her mouth. "You could still be wrong," I mumble, watching her head bob up and down, feeling like a pervert. The guy leans back against the truck, his hands weaving into her hair. I can't help but lick my lips, still tasting the salt from Henry coming inside my mouth.

"You like watching them, don't you?" Henry murmurs.

Is it wrong?

"Abbi...."

"Maybe," I admit shyly.

Henry's fingers curl around my skirt, pushing and tugging at the material until it's bunched on my lap and the cool night air is chilling my sensitive skin.

I swallow against my building anticipation as his hands slip around to pull my thighs farther apart. But he doesn't otherwise touch me yet.

I look down to see myself bared wide. "What if someone looks in?"

"We'll see anyone before they get here. Now watch them, Abbi."

The woman is back on her feet, pressed up against the guy and kissing him again. They both do a quick scan around them once again, and then the guy reaches down to hike the bottom of her dress up over her hips. She's not wearing anything underneath.

I startle as a finger slides over my clit and down through my slit.

"Stay still." He makes another pass, and then another one, and I can feel myself growing wet again.

I let out a small moan and try to adjust myself back. I want to feel Henry hard against me.

"You're not going to do as I ask, are you?"

"I'm watching!" I insist. The couple trade places, and the woman turns to face the truck. She spreads her legs apart and bends over, her hands bracing against the truck's frame. The faint light cast is enough to highlight her ample ass. "See? He's getting a condom out of his wallet."

"I see that." Henry pushes his thumb deep inside me, drawing a gasp from my lips. "Lean forward." I do, and he pulls his hand away, only to slide it in from behind, his long fingers easily reaching my clit again.

"If you squirm back again, it's going to be onto this." He prods against my tight hole with his thumb, slick from being inside me.

I flex instinctively.

"Now… watch," he hisses, running his fingertips over my slickness again.

I affix my eyes to the couple, waiting quietly until the guy has finally managed to roll on a condom. He positions himself behind her and then thrusts up and into her. She looks over her shoulder at him but it's too dark to see her expression. I find myself wishing I could see it.

Wishing I could feel that, only with Henry bending me up against the truck like that.

Henry groans. "Bullshit you don't like to watch. You're dripping." He holds his fingers up. I can just barely see the slick coating in the dark.

"That's because of you, not them."

With his free hand, he pulls one strap of my tank top down, over my shoulder and down around my elbow. He does the same with the other side, and then unfastens my bra, leaving me completely topless.

I tense as I look down at myself again, basically naked except for the skirt around my waist. There are about fifty people standing around the front of the bar and the row of bikes. What if Henry's wrong? What if they can see back here?

"Relax, they can't see you," Henry assures me, reaching up to slide a slick finger over my nipples a few times before shifting his hand back to my clit, though at a torturously languid pace.

"Faster," I whisper, doing my best to forget how vulnerable I am as I watch the couple fucking beside the truck.

He usually gives me what I want but this time, instead of speeding up, he stops all together. I let out a small mewl of complaint.

And he chuckles.

I gasp as he's suddenly pushing three fingers inside me, stretching me wide and filling me. There's a spot deep inside that he always seems to know how to touch, massaging against it with this delicious pressure that makes me start panting and my blood start rushing. I use the dashboard to brace myself as I grind against his hand. The fact that my breasts are on display for anyone nearby is no longer in the forefront of my thoughts.

Each time I bear down on his hand, Henry's thumb applies just enough pressure on my other entrance to make my muscles tense. Soon, I find myself wishing he'd push harder.

The guy pulls out of the woman.

"Is he done already?" I whisper.

"Doubt it. He's drunk. He's just getting started." Henry slides his fingers out and pulls them backward, smearing me with sticky liquid all the way along my crack, before pushing his fingers inside me again. "Take a deep breath." I do, and I feel the burn of his thumb slipping past the ring of muscle.

I swallow hard, waiting for my body to adjust to the intrusion. Ronan did this to me once before, but it was in the middle of sex, and I wasn't practically naked in a parking lot of a bar watching two other people have sex.

This seems so much more intense.

Maybe because it's with Henry.

The guy yanks the woman's top down, letting her breasts spill out. He spends a few minutes with his face in them, while his hand rubs her between her legs. She's pointing to a spot about twenty feet away from the truck, to where the gravel changes to grass.

Closer to us.

He nods and they stumble over to lie down together. The rig may still block them from view of the people on the bar's porch, but they're now in a stream of light.

I feel an odd mixture of dirtiness and thrill as she straddles his hips. She has large, heavy breasts and they bounce wildly as she starts riding him in the grass. She slows just long enough to glance around her—checking to make sure no one has wandered back here from the bar, I'm guessing—and then she starts bouncing again, this time reaching down between her legs.

"Make me come," I hear myself whisper out loud.

"Not yet." Henry forces his thumb in farther, countering the burn with his fingers deep inside me. I hold my breath and push against him until I can't take it anymore, earning his hiss. "Slow down. Fuck."

I reach down to grasp his wet hand, pushing against his fingers and grinding against him. "Please."

I hear his sharp inhale. "Okay, Abbi." His belt buckle starts jangling and I can't help but turn around, wanting to catch a glimpse of his beautiful cock before it's in me.

A dark, calculating look fills his eyes. His gaze drops to my lips and he smirks. "Admit you enjoying watching."

I do, but I won't admit it. Not just yet. I turn away from him to hide my smile.

The couple is changing positions again. She's now on her back with her legs splayed out on either side of his body, and he's lying on top of her. All I can see is his ass bobbing up and down as he thrusts into her, his pants bunched around his ankles.

Henry slips his fingers and thumb out of me, leaving me feeling oddly empty.

"Legs up," he commands, guiding me until my knees are bent and my legs are tucked back underneath me to either side of his body. He grips my hips tight, lifting me up just enough to line up his shaft against my opening, and then he pulls me down over him. I'm so wet that my body gives no resistance, accepting him all the way in.

I let out a small cry as I grip his legs and set to grinding against his cock, reveling in the fullness of having him inside me again. It barely lasts though, before he's seizing my hips and lifting me off him. "Lean forward." My mouth drops open when he grasps my ass, spreading my cheeks wide apart. A moment later, cool liquid drips along my crack.

"What is that?"

"Something to help ease me in." He shifts his hips a little to rub his smooth head against my entrance, smearing the liquid around. "Trust me?"

I swallow. This is really happening right now?

"Abbi?"

"Yes."

"Take a deep breath."

With a hand gripping his cock, he starts to push me down.

It's ten times as intense as his thumb was, going in, even with the added help of the lube.

"Okay, just relax."

I let out a shaky laugh. "I don't know if I can handle this, Henry."

He answers by reaching around to start rubbing my swollen clit. "How badly do you want to come?"

"So badly," I moan.

"Take a breath."

I do and he inches himself a little farther into me.

I close my eyes against the burn, focusing on his fingers sliding against my clit instead. When I open them again, I find a new view of the couple, of her on her elbows and knees, her ass in the air, and him behind her, fumbling with something.

"Looks like he has the same idea."

I watch as he tears a packet open and begins squeezing something out onto her backside.

"Ready?"

I nod, and Henry pushes in farther.

I focus on my breathing as Henry rubs me off and we watch the drunken guy line himself up with the woman's ass. She must have done this before because she's already bucking against him in no time. Meanwhile, the burn inside me is just barely fading.

Henry covers himself with more of my wetness, and then whispers, "Breathe," a moment before he pulls me down farther.

I can't help the slight whimper.

"Just relax." His fingers run up and down over my spine a few times, before returning to my clit. "I think they're almost done."

The guy is leaning over her, reminding me of those nature videos of rabbits on top of each other. A few seconds later, he slows, getting the last few pumps into her before he pulls out and flops over, onto his back.

"I doubt he even got her off." The scorn in Henry's voice is unmistakeable, his own fingers working relentlessly. Though, if he had wanted me to orgasm, I would have by now.

"Do you still want me to watch them?"

His hot breath trails against my spine. "Fuck them. I want you to watch us." He reaches up to angle the rearview mirror down, until it's reflecting a shadowy glimpse of my heavy, swollen breasts, all the way down to his fingers against my clit.

He grasps my hips, lifting me a little, only to bring me down. I gasp at the strange pleasurable pain.

I check the couple. They're on their feet, fixing their clothing and searching the ground—I assume for the woman's purse that she dropped by the truck. They still have no clue we were here, watching the whole time.

"It'll be good soon, I promise."

I rock my hips back and forth against him, acutely aware of how he's stretching me inside. It's not long before the pain is diminishing though, replaced by an odd pleasure. Tentatively, I pull my hips up and then gently slide back down, just an inch or so at first, then a little bit more.

Henry hisses, his hands grip my cheeks again, squeezing them almost to the point of pain. He starts helping me, rocking his hips against me, thrusting gently but deliberately. "I've imagined fucking your ass for months."

My muscles tense with his words, at the thought that Henry's been picturing this. "What does it feel like for you?"

"Fucking amazing. Tight. Sexy." His hands grip my rib cage and he starts thrusting in and out a little harder. I'm getting wet back there, too, now. I didn't know that was possible. I steal a glance in the mirror again, to watch my breasts bouncing like that woman's.

Everything within that SUV is so intense and intimate that I don't notice the two forms heading toward us until they're only twenty feet away.

"Abigail?" Jenny calls out.

I let out a cry of frustration and start to slow, to reach for my top.

"We're not stopping," Henry says through gritted teeth, pinning my hands down. "Where are your keys?"

"Clipped to my purse."

He reaches over, slowing only to hit the automatic car starter and unlock the doors on my truck. After a moment's pause, he starts the SUV, too. "They'll figure it out." He tosses my purse.

This is too much. I can't focus. "Come without me. I won't be able to."

"I'm not stopping until you do. Lean forward. All the way." His hand presses down against my back, forcing me forward until my chin is resting against the dash. He pushes my skirt up. "Fuck, this view…." He hooks his hands around my thighs and picks up his pace again. I cry out at the intensity, but he doesn't stop, thrusting hard and fast into me, as I watch Jenny and Veronica open the doors of my truck beside us and look inside.

"Are the doors locked?" I manage to get out through a gasp.

Henry hits a button and a click sounds.

"Hello?" Jenny's knocking on the passenger side window of the Suburban now. With the truck running, there are plenty of little lights on. It's no longer dark enough to hide completely.

She cups her eyes and looks inside.

An odd mix of exhilaration and panic set in as I hear her let out a yelp and call Veronica.

"Henry…."

"Almost there."

Henry's going to come inside me. Just the thought…. That familiar tingle starts at the base of my spine and begins spreading through my pelvis and between my legs.

Henry lets out a deep, guttural cry and I feel him begin to pulse inside me, setting off my own orgasm just as the passenger door flies open. With Veronica and Jenny standing there to witness, I scream as my wall of muscles spasm around Henry's cock, tightening against him in wave after wave of near-crippling ecstasy.

A beam of light shines on us. They've found the flashlight I keep in my console for emergencies.

Henry pulls my skirt down and snaps at them, "Close the fucking door."

They do, with a slam and a round of giggles.

"I'm sorry. I guess I accidentally unlocked it instead of locking it." His hand rubs over my bare back soothingly.

"It's okay." I say that, even as an edge of shame creeps along my spine.

Henry sighs. "Where do you have to drop them off?"

"Just in town."

He grasps my hips, ever so slowly sliding me off his cock. "You lead and then follow me back to the Inn."

# CHAPTER 14

"I wonder if Jenny will remember puking all over her mom's rosebush," I mutter, taking in the taupe and silver bedding and subtle floral accents of Henry's room. Mr. and Mrs. Rhodes gave him the one in the attic that spans the entire floor and overlooks the garden I used to maintain. Arguably the nicest room.

"She's not going to remember anything. I doubt she could even see straight by the end of it." Henry reaches back to pull his navy t-shirt over his head, letting me admire his chest and stomach, shaped by hard muscles and covered in smooth, tan skin. I didn't get to enjoy that sight earlier, my back to him the entire time.

When he sees me standing there, staring at him, he groans. "Don't look at me like that, Abbi. I'm too tired to do something about it."

The man is normally insatiable. If Henry is saying that, then he must be exhausted. My heart swells as I remind myself that he flew all the way from Alaska for one day, delaying his trip to Beijing. Yeah, he's the CEO, but I remember what a nightmare it was to move his meetings around. Miles is going to hate me.

"If you don't mind, I'm going to jump in the shower." I feel the need to get clean after tonight.

He reaches for his phone. "Go ahead. I have to cover a few things for work."

The bathroom is small but quaint, with a glass shower stall on the right. I strip down and climb in, reveling in the hot water. These last two days have been equal parts terrible and amazing. Henry showing up made me forget about the whole ordeal with Mama, but I'll have to deal with that at some point. It'll be a long time before I can forgive her though, both for risking her health in such a stupid way, but also for trying to keep Henry and me apart.

How do I convince her that he's not a bad man?

Because he's not.

He just likes to do bad things to me.

Was it right that we watched that couple? That we got off by watching them? Not that I wouldn't have gotten off anyway with Henry's hands on me. But he's right, I was dripping from the depravity of it all.

It just felt so… seedy, and dirty.

I didn't really enjoy what was going on in the pool room, but that's because that was uncomfortable. It didn't feel safe. And Henry wasn't there. Would it have been different, had he been there?

And then to get so out of control near the end that we couldn't stop? Knowing that we were about to have an audience? A drunken one, but one nonetheless. They stood there with the door wide open and watched and listened to us orgasm together. It was such an intimate moment and stupid Jenny and Veronica witnessed it.

My cheeks flush at the thought of that.

What does that say about me, that in the heat of the moment I allowed that?

The shower door opens behind me and Henry steps in,

taking up all available space in the stall. He leans down to lay a soft kiss on my lips, his hand sliding over my ass in a gentle manner. "Sore?"

"A little." The soap burned at first but I was fine by the time I finished cleaning myself down there. I like being able to feel him inside me.

"What's wrong?"

"Nothing."

"Abbi… I'm too tired for games."

I study him as he tips his head back to soak his hair under the stream of water. "What exactly have you done?"

He smirks. "Can you be more clear?"

"You know… sexually?"

"Right." He squirts a dollop of shampoo into his hand. "Ask specifics, and I'll tell you."

"Specifics?"

"If you're curious about something specific, I'll tell you if I've done it. But I'm not about to list all of my indiscretions as if I'm at a church confessional."

I have a mental flash of Henry sitting in that narrow wooden box, giving details in his way. He'd give the priest a heart attack. Okay…. "Have you slept with two women at once?"

He starts rubbing the shampoo into his hair. "Yes."

"How many times?"

"I didn't keep count."

I roll my eyes. "So more than a few?"

He chuckles. "Yes."

"What about more than two women at once?"

He hesitates.

"*Seriously?*"

"A few times."

I try to picture that. All those female body parts and only one of Henry. Even though his dick, hanging limp between his legs right now, is still an impressive five inches —at least.

He chuckles softly and I realize I'm scowling at his dick.

"Anything else you want to know?"

"What about men? Have you ever had sex with a man?"

"No."

"Have you ever wanted to?"

"No."

"Have you done *anything* with another man?"

"I've shared a woman, if that counts."

"Right." Margo. Somehow, I had forgotten.

How exactly did that go, anyway? Was it like with me and Ronan and Connor? My imagination travels to that day trapped in the truck with them. That was… intense but intimate, because I trusted them completely.

"Don't get any ideas," Henry mutters, as if reading my mind.

I quietly watch him rinse the suds out of his hair, the soapy rivulets running down his chest and abdomen. Curiosity finally gets the better of me. "Why not?"

"Why not, what? Let another man fuck you?" There's an edge in his voice.

I instinctively reach for him, tracing the ridges of his stomach soothingly. "I don't want another man, Henry. I'm just wondering why you wouldn't do it again."

"There are a lot of things I'll do with you and for you, if you ask me to, but sharing you with another man is not one of them."

"Why not?" I'm fishing for him to say the words. For him to talk to me, to tell me how he feels. He must know it.

He reaches for the bar of soap and begins lathering, saying nothing.

"You shared… *her*."

"She was nobody."

"And I'm…."

His jaw tenses. "Not nobody."

My heart squeezes. As terrible as Henry is at expressing his own feelings, I sense them. That'll have to be enough for me.

For now.

Leaning in close until my nipples are just barely grazing his flesh, I lift to my tiptoes and catch his lips with mine. He doesn't move to meet them, but he doesn't pull away either, his breath coming out in shallow pants as I run my tongue across the seam of his mouth, trying to coax him.

Finally, he lays a single, chaste kiss on my mouth. "You done in here?"

"Yeah."

His hands curl around my hips to spin me around. "I'll be there in a minute."

"You're kicking me out?" I pout.

"Cramped showers aren't my thing." He pushes the door open and slaps my ass, ushering me out.

Fair enough.

A minute is more like ten. Ten minutes to dwell on the entire twisted night—from being trapped in that pool room, to Henry showing up, to having us do things in his truck that I would never expect myself to do.

Henry seems to prefer risqué things. He likes watching and being watched. He's had more than one woman at a time. He's shared a woman, he's done God knows what else—the fact that I can't even come up with anything else to ask him about just proves how inexperienced I am.

What else is he going to want me to do?

Should I be worried that just having sex with me eventually won't be enough?

He says he doesn't want to share me, but what if there's a

time that that changes? What if there's a time when I have to share him to keep his appetite sated?

Just the thought of him inside another woman makes my chest hurt.

Is this really what everyone keeps saying, about me not being the kind of girl that can keep a man like him interested? Maybe it has nothing to do with money.

By the time I hear the bathroom door click open and watch Henry stroll out to crawl into the bed beside me, the glow from my lamp highlighting his beautiful naked body, I can't help but wonder how long I'll be able to satisfy him before I can't.

"Hey."

He leans over to kiss me and at the same time, switches my bedside lamp off, throwing us into near darkness, the only light a faint glow from a streetlight outside. "You were chewing your bottom lip."

"So?"

"You do that when something's wrong."

I hesitate. "What if I just want normal person sex?"

"Normal person sex?" His voice is laced with amusement.

"You know… In a bed, in the dark, by ourselves. Just you and me, being together and boring. Penis-in-vagina sex."

He sighs, sinking into the mattress beside me. "Then we have 'normal person sex.'"

"Yeah, but…." I swallow, afraid he'll chastise me for sounding insecure. "What if I'm not enough for you one day? What if you get bored?"

Silence hangs in the room for so long, I find myself holding my breath warily.

And then his large, warm hand seeks out my face, to cradle it, his thumb dragging back and forth over my cheek as he climbs on top of me, gently settling his body between my legs. I search the dark for his face but I can't make it out, so I'm left to just *feel* him.

Feel his weight pressing down on me.

Feel his minty breath skating across my face.

Feel his erection growing thick against me. Even with my soreness from earlier, my body automatically begins responding, growing slick. I stretch my thighs wide, opening up for him.

His fingers coil through mine and, lifting my arms above my head, he gently pins my hands down. He begins kissing me, his lips soft but forceful, leisurely but unrelenting. I moan against his mouth as his cock pushes into me.

The old bed frame begins to creak with his deliciously slow tempo and gentle thrusts. It doesn't take long before he's slipping in and out with ease, his pelvic bone rubbing against my clit with each pass to give me the friction I need.

I'm waiting for him to pick up the pace, to push harder into me, to release my hands so he can lift and bend my body for his pleasure. To turn the light on so he can watch my breasts bounce and me writhe beneath him. To start whispering dirty demands in my ear.

But he never does, his hips keeping that slow pace, his tongue sliding out every so often to catch mine, his breaths small pants, his thumbs rubbing back and forth over mine.

It's so intimate.

So consuming.

His fingers tense within mine and a few minutes later, with my name slipping from his tongue in a deep groan, he's pulsing inside me, filling me with his seed.

Releasing my fingers, he pulls out of me and begins shifting downward. I reach for him, toying with strands of his damp, silky hair, my stomach tightening with anticipation as his breath leaves a hot trail across my stomach. I hold my breath.

I have to smother my cries with a pillow when I come only thirty seconds later, not wanting the Rhodeses to hear me in the quiet of the night.

I'm panting when he returns to kiss me softly, his lips tasting like both of us. "How could I ever get bored of that, Abbi?" he whispers. Rolling off, he stretches out on his back, pulling me over to rest on his chest. I don't want to ruin the intensity of this by saying something stupid, so I say nothing, listening to his breaths, feeling his heart beat. Within minutes, his breathing has grown shallow.

"I love you, Henry," I whisper into the darkness, wishing I were brave enough to say it to him when he can hear me.

---

God, he's so beautiful.

Only once, in a plane thousands of feet in the air, with his legs sprawled out in front of him, have I ever witnessed Henry sleep.

He didn't look like this.

Peaceful.

Vulnerable.

I slowly roll onto my side, trying not to disturb the mattress, wanting a better look at this sleeping man. He's on his back, one arm resting on the pillow over his head, the other draped over his stomach. Long, dark lashes fringe his unmoving lids, so long they reach for his cheeks below.

His lips are parted just slightly. They really are the perfect lips, full and pink. I stay my hand against the urge to reach out and trace them with a finger. The things they've done… to me.

To others.

I let my gaze drift down, over his neck—even his neck is sexy—over his chest, down across his stomach, to where the white sheets bunch, the outline of his thick cock clearly visible.

I pinch a fold in the sheets and then, ever so slowly, begin pulling it back, until I've uncovered him.

I love his cock. I never thought I'd say that about a penis, but it's as beautiful and strong as the rest of him. And it's all mine. I don't have to share it with anyone.

Suddenly it jumps, startling me.

Henry's soft chuckles pull my eyes up to his now open but sleepy gaze.

"Good morning." I shift back up to drape myself over his chest and kiss him.

"What time is it?"

"Almost ten."

He groans.

"What time do you have to leave?"

"I have to be at the airfield by one."

It's my turn to groan. I have three hours left with him and then I don't know when I'll see him again. The dread of missing him is already settling on my shoulders.

He pushes my hair off my forehead. "I need to tell you something."

It sounds ominous and I instantly grow wary. "Okay?"

"I'm going to Margo's chateau again. The one she wants to partner with Wolf on."

*The place where you and her boyfriend fucked her?* "Oh?" What am I supposed to say? Don't go?

"I thought you might want to come with me."

"To France?"

"Yes. In three weeks."

I hesitate. "Will she mind?" Because I will sure as hell mind if he's with her there alone.

"She asked me to invite you."

"Really?" Is she aware of how jealous I am of her?

"There will be a few other people there as well." He slides out from under me. I lie on my stomach and admire his firm ass as he makes his way to the bathroom.

"I'd need a passport." And a million other things, like a new wardrobe, my hair redone, my body waxed.

Henry returns after relieving himself. "That's easy enough to get. So is that a yes?"

"I have to make sure Jed can manage while I'm away but… yeah." A trip to France with Henry. Excitement bubbles inside. I don't think I'll have the same resistance from Mama as I've had up until now, after what she just pulled. But who knows with her.

It'd be good to have Aunt May on my side for this one. "Are you hungry? We could go to the Pearl. It's just around the corner."

"Fine. I just need to finish something." He looks so serious all of a sudden.

"For work?"

He dives into bed, crawling up behind me, between my legs. His arms slide beneath me. I let out a squeal as I'm suddenly being dragged back and upward, until my thighs are sandwiched within his biceps and my ass is in his face.

"I was too rough last night. I need to make it better."

I gasp as I feel the first swipe of his wet tongue against me. "I don't…." Oh my God. He licked me there once before. I don't know if I can….

"Let go of your insecurities, Abbi, and look at how hard I am right now."

I manage to twist my body enough to see his rigid cock jutting out, beads of moisture rolling off the top. And then another long swipe of his tongue has me squirming and squeezing my eyes shut.

He doesn't relent this time, warm breath skating across my skin once before his mouth closes over me and that tongue of his both soothes and tortures me. I try my hardest to relax, to remind myself that he's doing this because he wants to.

Not four minutes later, I'm muffling my screams of ecstasy into Mrs. Rhodes's goose-down pillow as Henry brings me to a mind-bending orgasm.

---

HENRY SLIDES another piece of bacon into his mouth.

That dirty, filthy mouth that brings me so much pleasure. I can't stop staring at it.

"Abbi?"

It takes me a moment to realize he's asked me a question.

"Uh-huh?"

The corner of that mouth twitches. "What were you just thinking about?"

I duck my head as the blush creeps up my cheeks. "I don't know what's taking Aunt May so long. She must be busy."

I feel the weight of that gaze on me for long moment before he relents, letting it roam over our small family restaurant, a hub for Greenbank's gossip. "Well, it is packed in here."

I recognize several people from church. They're all watching, curious. I smile at them when we make eye contact, and they smile back.

I wonder how many of them have already heard that I stayed at the Inn with Henry last night.

The look on Mrs. Rhodes's face when I trailed him down the stairs half an hour ago in my skirt and tank top from last night was priceless. Henry was the only one renting, so any noises that might have carried through the house couldn't be blamed on anyone but us. She was professional enough to smile and nod, and ask when Henry was coming through again, that they may reserve the same room for his stay.

While Mrs. Rhodes herself isn't a huge gossip, she lives two doors down from Peggy Sue and, well… we all know that woman has a long wooden spoon at the ready to stir the pot.

"Have you spoken to that branding company yet?" Henry takes a sip of coffee.

"I'm supposed to talk to that girl on Monday."

He nods. "Good. Do it."

"Why did you go to that trouble, anyway?"

He shrugs nonchalantly. "I was on the plane. I had some time to kill."

I roll my eyes. "I don't have time for games, *Henry*." I drop my voice an octave to mimic him when he says that.

That earns me a smirk. "Fine. You said this was yours. Not your parents'. Not fuckface's. Just yours."

"Yeah…." I'm not following.

"And you were embarrassed to let me see it. Why?"

I shrug. "It's like running a five-cent lemonade stand at the end of the driveway in the summer compared to what you do."

He smirks, like he knew that would be my answer. "I want you to have something that's completely yours *and* that you can be 100 percent proud of. So, go… run with it. Take full advantage of them. They don't just do branding. They can help with company start-up, distribution, production efficiencies, forecasting. They're the best at what they do. You'll learn something and that's always useful, no matter where you end up in life."

I sigh. "How much do these people cost?"

"I'm not fighting over money with you," he mutters between mouthfuls. "It's my money and I'll spend it how I damn well please."

Impatient business tycoon Henry is making an appearance. I won't win against him, and I don't want to fight.

"Fine. I'll talk to them."

"Good. Let me know how it goes." Finishing his last mouthful, he wipes his mouth with his napkin, checking his watch. "I need to be leaving for my plane soon."

I reach across the table, placing my hand over his. "A few more minutes. She'll be out soon. She really wants to meet you."

His brow furrows. "This is your mother's sister, you said?"

"Yeah. But she's nothing like my mother."

As if summoned by our whispers, Aunt May pushes through the kitchen doors and makes her way over to us, her slender frame weaving through the tables. "Finally! I'm sorry, I had to prep the roast chickens for tonight's dinner and then it got busy and, you know.... Well, I'm here now." She heaves a sigh, smiling first at me, and then at Henry.

"Aunt May, this is Henry."

If there was ever a graceful way to get to a standing position from sitting at a small diner table, Henry has mastered it, smoothly getting to his feet to tower over the woman, offering her his hand. "Abbi talks about you a lot."

I think I've only ever mentioned her once to him, but that's the right thing to say.

"Oh, does she, now?" She chuckles. "All good things, I hope."

"Only."

"Can you sit for a minute, Aunt May?" *I need to beg for your help with Mama.*

"Sure, I'll just...." She glances around for a chair to pull up but they're all taken.

"Here, I'll find one for myself." Henry gestures to the chair he was just occupying. "I insist."

She takes it, giving me a wide-eyed look. Approval, I think. "So? How's your mother doing?"

"She's fine."

"Really? The Reverend was in here last night for dinner, saying how worried he was about her heart."

*That's because he doesn't know what she did.* "It's a long story that I can't get into right now, but we should be more worried about her head."

Her lips purse. "About *him*, I take it?"

I glance over to see Mrs. Baxter and her daughter preening over Henry as he asks to borrow their spare chair. "He makes me so happy. Why can't she see that?"

"I can tell." She pauses. "He's a lot older than you."

"Ten years."

"How long before he's looking to settle down, have some kids? Are you ready for that?"

Henry and kids? Her question throws me. I haven't given it a second's thought, too busy focusing on just keeping his interest. "We're far from that point, yet." Is he even the marrying kind?

"I suppose." She sighs. "Your mother called me this morning. Asked if I'd seen you. Said you were out *all night.* With him, I assume?"

"Yes. He flew in late and he has to leave soon. I won't see him for weeks."

She takes a sip of her coffee, pulling back in time to smile just as Henry settles in at the end of our table.

"So? Abigail tells me you travel a lot."

"Yes, too much sometimes. I'm actually on my way to Beijing now."

"And here I am, thirty-five and having never even left America. Sad, isn't it?"

"You'd be surprised how many Americans don't have a passport." He shoots a knowing look my way.

"I've never had a reason until now," I fire back.

May frowns curiously at the exchange, forcing me to explain.

"I'm going to visit Henry in France. In three weeks. *If* Mama doesn't pull anything else."

"Ah. I see." May takes another sip of her coffee, her gaze studying me. "Let me know how I can help."

I smile in relief. Not *everyone* in my life is against us being together.

---

"Not just yet." I slide his sunglasses back off him, the knot in my throat growing painfully hard to ignore. "Don't hide them just yet."

"I really have to go, Abbi." His hand rests on the top of the driver-side door. He has one foot inside.

"I know, it's just... it feels like I'm always saying good-bye to you." I would have thought it'd get easier each time, but it's the opposite.

His gaze drifts over Main Street, his jaw tensing. "I told you this was going to be hard."

He *did* say that, but I insisted that we try anyway. I don't regret that, even if it hurts.

I lean into him, memorizing the feel of his chest with my hand just once more. "I wish I could go with you."

The tension in his jaw slides off. "You don't have a passport."

I roll my eyes.

"And you're needed here, remember? With your parents. And fuckface." He seizes my chin with his thumb and index finger, and leans in to lay a soft kiss on my lips. "Three weeks. Miles will book your flight for you."

"Okay."

"So you'll come?"

"Yeah. Of course. I'll find a way."

He heaves a sigh and then climbs into the driver seat, hiding that handsome face behind his sunglasses.

"Henry?"

His brow tightens. "Yeah?"

I want to tell him. I want him to know how I feel about him.

The door is still open and so I scoot in close to him, my hand settling on his muscular thigh.

I open my mouth.

His slight headshake stops me. "Don't. It'll just make it harder on you."

The words die on my tongue as I step back, unable to ignore the hurt that I feel. Is this *only* hard on me?

The engine comes to a roaring start. "Keep yourself busy." He raises a severe brow. "And stay the hell away from places like Billy Bob's."

I manage to hold on to the tears until his SUV has rounded the street corner.

Three weeks. I just have to wait three weeks and then I'll see him. I know where my heart will still be.

But what about his?

# CHAPTER 15

Jed's pulling up in the baling tractor when I arrive home.

I'm not sure who I'd rather deal with right now—him or Mama.

I decide to face him first.

"Hey."

He looks up long enough to do a scan of my clothing.

"How was the morning?"

"We had three loads of hay picked up."

"Great."

"And another chunk of the barn came down. Didn't hit anything too vital."

I need to get that fixed and soon. "I'm sorry for not being around. I had… something."

"Yeah. We heard."

"You heard? Who told you?"

He shakes off his work gloves and tosses them onto the wagon. "Peggy Sue, I think. Or I don't know. One of them anyway." He digs a bottle of water out from the cooler. "So he's gone again?"

I hoist myself onto the wagon, squashing my overwhelming disappointment. "Yup."

Uncomfortable silence hangs between us.

"I really fucked up this time, didn't I?"

"Last night? No, Jed. That didn't change anything. It just proved what I already knew about you."

He chugs a mouthful of water. "That I'm weak?"

"And a liar. And that you don't love me as much as you think you do."

"That's not true!" he blurts out, taking offense.

"You don't love me the right way," I correct.

He sighs, but he doesn't argue. "It hurt, seeing you with him that night, and then knowing you were flying out to be with him."

"I do know, because I felt the same way every time I saw you with Cammie on campus. And even when I left for Alaska, knowing she was here with you. It hurt. So much."

He heaves a sigh. "I guess I just figured you and him would be over by now."

"Even if Henry and I don't last, you and I are better off being just friends."

After a long moment, he finally nods. "I think you may be right."

I hop off the wagon. "Guess I need to go and deal with Mama now."

"Can you not mention seeing me last night?"

"I'm not the tattletale."

He smiles sheepishly, his fingers going to his cheek where I slapped him. "I don't even know how I let last night happen."

"Because you knew it would feel good?"

He grins and nods toward the slogan on my tank top.

"I should get one for you, too, 'cause that's the only reason

I can figure for why you'd go into the men's bathroom with Beth."

He cringes. "I don't even like her."

"Well, word to the wise, I'd stay away from the lot of them. Especially Veronica."

"So I've heard."

I guess I'm the only one who didn't. "'Kay. Gotta go deal with Mama." I start moving toward the house but then stop. "Hey Jed? You should see about enrolling in class still."

"Nah… You know, I actually like farming." He slides his hands into his pockets, a smile of satisfaction touching his lips. "It's been fun, just like I always imagined. Well, minus the billionaire coming in to steal you away. But I know this is what I want to be doing. I don't even really care if I finish school." He shrugs. "So we'll see.'

"I'm glad you've figured that part out, Jed."

"Me, too. Abigail." He adds, a little more softly, "Abbi."

I hesitate. "Henry asked me to meet him in France in three weeks. I'm going."

Resignation fills his face. "I'll be here to take care of things."

For the first time in months, I walk away from Jed with a genuine smile.

Mama and Daddy are at the kitchen table when I step inside.

"Morning."

Mama gives my outfit a side-eye, while my dad's gaze shifts to the clock. It's just after one.

Henry's plane would have just taken off.

I push that thought aside.

"Jed said another chunk of the roof came off. We really need to get that fixed."

My dad sighs. "We should be able to scrape together enough for materials by early October. And your mother has been talking to a few people at the congregation who might be willing to lend a hand."

"I was actually thinking we could hire the Dorset Brothers to do it sooner."

"We don't have the money for that."

"I can pay for a new roof."

"You?" Mama's eyes narrow. "Or *him*?"

"I made a lot of money in Alaska." Not *that* much, but they don't need to know that.

Mama's already shaking her head. "No, I won't have that man paying for our farm. The next thing we know, he'll be trying to convince us to sell the land for condominiums! Or a hotel!"

"Which is exactly what we'll be doing if we don't start putting some money into the upkeep of this place!" my dad argues. "If Abigail says she has the money, then we need to use it and be thankful. I'll call Dorset just before dinner, when he's bound to be home."

Mama opens her mouth.

Daddy slams his good arm on the table. "Enough, Bernadette! She's with him, end of discussion."

Awkward silence hangs in the air.

I break it with, "I'm going to France in three weeks. Just for a few days. Jed said he'd take care of things while I'm gone." May as well get it all out there while we're fighting.

Mama heaves herself out of her chair and marches for the den. The rocking chair groans in protest under her weight.

"France," my dad murmurs. "That's exciting."

"It is."

He nods, though his smile is sad. "She's not gonna interfere none anymore. I'll make sure of it."

"Thanks, Daddy."

"It's your life. You should live it how you want to."

I plan on it.

---

"Farm Girl Soap Company?"

I'm sitting in our kitchen with my laptop open, frowning at the concept documents that Zaheera emailed me at the start of this meeting.

"It sounds organic and natural, but also fun. And it has a touch of personal flair, too. You live on a farm, right?"

"Yes, but—"

"It's a perfect fit. You aren't limiting yourself to specific blends and scents. I mean, Sage Oils is fine and all, but it makes your consumers think that they're predominantly getting, well… sage. But from the information we got, I see that you also have mint, and lavender, thyme… even some lemon. I'll need you to fill in some holes but for now, if you'll flip to page two, you can see some of the concept packaging we've come up with. Are you scrolling?"

"I'm scrolling." She's barely taken a breath. I think that's her way of stopping me from asking questions or disagreeing with her.

"So for packing, we wanted something contradictory. Simple paper wrap and twine, but balanced with upscale labelling. Natural, but balanced with a touch of class. The kind of stuff you might find in a high-end boutique hotel with personality. Also, great for gifting. Do you see the image?"

"I do. They look… great, actually." They've designed round embossed labels with "Farm Girl" in fancy font, the *F* and *G* much larger than the other letters. In her drawings are four square packages, each a different color. Even the colors she's chosen are striking. Considering I currently wrap my bars of soap in plastic wrap and buy small, plastic bottles from the Dollar Store for my moisturizers and oils, this is a huge step up. "How much will all this packaging cost though?" I can't see myself charging two dollars more per bar of soap to old Peggy Sue, just so she can rip the fancy packaging off.

"A lot less than you'd expect, especially as your production runs get bigger."

"Production runs?" I made a dozen lemon and thyme bars last week. Is that what she means?

"Yes. Don't worry about any of that right now though. First, we need to get the best product. And we were told you're eager to get started."

I roll my eyes at Henry. Everything is breakneck speed with that man. Then again, getting my mind involved with this will keep it busy while I wait for France. "Well, I definitely am looking to keep busy."

She laughs. "You will *definitely* be busy with this. Are you with me so far?"

I smile. "Yes. Absolutely."

"Okay, this is what I need from you...."

# CHAPTER 16

"Here, let me fix that." I lean over to pull the wheel of my dad's walker out of the crack between the porch boards. He's only just started using it in the last week, but it's good to see him mobile again.

He chuckles. "Who's gonna do that while you're away?" He must see my face fall as a pang of guilt hits me. "We'll figure it out. May will be here more than we need, I'm sure."

I rope my arms around his neck to give him a tight hug. "I'm going to miss you."

"You're only gone a week, Abigail. The trip will be over before you know it."

That's what I'm afraid of.

Grabbing the handle of my suitcase, I carry it down the three steps to the stone walkway. "Okay, well...." I glance to the door. Will Mama even come out to say good-bye? We've been on cool terms since the incident, our conversations polite but strained. I don't want to fly to Europe and leave things like this.

A moment later, the door creaks open and she wanders out, a cup of tea in her hand. Her blue and green smock dress hangs just a little looser on her, I notice. Probably because she's cut back on the coffee consumption, and my dad's been requesting fruits and salads for meals, forcing her to eat healthier, too. I don't know what happened after I left that night I discovered those pill packs in the trash, but I figure the two of them had an enormous fight. Regardless, Mama has been making an effort.

"Thank you, Bernadette," my dad murmurs, settling into the porch swing. "Abigail is leaving now."

"Yes, I see that. Have a safe flight."

The woman can hold a grudge with the best of them. If this is what she needs.... I'm not going to let her make me feel bad for being happy. "I'll text when I've landed in Paris, and send emergency info when I have it." With that, I turn and head toward the car Miles arranged for me, so I wouldn't have to deal with parking and traffic.

"Buy me something good," Jed jokes, standing by my truck, his arms folded.

I toss him the keys.

His eyes light up with recognition. "Seriously?"

"Don't go putting it up for auction while I'm away," I warn.

"Heck, no." He grins. "Thanks."

"No, thank *you*. Never thought I'd admit this but you really have been a godsend, Jed." Since our little truce, I'd actually call us friends again. I drop my voice a little. "May's gonna check in every day but can you keep an eye on them, too?"

He chuckles. "Relax. You're only gonna be gone for a week. Not even."

"I know." I roll my eyes at myself.

"So... excited?"

I nod. Excited, nervous, worried, terrified. How many words can I find to describe how I feel right now?

It's been three weeks since I've seen Henry. We've talked

when we could, but the time difference and his extra busy schedule has been a major hindrance. And then there's the fact that my parents are home, so video calls are out. At least, the ones Henry wants to have.

I've felt the separation. I'm trying to believe it's just the distance but, honestly... I don't know.

I guess I'll find out soon enough.

"Thanks, Jed." I throw my arm around his neck. "See you in a week."

---

"WHAT DO YOU MEAN, you lost my luggage?"

"I am very sorry, miss," the attendant says, her French accent polished and beautiful. Her words are the last ones I want to hear after flying all night and standing at the luggage carousel for a half hour, watching everyone else on my flight collect their baggage while mine, full of new clothes for this trip, never appeared.

"Well… do you have any idea where it is?" And, more importantly, when will I be getting it back?

She clicks a few keys on her machine. "It looks like it's in Madrid right now."

I can't help but laugh. Henry just left Spain to come here. His jet should be landing at a private airstrip just outside the city any minute, where he'll wait for me to board so we can continue to Corrèze. "We will have it transported on the next possible flight and bring it to your destination. *Bon?*"

I sigh, looking down at my leggings and t-shirt. I went for comfort over looks. I honestly think the flight attendant wanted to kick me out of first class for it. Either way, I have some toiletries and an outfit to change into for today, but that's it. "Will that be today?"

"It is hard to say. We will call and notify you."

"Thank you for your help." It's not her fault, I remind myself. *She* didn't lose my luggage.

She gives me a sympathetic smile and then quickly moves on to deal with another distressed customer.

"It's not the end of the world," I mutter to myself as I rush for the closest restroom to change and freshen up. "They'll find it and they'll deliver it and everything will be fine."

The important thing is that I'll be in Henry's arms within the hour.

My stomach stirs with butterflies at the thought.

---

"WELL, why don't I just wait for you at the airstrip then?"

"Because you could be sitting there all day."

"So?"

"No. Your driver is taking you straight to Margo's. I'll be there as soon as I can."

My head falls back against the headrest of the limo. First my luggage, now Henry's plane has been delayed because they've closed the runway he's taking off from for emergency maintenance, with no ETA for being finished. So far, this trip is not going as planned. Now I get to sit in a car for four hours, wondering what the hell I'm going to say to Margo when I see her.

"That means I'll have to be alone with her."

"Come on. You loved her before you found out about our past."

"Yeah... and there's that other part." The part where she and her boyfriend had sex in front of us.

"You'll have no issues with her. Just make yourself comfortable. Maybe have a nap so you're not so fucking cranky by the time I get there."

I scowl at the phone, even though there's humor in his voice.

"I haven't seen you in three weeks, Abbi. Keep your mind on what I'm going to do to you."

My cheeks flush and I glance at the driver, hoping he didn't hear that.

"And who knows? I might be there by the time you get there."

I hope so. "See you soon."

---

"Bonjour. Mademoiselle Abigail Mitchell est ici," the driver announces into the intercom.

The large iron gate creaks open and the airport limo crawls along the road, banked with a lake on the right and a crop of trees on the left.

"There is a lot of history here," he says as we round the tall stone wall and I see Margo's place for the first time.

My mouth drops open.

I've seen castles like this shown on TV, but for some reason I didn't believe that they actually existed. While it's not quite the same size as Wolf Cove, it's overwhelming in an entirely different way.

I'm in awe as we approach the massive, sprawling stone building, at its highest points four stories not including the numerous turrets.

"How old is this place?" I hear myself murmur.

"It was built in the 1400s. It is authentic in its design. Even the battlements." The driver points to something.

"What are those?"

"You know. The... how do I say... crenel and the merlons."

"The what and the what?" I know I sound like an idiot but I've never heard those words before.

He chuckles. "The top of the wall. The way it dips and rises in that pattern."

"Yes. Okay." He must be talking about the squared openings.

"Those are the original battlements, where archers hid and shot at invaders trying to steal the castle. Many died here."

My eyes roam the peaceful acreage. All I see are rolling green hills and trees. "It's a beautiful place."

"*Oui*. You are very lucky to be staying. Are you friends with Mademoiselle Lauren?"

"No, but my... uh... boyfriend is." That's the first time I've ever dared call Henry by that. Would he care?

"Oh, *oui*. Monsieur Wolf. I have met him once." The driver smiles, but says nothing else. I can't help but wonder what kind of impression Henry made on him.

Margo is already waiting by a set of solid wooden doors. There's no mistaking her, not even from a hundred feet away. Just the way she stands seems like a signature, her left hip thrust out slightly, her right arm raised as she leans against the frame, her gauzy white dress making her look like an angel. I know she's anything but. It's such a striking contrast to her shiny raven bob.

The driver—I was too frazzled about my luggage to remember his name—lets me out and then, with a nod at Margo, ducks back in his car and is gone.

Leaving us alone.

Henry said Margo would have other friends here, but I see no sign of them.

"Bonjour Abigail," she croons in that beautiful accent, seeming at perfect ease, even though the last time I saw her, she was naked and having sex with her boyfriend in front of Henry and me, all while eye-fucking Henry. Is she at all embarrassed by what happened at the club that night?

"Henry's plane was delayed," I blurt out, because I don't know what to say this woman.

She approaches slowly. "I heard. Henry called and told me." She leans in to air kiss both of my cheeks, just like she did last time, her light floral perfume catching my nostrils. It's a delicious scent and I want to tell her that I like it and ask her what it is, so that maybe I can match it with soaps, but I hold back.

She slept with Henry.

I don't want to like her, or compliment her.

"And they lost your luggage, too?"

I sigh. "Yes. Hopefully they'll find it soon." How often does Henry talk to her? Is it simply because we're on our way here?

"If they do not, I'm sure we can find something for you to wear." Her gaze drifts down, over the black one-piece jumper outfit thing that the girls in the department store convinced me to buy. "Size four?"

"Yeah."

She eyes my chest blatantly. "36D?"

I frown. "How can you tell?"

A tiny smile touches her lips. "I've been in the industry for more than a decade. You learn bodies well."

"Of course." *She's been modeling clothes for ten years, Abbi.*

She reaches up to touch a few strands of my hair, rubbing them within her thumb and forefinger. "You colored your hair."

"Yeah." Months of sun and washing had leached the vibrant copper and auburn highlights out of my hair, leaving it that dull ginger again. So I took a big risk, going to Pittsburgh to have it done again. I even showed them a picture of what that stylist did in Wolf Cove, praying that this woman could match it. While it's not exact, it's pretty close.

"It is beautiful." Something about the way she says that

feels oddly intimate. "Come, let me show you to your room. Henry suggested that you take a nap."

I roll my eyes, earning her melodic laugh.

I trail her through the main hallway, a wide corridor with arched white plaster ceilings and dark brown paneled walls, and many antique furniture pieces on either side. The air carries an odd scent to it. Impossible to describe, other than to call it "age."

"I will give you a tour later, when Henry is here. For now, this is the main hallway. It will lead to most rooms. The guest rooms are on the third and fourth floors. There are fifteen of them. A few will be in use this week."

*Wow.* "How long have you owned this?"

"My family purchased it one hundred and fifty years ago, and it has been passed down through the generations. I inherited it four years ago, when my grand-père passed away."

She reaches into a desk drawer for an old-fashioned wrought iron key, then begins climbing a set of steps, collecting the skirt of her gauzy dress as she goes. "Five of my dearest friends and Joel will be joining us this week. I'm sure you will get along. Here, this will be yours."

She's panting lightly by the time we reach the landing on the fourth floor. I trail her down another long hall, this one more narrow but just as aged, with the same ceiling details and gold gilded artwork lining the walls. I feel like I've been transported back in time.

I wish my parents could see this. Even Mama would have to appreciate it.

Margo uses the key to open the door. "There really is no need for you to lock it while you are here, but should you choose to, it is here." She hangs it from a hook just inside the door. "What do you think?"

In the far corner is a massive four-poster bed framed by

pale blue and white toile curtains. The draperies match the wallpaper that covers the entire room everywhere except the enormous white plaster fireplace. A stylish but not entirely comfortable looking blue settee sits on a rug, centered on that fireplace. Above us, an intricate pattern of beams and moldings decorate the ceiling.

To my left, is a bay of glass.

"You have a small terrace here." She leads me to a set of French doors where just outside, a wrought iron balcony has been affixed to the stone. It's just large enough for a bistro table and two chairs, and a planter over the railing.

I step out, my fingers instantly going for the long, silvery leaves. "Lavender."

"Yes. I love it. You will find sprigs in the dresser drawers and mist on the bedding, to help sleep." Her right hand ever so gently settles on my shoulder as she points to somewhere in the distance with her left. "There are lavender fields just over there. In the summer, the smell carries in the air."

Lavender fields. I've seen pictures—rows upon rows of bright purple bursts against vibrant green. "I would love to see that."

Her smile somehow grows wider as she gazes out over the property. "It truly is a different world here."

I step back inside, taking in the historical luxury of the room again. "Thank you for inviting me." It's the polite thing to say, even if I'm still wary of her.

"Of course. I wanted Henry to enjoy himself, and I knew he would with you here. I am so happy that you came."

I have to acknowledge that Margo could have made this a business trip and had Henry here all to herself. But she didn't. She's making it hard for me to stay bitter with her.

The sun streams in, through her gauzy white dress, showing me the curve of her breasts, and her long, taut torso.

She's not wearing a bra, and one dark pink nipple peeks through the sheer material.

I look up to find those cat's eyes on me, something secretive in that look. Does she know that her dress is see-through?

"Please make yourself comfortable. Do you need anything else from me?"

"I think I'm good. This is—"

A knock sounds on the door, and my heart jumps.

Henry?

My hopes are dashed a second later when a woman in a maid's uniform carries a tray of fruits and cheeses and other things in, setting it on the small dining table. She ducks out quickly and quietly.

"Some refreshments for you, so you don't starve. The croissants are freshly baked."

The way she says croissants makes me never want to try and say that word again. I'll only sound stupid in comparison.

"Eat, and then sleep." She gestures to the bed and I catch a mischievous twinkle in her eyes. "Henry asked me to make sure you are well rested."

She knows what kind of man he is.

And thanks to Henry, I have a good idea what kind of woman she is too.

Two men at the same time? One being her boyfriend?

I tamp down my jealousy and my judgment, because the past is the past and I have no right to judge her, given what I myself have done. "I will. Thanks."

She smiles as she kind of floats toward me in that ethereal way of hers, a genuine heartwarming smile. Seizing my arms with cool, gentle hands, she leans forward and presses her soft lips against mine. It's a closed-mouth kiss and it only lasts for a second, but I'm caught unexpected in any case.

If she notices my shock, she doesn't let on.

"We will see you later."

I watch her sashay out of the room, her hips swinging.

My mouth still tingling.

It wasn't entirely offensive. Actually, it wasn't offensive at all.

It was just... weird.

With a sigh, I connect to the place's Wi-Fi, only to see that Henry hasn't left Barcelona yet. At least he *says* he hasn't. Who knows with him, seeing as he doesn't like to warn me when he's coming.

Well... when coming means flying, that is.

Looking around me at the room I'm going to share with Henry for the next six nights, my blood stirs.

I smile.

These walls are going to see a lot.

I've been up for thirty hours. I'm hungry and travel weary, and in need of sleep and a shower. The last thing I want to be is tired when he arrives.

Wandering over to the windows, I admire the view again —gardens and a courtyard below, rolling hills of fields and crops of lush trees beyond. Off to the side, I can just make out a newly built pool, surrounded by stone to fit in with the style of the place. It's late September and still warm during the day, though maybe not warm enough to swim. Still, a couple lie side by side in lounge chairs, sunbathing. I can't tell their age from here, but the woman's skimpy royal blue bikini shows off a svelte, tanned body.

I can't picture Henry lying in a lounge chair all day, doing nothing. Maybe he'll surprise me though.

With a sigh, I strip off the only outfit I have to wear and carefully lay it over the back of the wing chair. Crawling into the silky sheets, I hit the button to draw the blinds and close my eyes.

I WAKE up to a warm hand slipping over my hip and my heart starts racing.

I know it's Henry before I even open my eyes.

I try to roll to meet him, but he's already right there, his chest pressed against my back, lifting my leg up to fit himself between my legs from behind. I feel his smooth, hard cock as it slides against my thigh and heat instantly floods to my core.

And then he's lining himself up and pushing inside me.

"Good sleep?" he murmurs, settling one of his muscular legs between mine. It changes the angle, giving him deeper access.

I reach back to curl my fingers through his hair, twisting my body just enough that I can see his handsome face. I never tire of it. "Kiss me."

He smiles and brushes my hair off my face. Leaning down, his tongue catches mine, giving me a taste of Scotch.

"Have you been drinking?"

"Just one on the plane, to take the edge off of waiting all day for this." He punctuates this with a hard thrust and I cry out against his mouth.

He smirks. And then he plunges again.

And again.

The arm hooked around my leg is like a vice, holding me in a perfect position as he pumps in and out of me relentlessly.

"I don't have enough hands," he murmurs, curling his fingers through my hair. "Use yours."

I reach down to start rubbing my clit, already slick and swollen and needing attention.

Thirty seconds later and without warning, he suddenly groans and shudders. "Fuck," he forces out between gritted teeth, pulsing inside me. "I'm sorry, I couldn't stop it this time. I've been thinking about it too much."

I sigh, my hand slowing. "It's okay. This time." Truthfully, he could come ten seconds in and I'd still be okay with it. I've never been so happy as I am right now.

"No, it's not." He slides out of me and climbs to his knees, leaning back on his haunches. Throwing the covers off, he rolls me onto my back and pushes my knees apart, spreading my legs wide. "Keep going."

"But you do it so much better," I tease.

He stretches over me just long enough to hit the button to the retractable curtains. They begin drawing open, filling the room with late sun. I squint into the brightness.

"I'm waiting, Abbi."

Keeping my eyes closed for the moment, I tentatively reach down, feeling his eyes on me even though I can't see them. I may have done this a lot on our video calls, but I've only done it once with him sitting and watching me like this. I still felt this strange mix of erotic excitement and embarrassment.

I let my fingers slip over my clit and then down, to where I'm slick and sticky with his seed as it leaks out. Back and forth, I draw slow circles, feeling my embarrassment slowly diminish.

"Open your eyes."

I do, letting them adjust to the daylight until I can easily focus on Henry kneeling in front of me, his naked, muscular body settled in a relaxed pose. His cock is jutting up from between his legs. He looks ready again, but he's not making a move.

He's just staring at me with that intense gaze of his—at my fingers between my legs, my breasts, my face.

I look down at his erection again, and my legs instinctively slide farther out, opening my body up more for him. God, I want him on me and inside me again.

His lips curl into a sexy smirk, like he knows exactly what I'm thinking. With his right hand, he runs his hand up and down his shaft twice before letting it fall away again.

He's teasing me now.

I move to sit up.

"No." He gives my shoulder a gentle push, sending me falling back. "I like watching you fuck yourself. In fact…." He stretches forward, reaching for the nightstand beside the bed.

I use this chance, curling my body and sliding under him.

He lets out a groan as I wrap my fist tight around his shaft and then open wide, letting my teeth scrape across his skin ever so lightly as I take him in. He freezes on his hands and knees, whatever he was going for temporarily forgotten.

I look up to find him watching me. I pull away just long enough to smile at him, earning an eyebrow spike. "You think you've won?" Even his voice is husky, though he tries his best to play cool.

I stick my tongue out and lick his tip like an ice-cream cone in answer, pretty sure that I *have* won. I ignore the rustling at the drawer and, closing my eyes, I fill my mouth with him again, reveling in the fact that I get to do this for six days straight.

He lifts to his knees, his hands on the back of my head, pushing himself farther into me. "Goddammit, Abbi," he hisses. He's swelling inside my mouth already, and I can taste beads of his cum on the back of my tongue. It won't be long before he orgasms again.

Suddenly he's gripping my hair and pulling himself out. I look up to find his heated eyes glaring at me, and his chest puffing in and out with his fast breaths. He's seconds away from coming and is deftly shifting me back to my original position, on my back with my legs spread.

He settles on his haunches again and tosses something long and black at me.

I recognize it immediately. It's just like Autumn's green dildo, only a little bigger.

"*This* was in the nightstand?"

He chuckles. "Margo makes sure her guests have everything they might need." The smile drops off, and a seriously intense gaze takes over. "I want you to fuck it, Abbi. I want to watch you do it until you come." He starts stroking himself in long, slow movements, waiting. "The sooner you do that, the sooner you'll get this."

*God, this man....*

It's been a while since I've heard him talk to me like that. I tentatively pick it up. It's almost as thick as Henry and just as smooth, except for the ridges around it. It has a slight curve, to it, too.

Henry takes it from me with a smirk. "I'll get you started. Sit up a bit so you can see."

I prop myself up on my elbows as he begins sliding it up and down my folds, twisting and turning it with each pass, until it starts to glisten.

And then he slowly begins to push.

It's not going in as easily as Henry does. He stops pushing and, with his other hand, starts rubbing my clit, his touch instantly making blood rush down between my legs.

He pushes it in farther. "Come on, Abbi. I know how wet you get for me. Open up."

I stretch my thighs apart. He pulls it back and then pushes in again, forcing it farther. I stop focusing on the black thing, and instead focus on his hand, gripped around it, strong and rough, and so skilled at delivering orgasms.

The dildo disappears deep inside me.

He pulls it in and out a few more times and then he releases it. Grabbing two pillows to prop my head up, he leans back, his hands at his sides again. "Your turn."

I reach for it, feeling the warmth of Henry's hand where he was just gripping it. It feels weird, having something foreign inside me.

I slide it out slowly, and then push it back in as he did.

Henry lets out a sigh, his cock bobbing once in anticipation. He runs his hand along his shaft once. "Keep going. Pretend it's me."

I close my eyes and do as he asks, imagining this is Henry inside me.

"You'll need to go faster if you ever want to come."

He's actually going to make me keep going until I come? How is *he* not coming? He was going to explode. With my other hand, I reach for my clit and start rubbing it.

"Look at it. Look how wet you are."

I open my eyes and look down. The black rubber only accentuates how much thick, white cream is coating the shaft now. Each push in makes a wet, slurping sound now.

"Fuck, I love seeing you like this, Abbi," Henry hisses through pants. They're matching my own, I realize, my breasts heaving up and down with quick breaths.

His words spur me on and I start pumping it in and out even harder, and faster, until the curved end hits against that spot deep inside that Henry loves to rub. An almost uncomfortable pressure begins to build.

The orgasm comes on hard and unexpectedly, bursting inside me. I'm still crying out when Henry yanks the dildo out of me and replaces it with himself, thrusting himself in and out of me at the same unrelenting pace until, only moments later, he's groaning and pulsing inside me.

I'm boneless as I lie beneath his body.

"Now you know how to get by when we're not together." His breaths are heavy in my ear.

"Somehow I don't think it'll be quite the same," I murmur. "And there's no way I'm doing that in my bedroom at home, with my parents downstairs."

"So get your own place."

I roll my eyes. "We're not all made of money."

Henry lifts himself off enough to peer down at my face. "You know that whatever you want, you can have. Right?"

"I'm not taking advantage of you."

"Why not? I'm taking advantage of you, right?" He lays a lingering kiss against the small of my neck, making me moan. "Preying on your virtue?"

I giggle. "According to Mama."

With a groan, he climbs off me. "We should get up. Margo said they were all meeting for drinks at seven. Dinner's at eight."

I roll over to glance at the clock. It's just after six. I can't believe I slept the afternoon away.

The nightstand drawer still sits wide open. Curious, I look inside. There's a basket filled with condoms and packets of lube, along with a bunch of other toys. "Anal beads?" I hold it up. "What is all this stuff?"

"Things we can try out when we don't have to be ready in an hour."

I frown, turning to take Henry in. He's standing in front of the bay window, unashamed of his nakedness as he peers out over the scene. "How did you know that *that*"—I gesture at the dildo lying in the sheets—"would be in there?"

"Just a hunch."

"You had a hunch that she'd put a basket of sex toys in our drawer?"

He smirks. "Have you not figured out that she's an odd one, yet?"

He's halfway to the bathroom when I remember and blurt out, "She kissed me. On the lips."

His feet slow for a moment before he continues on, disappearing behind the door.

I hear him chuckling to himself.

# CHAPTER 17

"This is the original cellar, five hundred years old." Margo's heels click on the uneven stone beneath our feet. "I've put off restoring it as it will take much time, but I will eventually. Of course, we cannot use this when we open as a hotel. It will be for my private collection." The word "collection" slides from her mouth so smoothly in her French accent.

I wrap my arms around my chest, fighting off the damp chill down here. "It's so narrow." And dark, the only light comes from a utility light that dangles above us on a wire.

"Yes, most of the servants' passageways did not leave a lot of room for maneuvering. There are still a few left behind the walls. I will show you tomorrow during our official tour. Henry, could you please reach those two bottles for me?" She points to the top of the wine rack.

Henry, who's behind me, shimmies past, his body forced to rub against mine on the way by because there isn't enough room for two people to pass each other easily.

"Which ones?"

"The two Beaujolais on the end. They are rare. I have been saving them."

He edges past her, and I imagine his groin presses against her ass like it just did to mine.

I grit my teeth. Henry's with me. That's in the past. He said so himself, he doesn't want to be with her.

Looking at her now, in a plunging, black, backless dress that looks more like a sexy nightgown, I'm having a hard time buying it.

"*Merci*, Henry. Now lead the way out." She smiles up at him.

He shimmies past me again, each hand filled with a bottle.

Her cool hand settles lightly on my shoulder. "Ready, Abigail?"

I steal one more look at her, to see her giving me that same broad, friendly smile. There's nothing overtly evil or flirtatious about it. Nothing that says she's plotting to steal Henry away from me.

Still, I don't trust her.

---

"WHAT IS IT?"

"A French 75. I think you'll like it."

I take the martini glass from Henry and hold it to my lips for a taste. "There's lavender in this?"

Henry smiles as I take a bigger sip, the sharp contrast of liquor and floral enticing.

From the other side of the garden terrace, Margo bursts out in laughter. She's talking to a couple who just arrived, the French rolling off her tongue with beautiful speed. She catches my eyes and then, reaching out with a guiding hand, ushers them over to us. "Henry and Abigail. This is Marc and Charlotte, two of my dearest friends. Charlotte and I used to do a lot of work together."

One look at Charlotte's high cheekbones and perfect,

svelte body and I can tell she's another model. She looks a little older than Margo though, maybe by a few years.

"This is Henry Wolf, owner of Wolf Hotels, and his Abigail."

*His Abigail.*

Okay, she just scored a point or two.

We exchange nods and smiles just as three more people arrive through the doors.

Another round of introductions, as I meet Annie-Claude and her husband, also Marc; a French couple who live in Paris, and Isabelle, a dear friend.

Not surprisingly, Margo surrounds herself with attractive people, all of them carrying that air of wealth that I can't fake. I hook my arm through Henry's, intent on attaching myself to him for the rest of the night. It's my only suitable disguise to hide the fact that I do not belong here.

---

THE TWO FANCY bottles of wine sit empty on the dining room sideboard, along with six more, polished off over a three course meal of partridge ravioli, rare tenderloin and a vegetable dish I can't pronounce. I'm all but licking the dish of the creamy dark chocolate mousse served for dessert.

"Good, yes?" Joel grins as he watches me, his elbows resting comfortably on the table as he sips his wine. He was the last to arrive tonight, and has been as easygoing and charming as the night we met, completely unfazed that I've watched him having sex. Am I the only one at this table who thinks this is strange?

"Yes. It's delicious." My cheeks flush. I probably look like a small child. Thank God Henry's attention is on Marc—the one married to Annie-Claude—or he'd probably be embarrassed.

Joel leans forward and lowers his voice, "If you ask nicely, Margo may give you seconds." I'm pretty sure he's drunk, but I can't tell if he's flirting with me or patronizing me, that accent too hard for me to read.

I set my spoon down and slide the bowl away, giggling at myself. I think the two glasses of wine I nursed through dinner have gone to my head. I've tried to pace myself but it's hard, sitting at a table with this group, which spontaneously switches to French and chatters on for minutes before remembering that Charlotte's Marc—who's from England—and I don't understand a word.

So I've spent a lot of time eating and drinking and just listening, learning what I can about them.

Annie and Marc have been married for two years, no kids and, from the sounds of it, no plans on having one anytime soon. Annie is a well-known—to everyone but me—fashion designer and Marc is an architect who designs large-scale buildings. It's not surprising he and Henry hit it off. He's attractive in a nerdy way, with short brown hair and designer glasses. But you can see he's well-built beneath his clothes. Married Marc is a nerdy muscular architect.

Charlotte and the other Marc have been together for ten years, but are not married. Both were models. Charlotte retired a few years ago but Marc still takes jobs, mainly for clothing companies. They live an hour away from here, where Charlotte is taking over her family's winery. Three of the bottles we had tonight were brought by her.

Isabelle and Joel actually dated for a short time, a long time ago. Isabelle is Isabelle Monteblanc, the famous ballerina—again, to everyone but me, apparently—whose career was cut short by a horse riding accident. I'm not sure what she does now, but it sounds like she comes from a lot of money.

"Abigail!" Margo calls out from across the table, suddenly switching to English. "Henry says you live on a farm."

Yes, within this mix of impressive resumes… I'm Abbi, who lives on a farm.

I haven't felt out of place over dinner, until now.

All sets of eyes turn to settle on me, and my cheeks begin to burn.

Henry's hand settling on my knee beneath the table does little to comfort me. "I do. It's my family's farm actually. I had to delay my last year of college to come back and run it for my dad while he recovers. He was badly injured in an accident not that long ago now."

"I am sorry to hear that." Margo smiles sympathetically.

"He'll be fine in a few months."

She takes a sip of her wine. "And then what will you do?"

Good question. "I'm not entirely sure. Finish school probably." I hesitate. "I'm actually starting up a small soap company so we'll see where that goes."

"Oh?" Her eyes, a little glossy thanks to the wine, light up. "Tell me more."

The others have been distracted by side conversations, but she seems genuinely interested so I do.

"Did you bring any of these soaps with you?"

I sigh. "Yeah. They're… in my suitcase." I brought the demos because I thought Henry might like to see them.

"The lost suitcase." Her shoulders sink with disappointment. "Well, if your suitcase arrives, I would love to see them."

*Really?* "Okay."

She smiles warmly at me for a long, lingering moment, and then claps her hands together. "The parlor for a digestif?"

"Depends." Joel looks to Charlotte. "When do you want to do this?"

She shrugs, glancing at Unmarried Marc. "Tonight?"

"Maybe after a few more drinks. She'll be more relaxed," he murmurs, his British accent thick.

"That can work." Joel turns to me, his hazel eyes dancing. "Will you let me photograph you one of these nights?"

"Me? Uh...." I glance over at Henry.

"No." Henry tips his head back and finishes the last drops of wine.

"You would enjoy them while you two are apart," Margo says.

"I have my imagination for that." He smirks at Margo, and it's not altogether friendly.

People start moving, glasses in hand and easy laughter flowing, out the dining room door.

"We're going to head up for the night," Henry says. "Thank you for dinner."

Margo turns back to pout at him, the look somehow downright sexy when it's coupled with that dress, the front of it low enough to highlight the fact that she's not wearing a bra.

"Abbi, can you not convince him otherwise?"

I look from her to Henry and back again, not sure what to say. It's obvious she's desperate for him to stay. Probably so she can screw Joel in front of him again.

He slides his arm around my waist. "Good night, Margo."

She sighs, then shrugs. "See you tomorrow. We are going to harvest grapes for our wine."

"I've got a few hours of work tomorrow but I'm sure Abbi will join you," he answers for me.

"Okay, then. Until tomorrow." She's gone quickly, her hips swaying seductively with each step.

Despite her likely intentions for having us stay, I still feel awkward. "Isn't it rude to eat dinner and leave?"

Henry settles his hand on the small of my back and guides

me out the other way. "Normally, yes. Here? It's fine. We'll see them tomorrow."

"Okay. You would know." I follow him up the stairs, the sound of laughter carrying down the hall. "Are you tired?"

"Exhausted."

I'm the one who got a four hour nap, I remind myself. Though, he wasn't coming from a six hour time change. "Okay, well. We can go to sleep now so you're well rested for—"

The door hasn't even shut and his hands are at the straps of my outfit, pushing it off my shoulders, letting it tumble to the ground.

---

I NEED MORE WATER.

It's one in the morning and the bottle of Evian by our bed is empty and I'm ready to peel my tongue off the roof of my mouth, thanks to the red wine. I tried drinking from the tap, but it has an odd tin taste that is making me feel ill.

Henry's still beside me, his beautiful chest rising and falling with shallow breaths. I slip away, trying my best not to shift the mattress too much. Throwing the robe that hangs on the door over my naked self, I tiptoe out of the room.

Margo showed us where the kitchen is, should we need anything when the staff has left for the day. I head down the stairs toward there now, my arms coiled around my chest, my steps quick. This place is eerie at night.

With a bottle in my hand, I make my way back.

Joel's voice carries from somewhere on the third floor, stalling my feet. He's speaking in French, his words tender, his tone soft.

A door sits open, the light beaming into the hallway.

"Back up just for a moment, Marc... yes." Several clicks

sound, and I realize that he's taking pictures. I know I should head to the safety of my room, and yet I find myself tiptoeing over, curious about what the famous photographer with his portraits hanging in galleries all over the world does.

And why Henry seemed adamant on Joel *not* taking my picture.

*Oh my God.*

Charlotte is lying on the bed, her legs spread and dangling off the edge. Marc is kneeling in front of her, his mouth between her legs.

And Joel is crouched in front of her, angling his camera at her hard nipple.

*Click.*

Licking his thumb, he rubs her nipple a little.

*Click.*

My mouth hangs open as I watch Joel shift around, aiming the camera at her body, taking close-ups from dozens of angles. And as he works with his lens, Marc works with his mouth.

Charlotte's chest is heaving.

"Not long now," Margo's voice murmurs in my ear, startling me so much I gasp.

I step back, out of the doorway where I'm spying like a pervert—though they did leave the door wide open—and hope she can't see my reddened face.

Margo doesn't move though, the light bathing over her striking face to show me the amusement that dances in her green eyes as they flicker between me and her friends.

"It is beautiful, no? Watching Joel work."

"*This* is what he does?"

She smiles. "His specialty is capturing the essence of a woman when she is about to orgasm."

*And he wants to photograph me....*

No wonder Henry said no. There's no way I'd be comfortable with that.

Charlotte's moans grow louder. Margo reaches for me, taking my hand, pulling me out of the shadows. "Come. You must watch. I insist." She's surprisingly strong for such a delicate woman and I find myself in the doorway again, just as Charlotte lifts her hips toward Marc's face, her hands on the back of his head, pushing him closer into her. Joel just keeps clicking as she moans and writhes, her lips parting and her breasts heaving.

Marc pulls his face away, his own breathing ragged, and Joel wastes no time sticking his long lens in between her legs to get a close-up. "That one's just for you," he whispers, winking at his friend.

"They have such beautiful bodies, don't they?" Margo whispers, lustful admiration in her eyes.

I step back into the shadow of the hall. "I need to go."

"Why? They don't mind." She edges in closer to me, into the darkness. "It is a turn-on, watching, yes? For them and for us."

It finally clicks.

Henry said there were places he could take me if *this* is what I wanted. Is that the whole point of this trip? Is this why he brought me to France?

I swallow.

He also said he didn't want me watching this alone. "I should go."

"Wait." Margo steps in close, so close that her breath skates across my lips. Somehow it's still sweet, even though it should be sour after all that wine.

"Henry wouldn't be okay with me being here, Margo."

Again, she laughs, and it sounds so musical. "With you watching people fuck?" God, even that word sounds like a song coming from her. "Henry has watched plenty, and he has been watched." There's just enough light to catch the glint in her eyes as realization sparks. "But he would not be okay with you watching without him." Her eyes skate down to my mouth. "I was wondering about you. You seem so innocent and young, but you are not. Not anymore, are you? Not with a man like Henry. He is… impossible to say no to." She says that like she knows.

Because she does.

"He has quite the appetite. He is not bound by traditional relationships."

"I know you slept with him, Margo. I've heard all the details."

She doesn't seem the least bit embarrassed by that. "It was one of the best nights of my life. He was… *incroyable*."

Jealousy tightens my gut. "I know he is. And I'm not sharing him with you."

"*He* is not who I want." Her fingers reach up to trace my jawline, her gaze dropping to my lips. "Would he share you?"

My mouth drops open.

Is Margo Lauren propositioning me?

Margo Lauren wants *me*?

"I… uh… I don't know. I mean, I don't think so."

She smiles. "Go to sleep, sweet Abigail." Leaning forward, she plants a kiss on my lips.

"Margo?" Marc calls.

Taking steps back into the light of the doorway, she slides the straps of her dress off her shoulders and it pools on the floor around her feet. She's completely naked beneath.

She stands there, unabashed, giving me a full view of her —of perky breasts that are the perfect size and have tight nipples that sit high and centered; of her taut, long torso; of the baldness between her legs.

I don't mean to stare so blatantly, but something about her makes it impossible not to.

"Good night." She smiles and turns to stroll into the room. And I see firsthand why people pay so much to photograph her body, slender and sculpted, the curve of her back to a hard, round, defined ass. Her legs are super slim and long, but so is her torso. Normally it's one or the other, but she's perfectly proportioned.

Joel rhymes off a bunch of things in French to her. She says something in return, and I hear packaging ripping apart.

I wait a few long moments and then, when that damn curiosity that gets me into so much trouble gets the better of me, I steal one more glance into the room.

Heat floods my body at the sight.

Charlotte is on top of a naked Marc on the bed, leaning forward, their lips locked in an intimate kiss. Meanwhile Joel is behind them, his naked lean body straddling Marc's legs. He's squeezing a pack of lube along her crack and himself, stroking it over his wrapped length. Chucking the empty packaging to the floor, he positions himself behind Charlotte.

And pushes.

She cries out against Marc's mouth.

It takes a few gentle thrusts with his hips but Joel is all the way inside. And so is Marc.

Charlotte lets out a string of French words and then she's crying out as the guys fall into a rhythm, stretching her body so wide that I don't know how she can handle it.

This is what Ronan and Conner were going to do to me.

And Margo stands next to them, her green eyes weighing heavily on me as her boyfriend fucks her friend—right in front of her—a seductive smile curling her lips.

I run the rest of the way to my room.

# CHAPTER 18

"Joel takes pictures of people having sex."

Henry blinks once… twice… before in a groggy but still sexy voice, he murmurs, "Good morning, Abbi."

"Did you know?"

"Of course I knew." He frowns. "How did *you* figure that out between last night and this morning?"

I tell him about my trip to the kitchen for water and stumbling upon the open door.

He shakes his head, but he's smiling. "How do you always get yourself into these things?" At least he's not mad.

"And then they all started having sex together. Did you know that they would be doing that, too?"

He sighs. "That's what they're into."

I hesitate. "Is that what *you're* into, too?"

His fingers weave through my hair. "I'm into you."

"But are you also into that?"

"I'm into a lot of things. I've told you that before."

"Is this why you brought me here?"

"You seriously think I'm going to let another man touch you?"

"No, but—"

"Why do you think we went up early last night?"

"And if we hadn't?"

He sighs. "The night might have gone very differently. And way out of your comfort zone."

"I'm not sharing you, Henry. I can't do that." I close my eyes tight against the thought of him being intimate with another woman at all, let alone me having to watch.

"I would never expect you to."

"Margo would still sleep with you. You know that, right?"

Pushing me onto my back, he pulls the sheet down and rolls over onto his side to graze my nipple with his teeth. Heat rushes between my legs "She'd also sleep with you."

"Yeah… she told me last night." I hesitate. Will he be mad? "And she kissed me again. I didn't have a chance to tell her to —" I gasp as he pulls my nipple into his mouth, sucking hard.

"It's okay, Abbi."

"You're not mad?"

He chuckles. "That Margo wants to fuck you? No."

"I just don't understand her. She has a boyfriend, and she watches him sleep with her friends while she's propositioning me."

"Margo is like no one you'll ever meet in your life. She loves the human body, male or female. She wants a front-row seat to people orgasming. The intimacy of it gets her off."

"That's…." I don't know what that is.

"That's a woman with no boundaries and full confidence in herself."

"You sound like you admire that?" Is that what he wants me to be?

"I'll admit, it's sexy." Henry's brow rises a notch. "What'd you say to her when she asked?"

"That you won't share me. What else was I supposed to say?"

His hand smooths over my stomach. He seems to be weighing his thoughts. "And if I said that I would share you with her… would that change your mind?"

"No."

He pulls the sheet down the rest of the way, exposing my body. "You sure?"

"Why? Is that what you want?"

His hand travels to my thighs to pull them apart. "You want complete honesty?"

"Yes?" I answer warily, because I'm not sure that I do.

His fingers slide through my folds, making my thighs clench. "Watching her go down on you would probably be the fucking hottest thing I've ever seen in my entire life."

"I'm not into women, though."

"You don't have to be into women to be into Margo." With his typical fluid grace, Henry slides down to place his head between my legs. "Lie back and close your eyes."

I do as asked, waiting with anticipation as his breath skates against my most private part.

"You've seen her mouth. I know you have. I've watched you stare at it."

Her soft, plump lips, painted in velvety lipstick. "So?"

"Do me a favor. Imagine it right here." His tongue dips into my opening, earning my gasp. "Do you think you'll care if it's my tongue or hers, once you're coming?"

I don't know, but I do know that his words alone are making me wet right now.

"Stop talking." I reach down and press against the back of his head, pushing his face into me. My muscles spasm as he chuckles once.

And then he grants me my request.

---

Henry's in the shower when the knock sounds on our door. I assume it's the staff, coming to take our breakfast dishes, so I holler, "Come in."

When I turn around, I find Margo standing in the doorway. She's wearing a fitted t-shirt and casual cotton pants today. Simple and casual, and yet still somehow glamorous.

She drapes a navy-and-white-striped cotton dress across the chair by the door. "A change of clothes for you. It should fit."

"Thank you."

"Have you heard from the airline yet?"

I shake my head. "Hopefully today."

She pauses. "How did you sleep?"

My eyes flicker to her plump lips, painted a soft pink today, remembering Henry's words. I flush with the thought. "Well. Thank you."

She comes farther in. "Henry mentioned that he had a few calls to make?"

"Yes." I groan. I hate that he has to work while we're here.

"Don't let that stop you from having fun. We'll be leaving shortly for the vines. Come with us. There is no point wasting your day inside."

It *is* sunny out. "Who's going?"

"Everyone but Henry."

Great. It was one thing to spy on that couple in the parking lot outside Billy Bob's, but I have to actually look these people in the eye for the next several days. Not that I haven't been in this position before, with Katie, Rachel, and Ronan. But this feels somehow different and I can't explain why.

She must be able to read my apprehension. "Please." She reaches out to touch my wrist. "There is no reason to be uncomfortable about what you saw, Abigail. We are not. It is not a big deal for us."

What about what she said to me last night? Is propositioning me not a big deal either? Does she do that with every woman she finds attractive?

The water shuts off in the bathroom, signaling the end of Henry's shower. He'll be coming out in a few minutes and I doubt he'll be wearing a towel.

Margo's eyes drift to the door, pushed shut but not closed all the way. "Please, come with us. We are meeting at the doors in ten minutes. We've packed a picnic." She ducks out the door, leaving the faint scent of her perfume behind.

I venture over to see what she brought, reveling in the feel of the material between my fingers. It's softer than normal cotton. Tossing my robe onto the hook, I pull the simple pencil dress over my head. It reaches halfway down my thighs, which makes me wonder how short it is on her. All in all though, it fits nicely.

"From Margo?" Henry asks, strolling out of the bathroom.

I admire the way his impressive length bobs between his legs as he heads for the dresser where his clothes are tucked away. "Yeah. She just dropped it off. She asked me to pick grapes with her and the others."

"You should go."

"But what if they... *you know,* out there?"

"Then leave." He chuckles as he pulls his briefs on. "I can't imagine fucking in between vines would be comfortable though. They're not animals. Either way, you're not going to have much fun here and I don't want you distracting me. I really do have to work."

"Will you come out and meet us?"

"I'll try." His phone starts ringing then and he sighs, checking the screen. "I have to take this." Grabbing my hips, he spins me around and ushers me toward the door. Opening it, he gives my ass a swift slap, just hard enough to make me yelp without it hurting. "Go on and have fun." He leans down to kiss me quickly on the lips. "But not too much, got it? Because I'm not there."

I sigh. I guess I'm going on a picnic.

---

"THE DRESS FITS NICELY."

"Yes, thank you." I shield my eyes against the sun as Margo stretches out next to me on the red-and-white-checked blanket that I pulled from the stack sitting on the wagon.

"You would pay to visit a place like this, *oui?*"

"Yes. If I could afford it." It's so peaceful here, lying in the grass, overlooking the rolling hills and valley below. We picked several bushels of grapes before breaking for lunch—a delicious assortment of freshly baked breads and cheeses and sliced meats. And wine, of course, which has left my cheeks warm and my shoulders relaxed. I think these people crack a bottle with breakfast.

She chuckles, her hand smoothing over her taut belly. "You are with Henry. You can afford anything your heart desires."

"His money isn't my money."

"But you two are serious?"

I sigh. "I don't know what we are."

"You would like to be, though, yes?"

"Yes." Is it wrong to admit it to Margo?

"He is an interesting character. Very open in some ways, and very closed in others."

She is right about that. The man will give himself over physically without hesitation, but to let people in to what he's feeling? He's a vault.

"Are you enjoying yourself so far, Abigail?"

I close my eyes and revel in the early afternoon sun beating down on my limbs. "Yes." Despite everything, it's been an incredible day so far. Margo was right, there's no awkwardness coming from any of them. They laugh loud and they joke frequently. It reminds me of my relationship with Connor and Ronan and, while I'm still an outsider here, they haven't made me feel uncomfortable for it.

Margo rolls onto her side to face me, her body close but not touching. "Did you tell him what I said last night?"

I can feel her watching me behind her dark sunglasses. "Yeah."

"And? Was he surprised?"

"No."

"Of course not." I hear the smile in her voice. Rolling onto her back, she sighs. "I see the way you look at me. You are curious."

If I'm being honest with myself, I *am* curious. At least, I'm becoming so as I spend more time with her, in this seductive fog that swirls around her, now that I know she's attracted to me.

What *would* it be like to have Margo touch me?

What would it be like to have her go down on me while Henry watched? If I were ever to allow a woman to do that, I have to think that it'd be Margo.

As the minutes go by and my thoughts spin and the smell of her shampoo and perfume waft in my nostrils, I feel my blood beginning to pulse.

I'm actually disappointed when Margo climbs to her feet. "We have one more bushel to pick and then we can go to the grotto to swim."

I frown. "The grotto?"

"Ah, you have not seen it yet. It is underground and the best part of this chateau. You will come, yes?"

Swimming sounds like heaven. "If my suitcase comes in time."

Another secretive smile touches her lips. She holds her hand out for me. "Come."

Hesitating for only a minute, I take it, letting her fingers slip through mine.

---

"MARGO SAID she'll send us a case of the wine when it's ready."

"Did she now?" I hear amusement in his voice.

I wander out onto the balcony, to where Henry sits at the table with his computer and a glass of Scotch. "What's so funny?"

"Nothing at all," he murmurs, but his eyes are twinkling in that way.

Coupled with that smirk and a fitted black long-sleeved shirt, he looks irresistible. I can't help myself, I drape my arm over his shoulders, grabbing his earlobe between my teeth.

"I have to get this e-mail out in the next ten minutes." He stops my hand before I can get it past his belt and into his pants.

I heave a sigh. "It's almost three o'clock. You've been in here all day."

"Almost done. Oh, your suitcase arrived."

I gasp. Darting inside, I dive for it, pulling the zipper to inspect its contents. Everything seems to be there.

Including the samples of the new soap packaging. I quickly gather them, bringing them out to show Henry. "Look at them! Aren't they amazing?"

He pauses from his work to flip them around in his hands. "They are. I like the name you went with."

"It's perfect, isn't it? Organic and natural, but also fun," I parrot Zaheera. "I wasn't sure about it at first but it's grown on me, and now I love it. And look! They even colored the twine!" I hold up the mauve string that wraps the lavender bar.

Henry leans back in his seat with a sigh. "Abbi, how much have you had to drink?"

"A few glasses. Why?"

He smirks. "No reason."

I roll my eyes. "I'm fine."

"Yes, I can see that."

I head back to my suitcase, where I packed a new bikini. "When will you be done?"

"Another hour. Two at most."

"*Seriously?*" I groan exaggeratedly.

He shoots a glare at me before shifting back to his computer, those fingers of his that are so skilled in getting me off typing furiously. "I think I liked you better when you were my assistant and scared shitless of me."

"Too bad." I stand in the doorway and peel Margo's dress over my head.

His fingers stall. "What are you doing?"

"Changing into my bathing suit."

I feel his hard gaze on me as I unfasten my bra. My breasts spring free. "No. You're trying to distract me."

"I don't know what you're talking about." I turn around to make an elaborate show of peeling off my panties, bending over to give him a good view.

And lose my balance trying to get my foot out. I stumble into our room.

His chuckles carry as he types.

"Don't worry, I'm not hurt," I mumble. Giving up on my attempts to seduce him away from his computer, I pull on my bikini.

"I'll do my best to be done in an hour and meet you by the pool."

"We're not going to the pool. We're going to the grotto."

The furious typing stops. "Who's going?"

"Me and Margo. I don't know who else. Why?"

He looks up from his computer at me, and his jaw instantly tightens. With a heavy sigh, he scans whatever he was typing, clicks something with his mouse, and then pushes his laptop shut.

"You're coming?" I exclaim excitedly.

"I'm definitely not letting you go there alone." Setting his laptop on the table, he grabs the robes from the hooks. His gaze wanders over my body like fingertips, sending shivers through me, making my nipples pebble. "New?"

"Yeah. Do you like it?"

"I do." He yanks on the strings until they unfasten and the bottoms fall to the floor. "But it's pointless wearing it down there."

I frown. "Why?"

Unfastening my top, he holds out the robe out for me. "Because nobody else will be wearing anything."

My mouth drops open as he fastens the belt around my waist.

"What do you mean? We're going naked? I don't know…." I'm shaking my head, even as nervous flutters course through my body. Skinny-dipping? I've never done anything like that before.

I quietly watch him strip. Heat pools between my legs as he drops his boxers. I'll never get enough of the sight of Henry's body.

He pulls the fluffy black robe over himself. "Do you trust me?"

"Yeah, but—"

"Do you trust that I know what you'll enjoy?"

"Yes."

He leans down and kisses me. "Then trust me now."

Nervous flutters explode in my stomach as he takes my hand and leads me out of the room.

---

IT TAKES a minute for my eyes to adjust to the dim lighting. "Holy…."

"This part of the castle was built over a system of caves. Margo's grandmother was Italian, so her grandfather built an underground spa reminiscent of the grotto near her childhood home." Henry's eyes skate over the stone ceiling above us. "Spent a lot of fucking money on this gem."

"But it is well worth it, yes?" Margo glides through the water toward us, her wet hair slicked back. "Henry, you should take Abigail to the real grottos one day. They are… *magnifique*."

He peers down at her. "Where's everyone else?"

"Napping or fucking. Not here. Annie complained that Charlotte's wine is too strong. "

He says something to her in French. I have no clue what, but the tone is dark, warning.

She only smiles. "Because I knew you would come." She stretches out to float on her back, her round breasts like two peaks breaking the water's surface.

She's taunting us.

Or Henry.

"Fresh towels are on the shelf and you can hang your robes there." She points to where a rack hangs, fifteen feet away from the steps.

I feel her hawkish gaze on us as Henry leads me over.

He slides his robe off his body without hesitation, tossing it onto a hook, giving Margo a chance to take in his nakedness fully.

"Come on, Abbi. You wanted to come down here." He smirks. "It's cold standing here."

I can't believe I'm doing this. Taking a deep breath, I unfasten my robe and let it fall from my body. Henry hangs it next to his and then, taking my hand again, leads me toward the steps.

Margo is appraising us without shame, her eyes drifting from Henry to me, where they linger.

I find myself wondering what she's thinking about my body.

Thankfully, the water is much warmer than the air, and it's a rush to get to my neck. The ground beneath my feet is uneven. In some places it's shallow enough that I'd be halfway out of the water if I weren't crouching. In other spots, I'm on my tiptoes to keep my head above water.

"We need to talk business, Henry," Margo purrs, wading over to stand in one of the shallow spots, the water reaching just below her belly button, her perfect breasts and taut belly on full display.

I steal a glance at Henry to see if he's watching. Relief overwhelms me as I meet his eyes, locked on me. "Later." His hand coils around mine and he begins pulling me through a small chasm in the rock, seemingly on a mission. I follow willingly.

The hum of jets churning water can be heard as we round the bend ahead. A wall divides us from the small, circular whirlpool that's obviously manmade, the sea-blue tile walls smooth. Steam from the heated water rises, giving the entire area a mystical feeling.

Without warning, Henry hoists me out of the water and

over the wall with no effort, dunking me into the much warmer water. I crouch down to completely cover myself. "Stay on this side, Margo," he warns, swinging his body over the wall gracefully, slipping in with a groan. He doesn't crouch though. He stands there, the water barely covering him. The tip of his erection pokes out of the water.

Margo, who's resting her arms on the edge of the wall, stares at it with hunger.

My jealousy flares.

"Hey." Henry seizes my chin between his thumb and forefinger, turning my face to his. "This is yours, not hers. She can't have it. No one can have it except you. Understand?"

I nod.

"Do you trust me, Abbi?"

Another nod.

"Good." He hoists me out of the water to sit on the wall. The steam from the whirlpool has warmed the air on this side, and yet goose bumps still dance along every inch of my bare skin on display. Oddly though, I don't feel the overpowering need to cover up, even with Margo next to us.

Henry closes his mouth over mine in a soft, intimate way. So not like his normal hungry style. Still, I'm hyperaware that Margo is leaning over the wall right beside us, watching as Henry's hand slides down my belly and his finger slides into my slit. Try as I might, I can't keep the light moan from slipping out as they dip into me.

Margo murmurs something in French. It sounds like a question. A few more moments pass.

"Henry," she murmurs again, this time almost pleading.

Henry dips down to catch my ear with his teeth. "You remember that bet we made that night? The one that you lost?"

"Yeah?"

"I'm about to collect."

"I don't even know what that means." But my stomach drops all the same.

He cups my chin within his hands, his eyes turning gentle. "Trust me?"

"Okay," I whisper, because I have to trust him or this will never work between us.

"Bring your legs up," he orders.

I do. He lifts me at the waist and turns me around to face the other way.

To face Margo.

He presses his chest against my back as his lips find my neck and his hands find the insides of my thighs. "Relax, Abbi."

I do my best to as he pushes my legs apart.

Spreading me wide in front of her.

Before I have a chance to say anything, his hand is on my cheek again, turning my head so he can reach my lips. Again, kissing me in that slow, lingering, intimate way that makes my blood rush and my heart swell with love for him. Still, I sense Margo shifting to position herself, her shoulders just barely skimming my knees.

His rough, callused hand slips down between my legs to begin working against my clit. He smirks against my lips and I know why. That slickness isn't from water. I'm completely turned on right now.

"She is so beautiful, Henry," Margo purrs.

With a deep breath, I dare look down to find her peering up at me with nothing but adoration in her eyes, her full lips parted. "Please, Abigail." The way she pleads, so seductively….

I'm so nervous, but I *am* turned on right now, I'll admit. That such a beautiful woman wants me boosts my confidence.

And Henry would love this. I'll do anything, at least once, for Henry.

Reaching down, I coil my fingers through his, pulling his hand away. And then I stretch my thighs farther apart for her.

A sigh sails from her lips to my skin and when she leans forward, when her tongue slides over my clit for the first time, I cry out.

"Fuck," Henry growls, his hands tensing over my thighs as he watches Margo's tongue slide back and forth.

It feels strangely different than when Henry is going down on me. Margo's tongue is smaller, her lips are softer, her skin is smoother. But, it's no less intense. Almost too intense.

"Watch her," Henry whispers.

"I am," I gasp, catching her green eyes as they glance up at me, the flat of her tongue pressing against my clit. She murmurs in French against me and Henry wraps his arms around the backs of my thighs to lift my legs up and farther apart. I lean back against his chest and close my eyes as the base of my spine begins to tingle, her tongue relentless in its swirls and curls.

"I'm going to come," I moan.

"And I'm going to fucking explode if I don't get inside you soon," he pants against my ear.

Margo's fingertips dig into my thighs, but it's easy to ignore the sharpness as heat floods downward between my legs.

Henry's hand grasps the back of her head, fisting her hair as he presses her mouth against me. It only seems to excite her, her tongue pushing deep inside me, just in time for my muscles to begin to spasm.

My cries echo off the cavernous walls around us as I buck against her.

No sooner have I stopped than Henry is lifting me off the wall and into the whirlpool. Pushing my legs apart and my back down to lean against the divide, bracing myself with my palms, his rigid cock is inside me in less than five seconds. His hands grip my hips roughly as he thrusts into me from behind.

Margo simply watches us for a moment, her eyes hooded and full of lust. And then she blows me a kiss and swims away, disappearing around the bend.

Henry comes moments later, his deep groans trumping the jets, his legs trembling from exertion against me. The pulsing seems to go on forever before it subsides and he pulls me up to a standing position, his arms roping around my chest, his heart pounding against my back. "Thank you," he whispers through pants.

"For letting her go down on me?" I can't believe I just did that.

And I enjoyed it.

He rests his forehead against my temple. "No. For trusting me so completely."

I turn to face him, to peer up in his eyes, my emotions suddenly getting the better of me. "I love you, Henry."

He heaves a sigh and somehow I feel like I've said the wrong thing.

I avert my gaze but he's quickly pulling my chin up to face him again. "Don't. I may not be ready to use those words yet but know I feel it, too." His hand brushes back wet strands of hair from my forehead. "You are *everything* to me. Christ, Abbi. You should have figured that out by now. Do you think I'd fly across the country for a night for just anyone? Do you know how much I dread putting you back on a plane at the end of this trip? How much I dread not seeing you for another three weeks. Probably longer? I hate it." His sigh skates over my face. "This is the first time in my life that I have all the fucking money in the world and I can't have the one thing I want."

My heart hammers in my chest with his words. I slide my hands over his chest, my thumbs stalling over his nipples, pebbled from the cold. "You have me. I'm yours."

"Not how I want you though."

"How do you want me?" I ask tentatively. He's finally opening up to me, but I don't want to scare him.

His lips twist. He's hesitating. "With me when I go to bed at night and when I wake up. When I'm stressed and I need to talk." The corner of his mouth curls. "Or not talk."

"Soon. I can be that soon."

"I don't like missing people. It's been a long time since I've missed anyone."

"It won't be forever, I promise." I stretch onto my tiptoes to kiss him deeply.

Laughter carries from the other side of the grotto.

I peer over my shoulder to make sure we're not being watched. "I guess the others are here now?"

"Perfect timing. Margo's going to need to get off after that."

"I think I want to go back to our room." I've had all the group excitement I can take.

"Good idea." Henry pulls me down until the water covers my shoulders. "I'll go and get our robes."

"Oh, so *now* you don't want me on display," I tease, sighing as I feel his hands cup my breasts.

"Not for those assholes. No fucking way."

"But women are okay?"

"Margo's different. I trust her and I understand her. It's hard to explain."

"I think I know what you mean." It's how I trust Ronan. Not that I'm going to mention him right now.

I watch Henry climb out of the whirlpool, the muscles in his legs and ass still extra taut from his recent exertion.

And accept that I will do whatever it takes to keep him happy with me forever.

Because it finally feels like Henry is mine.

# CHAPTER 19

"Shower with me?" My skin reeks of chlorine.

"Yeah, just a minute." Henry frowns at his phone.

"What's wrong?"

"Scott called me three times in the last hour. He never calls me."

I stifle my groan—if there is only one person I hate in the world, it's Henry's brother—as Henry puts his phone to his ear.

"Yeah, what?" Henry doesn't waste time with pleasantries. He hates his brother as much as I do.

I watch, as Henry's scowl slips away and his face pales. "When? No...." He turns his back to me, to face the French doors and the rolling hills beyond. "France... yeah... yeah.... No... You didn't call her, did you?" After a long moment. "I'll be there as soon as I can."

He hangs up.

"What's wrong?"

"My dad had a heart attack."

"Oh no. Is he okay?" I know William Wolf isn't in the best

of health, with terminal cancer. But to have this happen on top of all that?

"No." Henry tosses his phone to a table. "I have to fly back to start making funeral arrangements."

*Oh my God.*

I don't know what to do or say except, "I'm so sorry." I march straight for him, wrapping my arms around his shoulders. At first he doesn't make a move to meet the affection, but slowly, I feel his arms coil around my waist and his face bury into the crook of my neck, and soon his arms are squeezing so tight that it borderline hurts. But I just squeeze him against me tighter.

"He's all I had left," he whispers hoarsely.

I remember our roles being reversed, when my dad was knocking on death's door and Henry swooped in to take care of me. While I can't do anything to save the day, I can at least take care of him. "Why don't you grab a shower and get dressed. I'm going to phone Miles and have him make arrangements for your jet. I'll let Margo know that we're leaving. And I'm coming to New York to help you sort through this."

"You have your family to take care—"

"They'll figure it out. I'm going with you and don't you dare arg—"

"Okay." He shifts to rest his forehead against mine, his eyes shut. "I'm not going to argue with you, Abbi. I need you."

My heart swells. "Then I'll be here."

---

I ROLL both of our suitcases into the hallway. Margo said she'd have someone come and get them for us so we don't have to lug them down four flights of stairs. The one unavoidable problem of a chateau built in the 1400s is no elevators and no good solution for putting them in.

"Abigail?"

My breath catches with the sound of my name on her tongue. A tongue that brought me to orgasm only hours ago. Does she regret doing that? Do I regret allowing it? "Yes?" It takes me a moment to collect my nerve and look to her, my cheeks flushing.

I see nothing but concern in her eyes as she wanders into our room. "Your car is waiting downstairs."

"Thank you." I glance over to the balcony, where Henry stands, talking to someone. He's been on the phone most of the time since we found out. "I'm sorry to be leaving so abruptly—"

"*Non*!" Her hands rise in surrender as she approaches me. "Do not apologize for anything at all. I am so sorry that Henry must face this now. I remember when my father passed. It was heartbreaking for me."

"Yeah, I think he's pretty upset." He just doesn't know how to show it.

Henry comes in. "The car's here?"

"*Oui*. He is waiting outside."

He nods, his gaze drifting from Margo to me, and then back again. "We didn't really get to talk much business."

"Another time." She smiles a beautiful smile as she glides toward him. She cups his jaw in an affectionate way, murmuring something in French.

He responds in kind. She leans forward and kisses his cheek. Just one cheek, not in the French way, in a friendly but intimate way. Oddly enough, I don't find myself spiking with jealousy as I once did.

No, I don't regret allowing that to happen. It has bonded the three of us.

She leaves him to come back to me, the fingers of one

hand running through my hair, pushing the loose strands off my face, while the other one clasps my hands. "I know you will take good care of him." I get only a second's warning as her green eyes dip to my mouth, before she leans in to press her lips against mine in an unhurried kiss.

Releasing my hands, she strolls toward the door. Her eyes graze over the table, where I left the Farm Girl branding mock-ups. "These are for me?" she asks, lifting the note that says as much.

"You mentioned that you might like to try them." Was she just being polite?

She lifts the fuchsia-colored bar to her nose. "Mmm... rose and sandalwood?"

"Yeah. That's one of my favorites."

She closes her eyes with her sigh. "It smells like you."

Again, I blush, because Margo more than anyone except Henry would be familiar with what soap I'm using. "I hope you enjoy them."

"*Merci*. I will cherish them." She collects them all within her grasp. "Until we meet again." She disappears down the hall.

"That was smart of you, to give her samples. She has a lot of connections in the beauty industry. If anyone can help you sell your brand, it's her."

I grab my purse. "Let's worry about getting to New York right now."

"Abbi." He strolls over to me, his hands coiling gently around the base of my neck. "I just want you to know...." He hesitates. "You are everything that has been missing from my life. These next few days, with my brother and the media and *other* people... they aren't going to be easy. You don't have to put yourself through this for me."

I stretch to my tiptoes to press my lips against his. "You

are everything I didn't know was missing from *my* life, and I am not going anywhere, so shut up and let's go."

He heaves a sigh of relief.

I follow him out, wondering exactly what New York has in store for us this time around.

Whatever it is, I can handle it.

As long as I'm with Henry.

Did you enjoy Teach Me?

If so, please leave a ***review***!

Abbi and Henry's story continues in Surrender to Me, The Wolf Hotel #4, available *here*.

# SNEAK PEEK: SURRENDER TO ME (THE WOLF HOTEL, #4)

***The steamy and highly addictive Wolf Hotel series is available now! Enjoy this excerpt from Surrender to Me...***

The horizon is glowing with a faint pink hue as I step through the patio doors and take in the view of the Manhattan skyline, my eyes still half-closed thanks to terrible jet lag. It's promising another stifling hot day. "Record-breaking," according to the news. Thankfully, we missed the worst of it yesterday, our flight from France not arriving at the airfield until late in the evening.

I stroll around the rooftop pool—pristinely clean and so inviting—to the lounge chair where Henry is stretched out, wearing only his briefs, a glass of Scotch in hand, the half-finished bottle sitting on the concrete next to him. "Come to bed," I say softly, perching on the edge of the chair. "Get a few hours of sleep before the day has to start." It's 5:00 a.m. Henry has a meeting with the funeral director at ten to discuss arrangements for his father.

And he's drunk.

It's a long moment before his steely blue eyes break their lock on the sky to regard me, slowly drifting over the silky white sheet that I hug to my naked body. There's no hunger in that gaze though. "He was supposed to die of cancer, not while fucking a twenty-five-year-old," he murmurs, his attention drifting away again, to the city skyline this time.

When Henry shared the details about the cause of William Wolf's heart attack, I hadn't known what to say. It still feels like an awkward topic. "Did he have heart issues?"

"He had blood pressure problems, but he was taking medication for that. It was under control."

"And he was still feeling well?"

"As far as I know. He hadn't mentioned anything otherwise to me. And Scott said he hadn't talked to him all week."

I smooth my hand up and down Henry's muscular arm soothingly, fighting the natural urge for my fingers to wander over his bare flesh, memorizing each perfect curve. "Life isn't always fair."

"Don't get me wrong, of all the ways to go.... Just not yet," he mutters bitterly.

"How is the girl?" I can't even imagine what it'd be like to have the man you're having sex with die in the middle of it.

"Hysterical that night, but I'm sure she'll be fine."

"Did she know him well?"

Henry chuckles darkly. "Depends on your definition of 'well.' He'd been fucking her for a few weeks. She thought she was in love. Scott says she wasn't the brightest light bulb in the pack." He takes a sip. "Good for my dad."

"How old was he, again?"

"Sixty-three." He says that with a slight slur. I've never heard Henry slur, but then again he did crack this bottle of Scotch the second we walked through the door.

"He looked good for sixty-three." And dying of cancer. Granted, I only met him that one time, in Alaska for the grand opening of the Wolf hotel in Wolf Cove, and that was months ago.

Henry sighs. "When he told me about the diagnosis, he said he couldn't really complain, considering all the luck he'd been born into. He was bound to come up short somewhere. That was his logic."

All that luck he'd been born into.... A gold mine and the luxurious global Wolf hotel chain that has made Henry's family more money than they know what to do with. "It sounds like he had made peace with it, at least."

"He did. And I was getting there. I thought I had another few years with him. And then this happens." Henry's voice turns husky. "First my grandparents. Now him. He was all I had left and he's gone, just like that."

There's no point reminding Henry that he still has a brother, because Scott Wolf is a lecherous snake and not someone either of us wants around. And then there's his mother, but Henry's been estranged from her for almost twenty years, and it doesn't sound like there's any desire to reconcile there.

I swallow the lump in my throat. "You have me. I know it's not the same, but I'm here, whenever you need me. However you need me." I slide the glass out of his hand. "And maybe we should ease up on the Scotch for now."

Henry gives me one of those hard, unreadable stares for one... two... three seconds, and my stomach instinctively tightens, afraid of what dark thoughts might be churning inside that head of his.

And then he chuckles. It's a bitter sound. "You're right. I should save some for you. You'll be needing it more than I will...."

That's not the first time he's made comments about how the next few days will be an ordeal for me, which makes me more than a little nervous. I've already met—and now hate—his brother, who played a role in breaking us up with his lies and manipulation. But that was back when I was Henry's assistant and we had to hide our relationship from everyone, including Henry's father.

I no longer work for Wolf Hotels, and William Wolf is dead.

Abruptly, Henry leans in to grip the back of my head and plant a hard kiss on my mouth, the sweet, smoky taste of liquor on his breath. I half expect him to yank off my sheet and take me right here under the morning sky, but he pulls away just as quickly. Climbing out of the chair, he throws his arms above his head in a stretch. And then pushes his briefs off his hips, letting them tumble to the concrete. He's a little unsteady on his feet as he stalks to the edge of the pool, without so much as a glance around for onlookers. We're some eighty stories up in the Wolf Tower penthouse and it's still early enough that there *likely* aren't spectators in the few equally tall buildings around.

Not that Henry would give a damn if there were.

He smoothly dives in, sending a small splash in the air before emerging on the opposite side of the pool to grip the edge while thrusting a hand through his wavy chestnut-brown hair, pushing it back off his face. I consider dropping my sheet and climbing in after him, but then he begins swimming laps, his sculpted body moving swiftly and powerfully through the water.

And so I sit and quietly admire the indomitable Henry Wolf as the sun climbs the horizon beyond.

Wondering what fresh hell the next few days will bring.

---

I try not to fuss with the hemline of my dress as we step through the main doors of the funeral home. It's a modest black shift dress that I picked up at Saks yesterday, thinking it would be appropriate for the visitation. It, along with a pair of classic black pumps with a price tag that made me choke, complete the understated look I was going for. Still, I tried my best to look like I belong next to Henry, fussing with my makeup and hair for almost two hours.

Meanwhile Henry stands tall and sharply dressed—as usual—in a tailored black suit and tie. And matching socks, that I chose for him while he showered. "Ready?"

"Are *you?*" I peer up at his handsome face—a face that ensnares females of all ages instantly, I know because I've watched it happen from the sidelines countless times—and take in the steely mask. It's been firmly affixed since he swam some fifty laps in his pool and sobered up. That was the only time I've seen him let go of control. Since then, he's been in and out of the penthouse, but mostly out, splitting his time between the Wolf head office and making arrangements for his dad's burial. All business as usual, his emotions hidden from everyone.

Including me.

But I haven't pushed him to talk. I figure he'll talk when he's ready.

He slides a hand over the small of my back. I can feel the heat of it through the light material of my dress. With a heavy swallow, he leads me down the hall of the opulent funeral home in the heart of Manhattan.

Visitation hours don't begin for another twenty minutes, and yet there is already a stream of people of all ages milling about the entrance doors to Promenade Hall, where William Wolf's body awaits. I shouldn't be surprised. News of his sudden death made the New York Times.

Countless eyes veer our way as we approach, and my stomach twists with nerves. Most are watching the powerful mogul beside me, but more than a few curious onlookers are sizing me up.

"He knew a lot of people," I murmur, just loud enough for

Henry to hear, as my cheeks begin to burn from the attention.

"There will be a lot of Wolf employees here today to pay their respects. Plus business associates and media." Henry offers a reserved smile and nod to a middle-aged couple closest to us as we pass.

"What do you want me to say if they ask how I knew your father?" A question I *should* have asked him *before* climbing out of the limo.

"The truth. That you didn't know him at all, but you know his son *very* well."

"Is that a good idea?"

"Of course it is." Henry looks down at me, his eyebrow spiking with annoyance that I'm even questioning him.

"I'm just not sure you've thought this through." While we haven't been hiding our relationship, we have been keeping it low-key. But with a room full of Wolf employees, plus media, news of the woman striding in with "one of the world's most eligible bachelors," according to many—his ex-assistant—will spread like wildfire. Is Henry ready for that?

Am I?

"I'm quite sure that I have." The slightest smirk touches Henry's lips as he slips his strong, calloused hand into mine and leads me through the throng of watchful gazes to the set of heavy oak doors being manned by a solemn attendant.

I can't help the giddiness that surges through my limbs with this simple action, despite our surroundings. I know Henry. He wouldn't have done that if he didn't have serious intentions about me.

The doors close behind us with an ominous thud, sealing us inside the hall with William Wolf's body.

And Scott Wolf.

My tiny thrill vanishes instantly as I spot Henry's older brother standing at the far end of the cavernous room, where an elaborately carved wood coffin sits on a brass stand, surrounded by at least fifty elaborate bouquets—everything from the typical funeral white lilies to arrays of colorful sunflowers.

I fully expected Scott to be here and yet I can't help the visceral reaction at the sight of him. I haven't seen him in months, since the day he stormed out of Penthouse One at Wolf Cove, bleeding from several well-deserved punches delivered by Henry's fist.

Scott turns to watch us approach now, his gray-blue eyes widening at the sight of me by Henry's side.

"Huh," Henry murmurs.

"What?"

"I was sure he would have heard about you by now." There's amusement in his tone.

Unfortunately I can't match his joy as I watch Scott's face —not nearly as chiseled or handsome as Henry's—harden with the knowledge that he was duped.

Henry must sense my trepidation. His hand squeezes mine once in a sign of comfort. "Scott, you remember Abbi Mitchell."

"How could I forget?" An easy—fake—smile curls Scott's thin lips. "You're a better liar than I gave you credit for, *Abigail.*"

I'm assuming he's talking about the day he cornered me in an elevator and tried to manipulate me into admitting that Henry was screwing me, his assistant, in the midst of legal issues over screwing his last assistant. While he failed at that, he did manage to plant such toxic seeds of doubt and outright lies about Henry that I convinced myself that Henry was sleeping with other women. It was without doubt the worst day of my life. A thousand times worse than the day I walked in on Jed cheating on me.

I clear my throat. There are so many things I'd like to say

to this asshole—hell, I'd like to pick up that giant bouquet of white roses behind him and smash the heavy-looking white clay vase over his head—but this is not the time or place for vengeance. "I'm sorry for your loss."

His eyes shift to Henry. He isn't so adept at hiding the anger in them as his brother. "You son of a bitch."

"Now, now...."

"You have the nerve to bring your *whore* to his funeral?"

All amusement slips from Henry's face. "Call her that again, and you'll be joining Dad in that box," he warns, ice in his tone.

But Scott isn't so easily deterred. "You lied right to his face about fucking her."

"I told him about Abbi before he died. My conscience is clean. How's yours?"

I feel my own eyes widen with surprise now, as my attention veers to the left, to where the distinguished man lies. Still regal, even as a corpse. I didn't know Henry had told his dad about us.

Scott's eyes narrow as he regards his brother for a long moment, as if trying to read something between his words. "You lied right to Dad's face and yet I'm the one who took all the heat."

Henry releases my hand and steps forward. He's easily six inches taller than his brother, and now he towers over him. "You took heat from Dad because you tried to have me framed for rape so you could take over Wolf Hotels," he hisses through gritted teeth, his fists clenched at his side, looking ready to punch Scott again.

"I was just making sure Dad knew what kind of man his precious boy really is," Scott throws back, puffing out his chest to compensate for their size difference.

"A man who will run the family business with integrity?" Henry takes a step forward until they're toe-to-toe. Scott refuses to give ground. "Who has no problems keeping the women in his life satisfied? Who's always honest with them?"

The two Wolf men have somehow managed to fill this cavernous hall with tension. I'm torn between jumping between them to stall the explosion, and hiding behind the casket to avoid the shrapnel.

The door behind us creaks open and a man in a suit passes through. "Excuse me, but the crowd outside is quite large. Would you mind if we begin moving people in now to help clear the lobby? If everyone is ready?" He sounds skeptical. He must sense the impending doom in the air.

"Yes, we're ready. Thank you." Henry takes a deep breath and then two steps back, muttering under his breath to Scott, "Stay the fuck away from us."

I breathe a sigh of relief. Belinda, Wolf Cove's general manager and a woman who seems to know the Wolf men well, once commented on how Henry and Scott can't be in a room for more than five minutes without erupting.

Now I understand.

It's going to be a *long* three hours.

---

I settle a hand on Henry's shoulder, grabbing his attention before the next well-wisher steps up. "I'm going to get you water. I'll be back in a sec." We've been standing in this same spot, to the left of the casket, for two and a half hours now, greeting countless people. All strangers to me, though I smile and accept their condolences as if I'm a part of the family, because what else am I supposed to do, standing next to Henry?

"Thank you," he answers, his voice hoarse from talking.

I edge my way through the crowd, happy to be moving my legs, though my feet throb from these heels. Thankfully,

Scott has stayed on the other side of William Wolf's body, some distance away and suitably occupied by visitors and unable to cause more problems. Right now he's consoling a sobbing Becky, the woman William was with the night he died. The woman is everything I would expect of a rich older man like William, and yet at the same time not. She's stunningly beautiful and young, with evenly tanned skin, plump red lips and high cheekbones, and an hourglass figure. I'm 90 percent certain her waist-length platinum blonde hair is the result of high-end extensions.

She is the reason William apparently took a Viagra pill the night he died, something the preliminary autopsy report revealed. Henry threw a glass across the living room to hit the wall and shatter into a hundred pieces when he found out. William knew he couldn't take those pills because of his blood pressure issues, Henry said. But he must have taken one anyway, the need to enjoy his twenty-five-year-old plaything outweighing the dangers. He obviously didn't expect the consequences to be so severe.

I find a service area outside the hall, near the lobby, stocked with carafes of hot coffee and tea, along with a fridge full of cold beverages. I fish out two bottles of cold water, cracking one for myself and taking a big gulp.

"Is working for Mr.Wolf always so chaotic?" Miles asks from behind me, making me jump.

I offer Henry's assistant a sympathetic smile through my swallow. "Yes. It is."

He heaves a sigh and takes a sip of water from his own bottle, only to catch a dribble as it escapes his mouth and runs down his chin. "You'd think he'd slow down, with all *this* going on." He gestures toward the visitation room. "But the guy's actually working *harder*."

"It's just his way of coping. He'll ease up soon." *I think.* Henry has been sliding into bed after I've drifted off every night, and is either sweating his tension out in his home gym, or on the phone when I wake. The only proof I've had that he's actually slept is his gold watch sitting on the nightstand and the delicious smell of his cologne on his pillow.

We've shared nothing more than tender kisses since France.

For Henry to go four days without sex, with me ready and willing to give him whatever he wants?

He's hurting.

Miles runs a hand through his mop of curly brown hair. "He asked me to do, like, a *thousand* things and now I have a thousand follow-ups for him. I don't want to bug him, but at the same time, I know he's going to ask for a status update as soon as he walks into the office and expect it to be taken care of, and I'm not going to have any answers for him and he's going to think I'm an idiot and fire my ass. I don't want to get fired. I *like* working for him!" His face is pinched with stress.

I remember this feeling too well, back when I didn't think I could do anything right where Henry was concerned. "I'll ask him to carve out some time for you as soon as he's ready, so you two can sort out any questions you might have."

Miles sighs with relief. "Thank you. I guess it must have been a lot different for you, working for him. You know, because you two were...." His gaze drops to my ample chest, which, while it's well-covered by this shift dress, is still noticeable. "I mean, because he obviously had a hard on for you so.... No, wait! I mean...." His face screws up.

I can't help but laugh. I've only ever talked to Miles when he's confirming Henry's schedule or booking flights for me. On email and text, Miles seems so professional and smart. I wonder if he's always so frazzled in person, or if it's just because of the current situation. Something tells me it's the latter, because Henry wouldn't tolerate a bumbling fool assistant for long.

He gives me a sheepish smile. "I think it's cool. You know, that Wolf would fall for you. He could have *anyone* he wanted. Gorgeous women are throwing themselves at him *all* the time, but he's completely into *you*. I mean, not that you're not gorgeous, because you *are*, too. Like, *really* hot. But you're different than all the others. You're normal. Fuck, I need to stop talking. Please don't tell him I said anything. He'll fire me."

I giggle. "He won't hear it from me."

Miles sighs. "Fuck, I'm going back to the office. He can find me there."

I watch the tall, lanky guy speed away, amusement on my face.

"He's certainly in a rush."

I turn to find an attractive older woman—mid-fifties, maybe—filling a mug with coffee beside me. She's dressed in a well-cut black pantsuit, emphasizing a trim waist and appealing curves. Her hair, the color of spun gold, settles on her shoulders in a sleek bob.

"He's just a bit overwhelmed right now. He's Henry Wolf's assistant." I don't know why I add that last part.

The woman's piercing blue eyes flash with recognition. "He's not going to last long working for a Wolf if he can't find some decorum."

Something about her is so familiar, but I can't peg it. "Do you work for Wolf Hotels?"

"I used to, for a short time. A *very* long time ago, now." She chuckles as she stirs the sugar through her coffee, the metal spoon clanging softly against porcelain. "And you? Do you work there?"

"I used to. Also for a short time."

"Well, it's nice of you to pay your respects. Did you know William?"

"No. I mean, I met him once but I didn't know him. I

know his son. Henry. I know him well." I stumble over the answer Henry prescribed earlier. I haven't had to use it yet.

The woman pauses in her stirring, her curious gaze skating over my features, as if really taking me in for the first time. "And how is Henry taking his father's passing?"

"As well as can be expected."

"Working a lot?"

"Day and night." I frown slightly. "Do you know Henry?"

"Not really." She smiles sadly. "I'm guessing he's a lot like his father, though."

"So I've heard." The water bottles are beginning to sweat within my grasp. I've been gone too long. "Speaking of Henry, I need to get this to him before he loses his voice." Somehow, "enjoy the visitation" doesn't sound right. So I simply hold up the water for emphasis and then, with a smile, I turn and head back toward the room.

The crowd has thinned out somewhat, with only half an hour left before the room closes to visitors. I weave through the staggered groups of two and three until I reach Henry's side to wordlessly hand him his bottle and set a hand on his bicep in comfort.

He abruptly stops talking. And suddenly I feel like I'm interrupting a private conversation.

When I turn to take in the woman's face, I'm *sure* I've interrupted a private conversation.

Whoever she is, she's stunning. Her long brunette hair hangs like sheets of silk over her shoulders to reach halfway down her back. Her eyes remind me of cat's eyes—wide, almond-shaped, and bright green. And her legs... they're obscenely long. Like, unnaturally so.

And the way she's looking at me from beneath that thick fringe of eyelashes, the corners of her full mouth turned downward with a hint of distaste? She's sizing me up as competition that she can easily squash.

Henry clears his throat. "Abbi... this is Kiera. Kiera... Abbi Mitchell."

My chest tightens.

*This* is Kiera? *The* Kiera. Henry's ex-assistant. The one who he had an affair with. The one who falsely accused him of rape. The one who is obviously still madly in love with him, by the look in her eyes.

My fingers dig into Henry's bulging muscle. "You have a lot of nerve," I begin in a whispered hiss.

"Abbi... remember where we are," Henry warns softly.

Right. At his father's visitation. Slapping her across her pouty face—as much as she deserves it, as badly as I want to do it—is the wrong thing to do.

So instead of that, I press into Henry's hard body and force a wide, fake smile. "Hello, Kiera. It's *so* nice to *finally* meet you." I sound like Tillie, the catty southern bell from Wolf Cove who is masterful at delivering sweet words laced with cutting bitterness. I release Henry's arm long enough to offer my hand.

She responds with a limp shake—which I squeeze—and a tight smile behind her wince. I notice there isn't a wedding band on her left ring finger. I guess her husband didn't stick around after finding out the sexual relationship she'd had with her boss was 100 percent consensual.

"Let me know if you think that could work," she purrs, her eyes locked on Henry, ignoring me.

"Thank you for coming," he answers smoothly, seemingly unperturbed by her presence.

Henry may be mine, but I still feel like vomiting as I watch her turn and stroll away, her mile-long legs emphasized by the tight black skirt. "I'll bet she can't even find pants for those things," I mutter.

Henry chuckles. "Don't be petty."

I sigh, reminding myself that Henry's not attracted to insecurity. "What does she need your help with?"

He cracks open his water and takes a swig. The line to pay condolences has dwindled, and he has a break finally. "She wants to work for me again."

My mouth drops open. "For Wolf Hotels?"

He pauses, as if deciding what to say. "For me. As my assistant."

"Are you fucking kidding me? The nerve!" I blurt out, a touch too loud. "Well... you have Miles, so... you're good. You don't need another assistant." The last thing I care about right now is Miles's job. I don't want that woman anywhere near Henry.

"I do have Miles," Henry agrees, taking another long sip. I can't read his tone, and that makes my paranoia begin to grow.

I drop my voice to remind him, "And she accused you of rape."

"She did," he says too calmly.

"Henry!"

He turns to cup my cheek with his warm palm, his crystal blue eyes locking with mine. "I don't need a new assistant, and she accused me of rape, and I know you wouldn't be okay with it, so, no, there's no way in hell Kiera's coming back to Wolf in *any* capacity."

"Oh." I breathe a sigh of relief. "You handled her well."

"I humored her to get her the hell away from me. I wasn't going to cause a scene here." His lips curve into a sexy curve. "You, on the other hand.... I thought you were going to claw her eyes out."

I offer a sheepish smile. "Sorry, I saw red. I wasn't thinking."

His hand settles on the small of my back. "That's okay. I think I liked it." His fingertips slide down to trace the elastic waistband of my panties through my dress. "My money'd be on you, too."

I clear my throat and give him a cautionary look. There are undoubtedly people watching. "By the way, you need to make some time for Miles."

Henry's brow rises in question.

"I ran into him in the lobby. He looked overwhelmed."

He sighs. "I've probably been overworking him."

"You've been overworking, period."

Another sigh. "I don't want him quitting on me. He's good."

I wonder what Henry would say if I repeated Miles's words. Either laugh it off or fire him. There's rarely an in-between with this man. "Just give him some of your time so he can ask his questions and do his job. Let him know that you appreciate him, and he won't be going anywhere. For some strange reason, he likes working for you," I add wryly.

Henry grins, the first real amusement I've seen on his face in days. "You sure you don't want your job back?"

"I'm positive. The boss can be a real tyrant."

"A tyrant." He leans in closer to me, and drops his voice. "Tell me... what kinds of things did he make you do?"

This is *so* inappropriate, but I'm guessing Henry needs this bit of reprieve. I bite my bottom lip in thought. "Well, there was this one time he tied my hands up and...." I sense a figure hovering, waiting for us to break our conversation. My mouth clamps shut and my cheeks burn, embarrassed at the prospect of being overheard, especially given our surroundings.

It's the woman I met at the service area earlier.

Henry leans into my ear and whispers playfully, "I remember that day. We'll have to reenact it later." But when he turns to greet his latest visitor, his entire body stiffens.

"Hello, Henry," the woman croons in that same soft voice.

She's an inch or so shorter than I am, and is forced to tilt her head to peer up at him.

He doesn't answer for a few beats. When he finally does, his voice is curt. "Thank you for coming."

I feel Scott's beady eyes on us, but I'm unable to peel my attention away from this uneasy exchange.

She offers a wide smile, as if nothing is wrong. "How have you been?"

"Fantastic."

"Good. Well, I was hoping you'd be here."

"Of course I'm here. It's my father's visitation."

"Yes, I realize that. But I was hoping we could talk."

"So talk." Nothing about Henry's tone invites conversation.

After a moment of awkwardness, she turns to me and holds a hand out. "I'm sorry, I didn't catch your name earlier."

"Um...." I glance at Henry's stony face. "It's Abbi Mitchell."

"Hi Abbi. I'm Crystal McGuire." She meets Henry's gaze. "I'm Henry's mother."

Continue on with Henry Wolf

# ALSO BY K.A. TUCKER

*The Wolf Hotel Series*:

Tempt Me (#1)

Break Me (#2)

Teach Me (#3)

Surrender To Me (#4)

*Dirty Empire Series:*

Sweet Mercy (#1)

Gabriel Fallen (#2)

Dirty Empire (#3)

Fallen Empire (#4)

For Contemporary Romance, Women's Fiction, and Romantic Suspense by K.A. Tucker, visit katuckerbooks.com

# ABOUT THE AUTHOR

K.A. Tucker writes captivating stories with an edge.

She is the internationally bestselling author of the Ten Tiny Breaths and Burying Water series, He Will Be My Ruin, Until It Fades, Keep Her Safe, The Simple Wild, Be the Girl, and Say You Still Love Me. Her books have been featured in national publications including USA Today, Globe & Mail, Suspense Magazine, Publisher's Weekly, Oprah Mag, and First for Women.

K.A. Tucker currently resides in a quaint town outside of Toronto. Learn more about K.A. Tucker and her books at katuckerbooks.com

Printed in Great Britain
by Amazon

84441765R00171